Memories

of

Chronosalis

Memories

of

Chronosalis

Ceara Comeau

ISBN 978-0-578-19818-7 (Paperback Edition)
ISBN 978-0-578-19858-3 (Hardcover Edition)
ISBN 978-0-578-19859-0 (eBook Edition)

This novel's story is a work of fiction. Names, characters, events and incidents are the products of the author's imagination. Certain long-standing institutions, agencies, and public offices are mentioned, but the characters involved are wholly imaginary.

Edited by Julia Purdy

Cover Design copyright © JD&J Design LLC 2017

Published in 2017 by Ceara Comeau
www.amberoakmysteries.com

৵৽৶

In memory of
my friend Tyler Woods
and
my grandfather Rev. Robert F. Dobson
my first number one fans

1

Another dream. Ever since her sixteenth birthday, bizarre dreams of terrifying alien-like creatures haunted Amber. Their formless, blue, jagged glass bodies that always floated and their eyeless sockets that bore deep into her soul appeared frightening enough. But in every dream their mouths hung open constantly, revealing sharp razor like teeth ready to sink into her flesh. Usually, beautiful far-off places complete with friendly wildlife filled her dreams. But these other dreams seeped into her waking life, tormenting her relentlessly.

Although she desperately wanted to get to the source of the matter, the calendar reminded her that an especially important English paper needed to come first. Fortunately for her, only seven hours remained before the start of a research-filled weekend. But with her brother around, time became her worst enemy.

Chris always supported any hobbies Amber enjoyed doing, but as she grew older, he became snoopy and overly protective—more than she wanted. Since their mom, Holly, always took extra shifts at the hospital, Chris' near constant presence provided a way to lessen any of Holly's concerns. Amber found no fault with her mom because of her frequent absences. Holly worked as a nurse, but her income barely made ends meet to support the entire family and keep their beautiful Victorian house. Due to the strenuous financial circumstances, Chris searched for a job as soon as he graduated. He later became a mechanic and received quite a bit of money for the type of work he did. For as long as Amber remembered, her family life consisted of only the three of them. She knew that her dad lived elsewhere, but her mom never went into much detail about it aside from the fact that their relationship didn't work out and he lived with his family.

After contemplating her plans for the weekend, Amber swung her legs over the side of the large antique bed–her bare feet brushing the cold wood floor. She shuddered as chills went up her spine. Suddenly, she felt something warm and soft rub up against her arm. Amber turned her head and smiled down at a rather large creature whose fur was brown and black striped. Her beloved cat, Sphinx, stood on her bed, vying for her attention. She remembered getting the friendly feline when she was only four years old.

The occasion when she got him was a little fuzzy. A few times she asked her mom why he never seemed to grow or even age, but her only response was that Sphinx was a special breed of Maine Coon and they were naturally large cats. But Sphinx was unlike any cat Amber ever saw. He never ran around the house in the middle of the night as most cats should, and he was generally quiet. Those who knew the family immediately saw an attachment between the cat and his mistress, but despite their connection, he was the family cat and only occasionally looked to Amber's mom and brother for attention. Often, Amber saw Sphinx as a great listener and confided many secrets in him—mostly those involving her bizarre dreams.

Amber watched as the cat lazily walked away and nestled down into her now empty pillow. His bright blue eyes slowly closed. She shook her head and quietly laughed to herself. Casually looking away from the cat, she noticed her alarm clock sitting on her nightstand. Her eyes widened in panic as the black digital clock glared 7:30. School began in less than thirty minutes! Amber scrambled around the room, shoving books into her bag. She threw on a pair of jeans and a plain t-shirt before running out of the room. The sounds of her pounding feet echoed throughout the house as she made her way down the old wooden stairs. Amber almost jumped the last few steps when Chris came around the corner, a steaming mug of coffee in his hand.

Chris held the mug out, preventing the hot liquid from splashing onto his hand, and exclaimed, "Whoa! Amber, slow down!"

Amber latched onto the banister to steady herself and replied, "Sorry, Chris. I'm going to be late. Why didn't anyone wake me?"

Chris brought the mug to his mouth but then paused. He lowered it slowly, staring at Amber with a confused expression, "We thought you were already awake."

She lowered her eyebrows in confusion and continued staring at Chris, "What would make you think that?"

"Mom and I heard you talking, we figured it was Sphinx," he replied, his last words muffled by the mug.

Uncertain of how to react, Amber fidgeted nervously where she stood. She never talked in her sleep before or if so, no one ever mentioned it. It made her curious as to why it would suddenly happen now, "It hasn't been happening a lot, right?"

"Today was the first I heard, I don't know about mom, though," he replied, starting toward the living room. "Don't worry, I didn't hear anything you said."

His last words comforted Amber a little. If Chris knew what she dreamed about, he would undoubtedly call a psychiatrist. Brushing off the encounter, Amber made her way toward the kitchen where she found her mom making lunches. Holly stood by the counter in her pajamas while her blond hair threatened to fall from its messy bun. Amber grabbed a pastry from the counter then made her way to the table. Sitting down, she watched as her mom finished.

Sleep deprivation masked Holly's beautiful face, and a large yawn revealed rows of perfectly white teeth. "Hi honey!"

Amber smiled. She always admired her mom for all her hard work. Sometimes she felt guilty for not doing enough around the house like Chris. Amber watched as her mom wearily walked over to the table with a mug of hot coffee. Strands of hair danced in the light breeze. Holly sat down next to her daughter, her pale blue eyes meeting Amber's green eyes.

Amber shifted uncomfortably in her chair and replied, "Morning, Mom."

Concern filled Holly's eyes, and she placed a delicate, caring hand on Amber's shoulder, "Are you okay?"

"Yeah, just tired. I haven't been sleeping well, I guess," Amber's voice trailed off as her eyes glanced away from her mom.

Holly's thin eyebrows raised at her daughter's response. She knew Amber better than anyone—including her secretive poses. "Amber, what's wrong?"

Amber reflected back on last night's dream. That dream consisted of two creatures instead of the usual one. Hatred emanated from them both as their cold bodies seemingly wrapped around her, suffocating her mind in a frozen tundra. But in the midst of their icy grasp, human faces appeared in her line of sight—familiar faces at that. No matter how hard she tried, she couldn't remember why. Amber peered back at her mom whose expression was a mixture of concern and curiosity. A small smile formed at the edges of Amber's lips. "I've just been having bizarre dreams. It's really nothing, Mom."

Holly put her coffee down and shoved it aside, giving Amber her undivided attention. Amber heaved a great sigh. She wanted to tell her mom about the strange dreams, but even she found them difficult to comprehend let alone explain. Besides, burdening her mom with such trivial things seemed too selfish. Holly saw Amber's hesitation and decided not to press the matter further. She knew Amber always came to her in her own time. Her eyes glanced at the large clock on the wall, "This can wait another time. Right now, you need to get to school."

Amber shot out of her daze as she bolted from her seat, "School!"

"Relax, I'll take you," Chris announced, coming in with a now empty mug, "I have to head to work, anyway."

Suspicious of his sudden generosity, Amber took her backpack from the hook on the wall and replied, "Thanks, Chris, but I can just walk. It's no big deal."

Chris rolled his eyes and grabbed his keys. "I insist, it's not like it's out of my way."

Amber nodded, getting up from her chair. Holly quickly pulled out a hair tie and started pulling Amber's hair back in a pony-tail, "Mom, my hair's fine. You're going to make us both late!"

Chris chuckled at the regular morning routine. Holly always disliked seeing Amber's hair covering her face, but Amber loved it. Her hair provided a shield to hide from judging eyes at school. Straightening his posture, Chris' tone became mildly serious, "She's right, Mom. We need to get going."

Holly sighed in mild frustration and let Amber go, her dark brown hair bouncing freely in her wake. Chris already left the house before Amber muttered a quick goodbye to Holly. She raced outside into the cool, mid-September morning. She loved this time of year in Wisconsin. Not too hot or cold—just right according to Amber. She looked around her at the other Victorian houses on her street. Fall decorations adorned each one, and in just a few weeks Amber envisioned her street littered with the forgotten candy of the trick-or-treaters. She eagerly looked forward to that time of the year as the high school always put on the best Halloween party in all of Madison. It was a modest party compared to those of surrounding high schools, but it was just the right size for Amber.

Chris honked the horn of his silver pickup truck and poked his head out from the window. "You coming, Miss Dreamer?"

Amber laughed and then shook her head. "Can't I admire the beautiful fall surroundings?"

Impatiently, Chris glanced around the area, not seeing her interest, "Yeah, beautiful. Can we go now?"

She rolled her eyes and hopped in the truck. The trip usually lasted only ten minutes—five if Chris drove. Amber tried striking up a conversation with him, but for some reason, his mind seemed far away. This seemed abnormal to her. Occasionally she stole a glance, but every time his expression remained the same—frozen in a state of concentration. Something bothered Chris, but just like Amber, he never expressed his problems. She always figured that commonality made them closer as siblings. Soon the truck crawled up to the curb—Chris peered out the window, making sure nothing hit his vehicle. Amber stifled a laugh. Of all the guys she knew, only Chris treated his truck in such an overprotective way. When it rolled to a stop, Amber jumped out.

Chris rolled down the passenger window as Amber started for the school's doors, "Don't do anything I wouldn't do!"

Amber turned back and smiled as she opened up her arms in a challenge. "Then that should give me plenty of room!"

Chris stayed a while longer, watching his little sister enter the building. He put his hand on the gear shift as his expression grew solemn. He closed his eyes for a moment trying to brush a thought away. "Amber, you have no idea."

As Amber walked into the school, a feeling of dread instantly overwhelmed her. Students began walking into their classrooms, nearly emptying the hallways. She looked at the clock on the wall—a few minutes remained before the final bell would ring. Adrenaline coursed through her system as she ran through the halls, not caring about the rules.

With her mind so focused on getting to her English class, she accidentally collided with the last group of people she wanted to see. Books and papers fell out of her bag and scattered everywhere as Amber landed on the ground. She looked up to see James, his younger brother Jacob, and their friend Adam. The poster students for the high school, as Amber often liked to joke. In the eyes of the teachers and students, this trio epitomized perfection. But Amber saw, behind their façade, cowardly bullies.

James smirked at Amber's pitiful appearance, "Well, it looks like someone's going to be late. What's the rush, Amber? Is there a ghost behind you?"

Amber looked away from him as they laughed. She had grown accustomed to crossing paths with these boys. They always made fun of her for her unusual interests. Of course, their latest amusement came from the strange images from her dreams which they saw her sketching in her notebook. That just added to their fun. Still on the ground, Amber began collecting her papers and books. Her hands shook with anger as she shoved the papers in the bag.

Jacob kicked some straggling papers out of her way, "There's no point in hurrying now; you're already going to be late."

Amber put the last book in her bag as the final bell rang. She stood up, dreading the inevitable scolding from her teacher. Suddenly, a strange wave of confidence overcame her. "Guess we're all going to be late then."

Surprised, Jacob narrowed his eyes slightly. Amber never retaliated in any way before. Unfortunately, this just gave James more ammunition. "Don't worry about us, freak. We've got the teachers wrapped around our little fingers."

Amber knew that James had stayed back a year. A devious smile formed at the corners of her lips as she began walking away, "Let me know how that works out for you when you get a job—that is, if you ever graduate."

James came up behind her, grabbed her backpack, and jerked her back. Pushing her against the lockers, he growled, "You may be the smartest kid in school, but remember your place. You're just a loser, Amber, and nothing more."

A wave of relief swept over Amber when a teacher came out into the hall. He heard the commotion and broke James' vice grip on her, "What's going on?"

James saw some papers sticking out of her backpack and quickly snatched them, "She tried to steal my English paper, Mr. Turner."

Amazed at his blatant lie, Amber gave her side of the argument. "What? No, I didn't! That's my paper. I was going to turn it in before James attacked me."

Not even checking the paper, Mr. Turner chuckled, "I highly doubt Mr. Colbert would be so violent. You must have provoked him."

"Oh, like he needs any provocation!" she hissed taking them all by surprise.

Mr. Turner raised his eyebrows at Amber. "I think Principal O'Connell would like to have a word with you."

"Not again," whispered Amber, recalling back her previous visits to his office.

As Mr. Turner walked Amber toward the principal's office, she turned back and saw James crumple up her paper. He smiled and said in the most innocent tone, "I hope you can get your paper done, Amber."

Amber stopped suddenly. Mr. Turner grabbed her arm as she struggled to get free. Another outburst of anger erupted. "You know what, James? One day you will need a freak like me—one day you'll end up in a sticky situation, and I won't be around to help you!"

The teacher stared at Amber in shock. "Miss Oak, are you threatening Mr. Colbert?"

Amber looked back at the shocked faces. "Not if it comes true, sir."

The teacher forcefully led Amber away, muttering something unintelligible under his breath. Amber's heart pounded as she got closer and closer to the principal's office. Getting in trouble with the principal never really bothered Amber; she only worried about her mom and brother's reaction. Talking with the principal went as Amber expected. He rubbed his temples, trying to rid himself of an oncoming headache that always came whenever she sat in his office. Instead of reprimanding her as Mr. Turner had done, Principal O'Connell found it a waste of time after her first four offenses. With tired eyes, he looked at Amber and asked in a resigned tone, "Who should I call this time?"

Amber felt a twinge of guilt at the thought of interrupting her brother and mom. Since her mom picked her up the first four times, she thought it best to give her a reprieve. Writing down his number, she slid the paper across the desk. "Just call my brother."

As the principal picked up the phone and began dialing the number, he looked at Amber with eyes full of disappointment. "You're a really smart kid, Amber. Please don't waste your life by making foolish choices."

Since when is standing up for yourself a foolish choice? thought Amber grimly as she crossed her arms.

About ten minutes after getting the call, Chris came to pick her up. Amber waited outside the office. Chris and Principal O'Connell's voices resounded loudly throughout the abandoned hallway. When Chris emerged from the office, he seemed even more upset than Amber suspected. Amber followed him down the hall, grateful that his anger came from the conversation with the principal. As they left the school, Chris muttered something about taking the rest of the day off from work and wanting to get to the bottom of these suspensions.

As Chris drove home, his facial expression grew even more severe than earlier that morning, "Amber, the principal said if this happens again you'll be expelled."

Despite the fact her principal thought she instigated the whole encounter, Amber knew she had done the right thing. "It wasn't my fault."

He sighed in slight irritation, then replied, "Can you tell me your side of the story? I know you worked hard on that paper and I know you didn't steal anything from that James kid."

Amber pulled her knees in toward her chest. "James did his usual thing and called me a freak. He didn't like how I stood up to him, so he pushed me against a locker. Mr. Turner came out, and James lied to him, saying that I stole his paper. I got mad and yelled at James, saying that he might find himself in a sticky situation that only a freak like me could help with. They took it as a threat."

As Chris parked the truck in the driveway, he turned and stared at Amber. Concern filled his face, and his eyes grew wide. For the first time in her life, Amber saw her brother speechless. She turned toward him, tears slowly falling down her cheeks. "Maybe he's right...maybe I am a freak."

He shook his head from his daze and gave her an apologetic smile, calmly replying, "No, Amber, you're not. You're smarter and braver than he is, which is what makes him feel so insecure."

Releasing her grip on her legs, Amber turned toward her big brother. "That's funny; when he threw me against the lockers, I felt pretty insecure."

He unbuckled his seatbelt and started opening the door. "I know it doesn't seem it right now, but life's got a funny way of showing us how strong we really can be. Come on, Mom's going to want to hear about this."

While Amber nervously relayed the story to her mom, James and his brother sat at their home concocting a devious plan for three unfortunate fourth grade boys. In the last few weeks, James caught these young kids throwing mud at his new sports car. Instead of dealing with them like a mature young adult, he decided to take revenge. Unlike most of James' plans, Jacob saw this plan only ending badly, possibly even in injury. This was only part of the reason why Adam decided not to join in on his friend's fun. But unlike his friend, Jacob found no way to successfully argue. James' plans always worked out in the end. Jacob watched from a distance as James spoke to the parents about taking their children off their hands for a bit. Unsurprisingly, these parents knew of James Colbert and his excellent reputation around the town. They even seemed relieved at his kind, spontaneous babysitting offer. He then approached the children and cleverly reeled them into his trap. They followed James toward the woods. Jacob followed closely behind becoming, increasingly paranoid about the whole idea.

About ten minutes later, they came to a large, barren field. Typically, tall, weedy grass filled the area and spread as far as the eye could see, but frost had slowly crept in. Everything looked dead, including the trees. The children grew wary of what James told them regarding a secret Halloween surprise and looked around nervously. When they reached an old, partially dilapidated building, the children became eerily quiet. They stopped and stared at the creepy structure, bricks and glass shards haphazardly strewn about everywhere.

Noticing their sudden hesitation, James' gestures became wild with excitement. "Oh, come on! It's no big deal."

"I've heard about this place. My mom told me it wasn't safe," a young red-headed boy stuttered, looking nervously to his other friends.

A sly smile flashed across James' face. "Well, she doesn't know about the huge candy stash we have in there. You want to get ahead of everyone on Halloween, right, Caleb?"

Caleb fearfully looked to his friends. They too knew about the dangers of this place. He hesitantly looked back to the building. "I guess it's okay."

James smiled and glanced at his brother, who seemed rather unsettled about this whole plan. However, James quickly shot him a warning look before replying to the boys, "There's no time to wait, let's go in!"

James and his friends often visited this location. They never used it as a place to pull a prank, but rather as their own little secluded hideaway. Rumors flew around the surrounding towns about this building and what it once was used for. But the boys never really paid any mind to those. History merely told them the building acted as a hospital of sorts years ago. The forgotten furniture and medical equipment disturbed them a little, but they found no way to explain it. As James hopped over fallen chairs and carts, he completely ignored the other surroundings. The children, on the other hand, trembled with terror—yet at the same time their new discovery completely fascinated them.

"Hurry up!" James called impatiently.

Jacob hid his nervous glances from his brother, not daring to ruin his excitement, but an uncomfortable feeling in the pit of his stomach warned him of ensuing danger.

Jacob started looking off to the side, waiting for an unexpected part of the prank to come, but something else caught his attention. He slowed down by a doorway and stared in, his face growing pale. He gulped and nervously called to his brother, "Dude, you're going to want to see this."

James, annoyed by the interruption, turned around and stared at Jacob. But when he saw his expression, he quickly changed his attitude. James went to the doorway as the children stood far back in fear.

Knowing how terrified the kids were, Jacob wanted to avoid any unnecessary panic. Through a fake smile, he whispered to his brother, "Wasn't this room caved in before?"

Then James nodded silently, completely amazed at the now empty room. Impossible! This single word flashed across both of their minds. Only hours had passed since they had last visited the building and rubble, among other things, blocked the entrance. Removal of the debris would require a small tractor, but now the room sat entirely empty. Being the daredevil of the two, he bravely entered—curiosity and adrenaline driving him.

James nodded his head, trying to convince himself more than the others. "This is actually kind of cool."

They cautiously entered the windowless room as the children backed away from the room. Jacob scanned the room, trying to figure out its possible use long ago. From what he could see, no fixtures or even traditional outlets marred the walls. The clean floor appeared vacant of the memory of dragged equipment or bed frames. He quietly moved over toward James. "Something's not right. We shouldn't be here."

Irritated, James sighed and whispered through gritted teeth, "Shut up! Don't blow this!"

Jacob rolled his eyes as he grew even more uncomfortable with the room. One of the little boys saw the look on Jacob's face and began to back away. His heart began to race as he stammered, "Jake's right, something's fishy."

James' entire plan fell through; taunting became his only resort. "What, are you scared, Bobby?"

A strange sound came from above and grew into a loud roar as debris came crashing down, blocking the doorway. The two boys dove out of the way, covering their heads with their arms. As they heard tiny pebbles hit the floor, they opened their eyes and waited for them to adjust to the dim lighting. The sound of running footsteps echoed throughout the hall. As those diminished, the boys heard the sound of their own terrified screaming thoughts reverberating off the walls of their minds. They were trapped, and only the children knew of their location.

"What do we do now?" Jacob's voice echoed off the walls.

James tried to look for another light source—the only glimmer of hope leading to their escape. Sadly, the only way out happened to be the way they came. "I...I don't know."

Jacob's heart sank. His older brother always invented a backup plan. Hoping to be of help, he asked, "Can't we try to move some of this stuff?"

James tried lifting some of the debris, but stopped when he realized the weight of the mess. "With what, Jacob? It probably weighs more than both of us combined!"

James started backing up toward the middle of the room, trying to get a better view with what little lighting they had. He quickly stopped as a bright light glowed from behind him, followed by intense heat. With his heart racing, James knew that there was nothing else in the room. He closed his eyes, took a deep breath, and then turned around.

In the middle of the room, dressed in a gown made

completely of fire, stood Amber. Her exposed skin revealed veins as red as her outfit. Her crimson red eyes matched her entire ensemble, but her hair fell from her shoulders and halfway down her back in a waterfall of gold. The heat emanating from her body nearly scorched the boys' eyebrows and the flames lit up the entire room, as if the sun itself broke through a transparent window. The boys jumped away from her as her cherry red lips curved into an almost wicked smile. Then a golden glow emanated from her outstretched hands, striking the debris in front of the door. A golden light as bright as molten lava spread throughout the debris and pieces of cement as it effortlessly shattered the pile into smaller pieces. Neither of the boys questioned why Amber decided to spare their lives as they dashed out of the room to safety, both with the same question in their mind. What in the world just happened?

2

Amber ran down the stairs the next morning, filled with excitement. She jumped down the last two steps and dove into the kitchen, attacking her mom with a massive hug. Holly hesitantly wrapped a comforting arm around her daughter and said, "Good morning to you too?"

Amber released her grip and grabbed a banana from the fruit bowl. She went over to the table and sat down. Her mom slowly approached the table, wary of Amber's new attitude.

"Isn't it a great day?" asked Amber in a half-dazed voice.

Holly eyed her daughter suspiciously and replied, "Fabulous, what's wrong?"

Amber sighed in relief. For the first night in days, she slept all the way through the evening, without the hindrance of the terrifying creatures. She found it odd that the dreams suddenly stopped, but why question it? Since she never told her mom anything about the dreams, Amber thought it best to keep that to herself for now.

"I just had a really good night's sleep, that's all," replied Amber carefully.

Chris sleepily came into the kitchen and leaned against the doorframe as he tousled his short blond hair. His blue eyes still crusted over from his interrupted sleep. Amber stared up at him, smiling, and said, "You look like how I felt yesterday!"

A giant yawn stifled Chris' reply as he lazily walked over to the coffee pot. He blindly reached for a mug in the cupboard and poured the hot liquid. As he finished making his coffee, he joined his family at the table. After a few sips in silence, he started waking up and questioned, "How can one good night's sleep make you so happy? Did you forget what happened yesterday?"

Yesterday's unforgettable events constantly pestered Amber. It still made her angry whenever the thoughts reared their ugly heads. Not having to see the boys' smug looks for a few days only added to her relief. "No, I remember, but I'm trying to have a better outlook on things. Plus, it's not like they could cause me any more trouble while I'm at home."

Suddenly, the doorbell rang, interrupting Chris' next comment. Amber looked toward the entryway, confused by the sudden noise, "Are you expecting anyone?"

Holly and Chris simultaneously shook their heads, their expressions equally confused. The doorbell rang again as Amber approached the door, ready to slam it on an unsuspecting salesman. When she opened it, her heart sank. Adam stood in the doorway, one arm holding up the other while he rubbed his eyes. James and Jacob stood in the yard behind him, nearly shaking from fear.

"This better be important," snapped Amber. She didn't want to give any of them the pleasure of seeing her vulnerable—again.

"Look, this is embarrassing," said Adam awkwardly, "but were you by chance out at the old asylum at Baker's Field last night?"

Amber looked at the other two boys in the yard, neither of them willing to even look at her. She then looked at Adam, who looked as if he'd rather be anywhere but at her doorstep. With a shake of her head and roll of her eyes, she replied, "I don't generally take a stroll through condemned and private property. Find someone else to bother."

Adam opened his mouth to speak when Amber shut the door in his face. She refused to entertain their immature behavior. As she turned away, Holly came out of the kitchen, mildly concerned about the conversation she just overheard. "Amber, who was that?"

"No one important, just those three guys from school," she replied, starting toward the living room.

Holly glanced toward the door, a puzzled expression crossing her face. "What did they want?"

Amber stopped and heaved a frustrated sigh, "Don't know, they wanted to know if I was out at Baker's Field last night. Probably just some stupid prank."

Chris walked over to join them, his hand now empty of the mug. He crossed his arms and remained silent. Amber noticed his behavior, thinking that under any other circumstance a sarcastic comment usually escaped his lips. But today he seemed almost indifferent.

"Maybe you should give them another chance. Maybe they want to apologize," suggested Holly kindly.

Amber shook her head in disbelief, "You heard what they did, right? People like them don't apologize."

"Prove to them they're wrong about you," Chris blurted out suddenly.

Amber gaped at her brother, surprised by this remark. Aside from his wisecracks, Chris never liked confrontation. Challenging these boys had never seemed like a viable option to him. "What would it matter?"

Holly's eyes shifted from Chris to Amber and said, "Well, you could always ignore them. But, if you do help them, they'll owe you."

"Guys like them don't keep their word, Mom," said Amber, plopping down on the sofa.

Holly sat down beside Amber and leaned in toward her daughter. Their noses nearly touched as she whispered with a knowing smile, "You never know, Amber. Things aren't always what they seem."

Amber gazed into her mother's pale blue eyes. They saw so much and held so many secrets—a common thing Amber always saw when their eyes met. At this moment, Holly's eyes seemed to silently tell Amber something—something that was still too far out of reach. Amber closed her eyes and nodded, "Okay, I'll give them another shot."

"That's my girl!" said Holly as Amber walked toward the entryway.

"If I'm not back in two hours, call the cops," Amber warned as she closed the door behind her.

Amber stood out in the cool Saturday morning air and saw three retreating figures at the end of her driveway. She hesitated, not certain if she wanted to call out to them. Every part of her screamed to go back inside and forget the whole mess. Then, another part of her rose to the surface, which desperately wanted to prove herself. She bit back all her fears and called, "Hey! Wait!"

The boys slowed their pace but continued on their way down the road. Amber jumped off the porch steps and ran to catch up with them. Just as she neared them, she slid on a wet leaf, almost running into Adam. With cat-like reflexes, he turned around and grabbed her wrists to steady her. She looked into his brown eyes. She stared at him completely frozen in shock. He let Amber go when she regained her balance, but her hands remained up in a defensive position. She quickly glanced at the other two, who stared at her apprehensively. As she slowly put her hands to her side, she said reluctantly, "I'll help you."

After about twenty minutes of silence went by they neared the barren field. While they walked, Amber began to notice more things about the boys than she had before. She saw how Adam's long brown hair brushed his tan skin whenever the cold wind blew. Of the three, she always thought he acted more down to earth and relaxed. It completely boggled her mind how someone like him ended up with friends like James and Jacob. Her eyes moved over to Jacob, the younger of the two brothers, although they looked more like twins than anything else. From what Amber knew of him, Jacob often tried getting out from under his brother's thumb and often disagreed with James' decisions—although most of the time he kept his opinions to himself.

As Amber's eyes drifted over toward James, she noticed his handsome, chiseled features and clear complexion. The light blue windbreaker he wore flapped in the wind, defining his large muscles. The perfect amount of gel matted down his blond hair. He turned his head slightly and Amber caught a glimpse of his light blue eyes. But something seemed rather odd—something beyond just his appearance. In his eyes, Amber could almost see the various emotions that raced through his mind. Anger and frustration swarmed around in his mind, but, primarily, fear. Amber looked away as confusion entered her mind. Normally, she tried to ignore her surroundings and people, but now it seemed like those details shouted out to her.

Her attention was suddenly diverted when they reached the old building. Amber stopped and stared at the toppling structure. Her face went white as snow. Her stomach churned at the sight of the old hospital. Something felt off, well, a little more than usual. James happened to look back and saw Amber's reaction. Nervously, he asked, "What's wrong?"

Ignoring his question, Amber remained silent. She continued looking at the old building, trying to recall what she read about it, wondering if its history is what disturbed her. According to all of the town history books, Greenwood Sanatorium made everyone's skin crawl, even during its prime. Originally, the small, one-story building served as a tuberculosis hospital back in 1911. It only held a maximum of twenty patients, all with no hope of recovery. The most disturbing aspect of its past came after the tuberculosis epidemic left Madison. Greenwood then became the home for the clinically insane. Most of the patients during this time were a danger to society, and the asylum acted as their prison. Fortunately, this part of the building's history lasted only a few years. Some of the things done to the patients ranged from unethical to downright sadistic. Upon this discovery, the authorities came in and shut them down immediately. They moved the patients to a different hospital nearby while the equipment and furniture lay forgotten and rotting, along with the building.

Residents of Madison only remembered this last part of the building's past. Because of that, parents always warned their children not to go near the place. Most often, their excuses focused on the fact that each year another part of the building fell to ruin and no one wanted their children harmed by falling debris or injuring themselves on the rusty equipment. But Amber's reasons for not wanting to go there sounded strange in comparison. To an extent, she believed in the supernatural and thought it unwise to disturb places with violent pasts.

Adam came over to Amber as she continued to stare at the messy site. He repeated his friend's question, "What's wrong?"

With her eyes still fixed on the structure, Amber replied, "I'm not sure, it feels different for some reason."

"Well, it's probably a little more decrepit than the last time you were here. Could that be it?" asked Adam, hiding the events that his friends experienced.

Amber looked at Adam, then at the brothers, who appeared even paler than when they came to her house. Her eyes drifted back toward the building. James and Jacob saw something, that much she knew, but a part of her wondered what could be so terrifying that it would silence them. She shook her head and continued on as she replied, "Maybe?"

Adam looked at his friends. He returned his gaze to Amber, concerned about her reaction. Adam knew what his friends thought they saw, but couldn't bring himself to fully believe that Amber had magical powers and that her body could withstand fire. None of it seemed logical to him. He resumed walking toward the old sanatorium, growing more concerned with each step.

As Amber neared a set of doors, another strange feeling suddenly came over her—like an invisible force pulling her in. She wanted to run away, but her curiosity was too overwhelming. Her feet crunched shards of glass as she came closer to the entrance. "Greenwood Sanatorium," the engraved words were still visible, in weathered stone above the door. A sudden cold breeze swept over her as she cautiously stepped through the remains of the doorway.

The inside of the building appeared in far worse disarray than the outside. In front of her was a short entryway that led into the crumbling remains of a circular atrium that doubled as a dining hall. Although the ceiling had fallen in, some dining tables peeked out from under the rubble. As she approached the entrance to the atrium, she noticed a single hallway that ran left and right which spanned the entire building. Oddly enough, this part of the building seemed free of any debris. Dozens of rooms lined both sides of the hallway. Amber assumed most of the doors opened into patients' rooms. She wanted to imagine that at one point the patients found their living quarters quite comfortable, but it probably just served as a safe haven for them in comparison to the treatments they endured. She walked further into the atrium while noticing that the boys were heading down one of the hall.

She grew suspicious of them and said, "Wait, where are we headed exactly?"

Knowing she would be incredibly reluctant, Adam knew the truth needed to come out. He hesitantly said, "I'm not exactly sure, but the guys saw something really weird in one of the rooms down here. They think you might know what it is."

"I'm out!" she exclaimed, expecting to be the next victim of one of their twisted pranks. She turned to leave. However, an alarming sight immediately stopped her, one which apparently only she saw.

Standing outside the entrance, not ten feet from where she stood, was the most beautiful woman Amber had ever seen. She stood at least seven feet tall, and her slim figure seemed almost otherworldly. But her outfit reminded Amber a lot of what fairies in mythology wore, a floor-length, lilac-colored dress that was made of a flowing material, the straps of the dress hanging off her shoulders. Her straight, pale lavender hair cascaded over her shoulders like a cloud landing at her waist.

A simple circlet made of various leaves and plants sat on top of her head and a single flower petal dangled down her small forehead. Her eyes revealed her otherworldliness as they glowed the same color as her hair and dress—the iris and whites of her eyes included, her thin lips coated in a dark purple with faint lines of lavender coming down in stripes. Chills ran up and down Amber's spine as the figure turned and silently slid from view. Was it a demon? Not a chance, they looked nothing like this strange creature—well, those that she had heard of anyway. Its presence seemed out of place, completely disconnected from the building or surrounding areas.

Still nervous yet becoming a little braver, James said, "Are you coming or what?"

Amber blinked a few times, searching her mind for a logical explanation as to what she just saw. But nothing came up. The sinister figure stood in the doorway well in sight of the boys, yet only Amber saw her. Her strange feeling of fear quickly turned into dread. The character's appearance only meant to warn her, she just somehow knew it. Amber brought her attention back to the boys and followed them down the hallway to the mysterious room. When she entered, she looked around the empty room, wondering whether her "prank" theory was true. However, the boys' fearful expressions showed no signs of this possibility.

Feeling slightly awkward, Amber scanned the room again, then said, "Um, what am I supposed to be looking at?"

"That's what we wanted to know. We saw you here, but it wasn't actually you. You had creepy red eyes and fire flickered all around you. And...and you had a crazy golden beam of light coming from your hands. We're sorry, okay? We were jerks about the whole English paper thing, but was it really necessary to try and kill us?" exclaimed James in panic.

Surprised by his response, Amber stared at James in concern. She never heard him react that way or make a stupid accusation like that. The other two just stared at James. Jacob's expression seemed to agree with the comment while Adam put a hand to his forehead as he shook his head, his face growing red with even more embarrassment than before. Although frustrated and annoyed by James, Amber ignored him and pressed on with her investigation, walking toward the walls, scanning them for any clues. She put a hand on the cold cement, trying to feel for any unusual indentations. Still looking at the wall in front of her, she asked, rather annoyed, "What is it that you saw?"

"Something like that," whispered Jacob, fear shaking his voice.

A little alarmed by his response, Amber turned around. The cold immediately overwhelmed her at the unexpected sight of a strange young man. Well, it sort of looked like a man. He stood in the same place where the boys had seen Amber's Doppelgänger. In some ways, he looked very much like Amber, with the way he stood, his height, and even his facial structure. But with everything else, he looked the complete opposite. Instead of fire, he looked mostly like water, with his shirt flowing the way gentle ocean waves would. His black pants clung tightly to his legs, emphasizing his jersey and its various shades of blue. His short, blackish-blue hair spiked in the front, accenting his pale skin and bright blue eyes. The young man looked absolutely terrifying, and Amber thought that if she looked anything like him, it was no wonder James and Jacob ran away nearly hysterical!

Dark blue energy formed into a circle in the center of the man's hand and inched toward Amber. She yelled for the others to run as she made her way toward the door. The man let the boys leave the room, but as smoothly as his element, he made his way swiftly over to the door, stopping Amber from leaving. In a non-threatening way, the strange man held up his other hand, silently telling Amber to wait as he lifted his hand with the dark blue energy. It formed into a circle and the center became reflective. Amber stared into the mirror and stifled a scream as she saw exactly what the boys had seen only a day before: glowing red eyes, long blond hair, pale skin and even her veins, showing faint signs of red blood, not blue like a normal person would see. Flames licked her reflection's chest, not even burning the flesh.

Amber peeled her eyes from the horrific sight and returned her gaze to the man, who now stood mere inches from her, his blue veins quite distinct. Amber waited for him to kill her in a gruesome way, but he just disappeared without a trace. Suddenly, the barrier blocking the exit lifted back up toward the ceiling as if on rewind. Only Adam was waiting for Amber.

"Hurry up!" exclaimed Adam. He grabbed her arm and pulled her out of the room, practically dragging her out of the building itself.

The group ran out of the building, finally coming to rest at a massive maple tree, which stood tall in the center of Baker's Field.

"So, I take it you had nothing to do with that?" Jacob asked sarcastically in between gasps of breaths. Amber's sudden expression of disbelief just reiterated what he already knew. "Sorry, thought I'd just ask anyway."

"Who...who was that guy? He looked just the opposite of you...well, the freakish-looking you," said James, trying to find his words.

"Yeah, do you have another brother we don't know about?" asked Adam half-heartedly.

Amber shook her head as her eyes glanced back to the empty building and said, "Not to my knowledge."

"Amber, not to point fingers, but from what little I could tell, it doesn't seem like those things are after us...they're after you. Can you think of why that'd be?" asked Adam calmly.

She tried to think of anything in her life that would lead up to this, but nothing came to mind. Her life always seemed normal, almost dull at times. But if there was one thing that remained constant in her life, it was her mom's knowledge. She was practically a walking encyclopedia for Amber, no matter how weird the situation was. Amber nodded and replied, "Yeah, I think I know someone who can help. Come on, follow me!"

For the first fifteen minutes on their way back, the boys pelted Amber with questions. It wasn't necessarily that she ignored them, but rather she was lost in her own world—trying to sort out everything that happened. First, it began with the bizarre dreams of the glass-like creatures, then they stopped, and suddenly she sees a guy that could easily pass for her twin, showing her a different and scary version of her. Adding all that up just seemed more of a bad omen than anything else. Were the creatures threatening to kill her? Was that guy real or was he just an image merely meant to scare her away from something? Regret filled her mind as she reflected back to the day before when her mom inquired about the dreams. *I should have said something! How could I have been so stupid!* She scolded herself. Just as the boys' incessant questions finally started to annoy her, they came in view of her house. She almost turned around to tell them to stop talking when suddenly a strange muffled sound came from within the house.

Amber stopped and held up her hand, silencing the boys. As she slowly moved closer, trying to get an angle on what direction the sound came from, the boys followed closely behind. The sounds seemed to be coming from the living room. Amber heard Chris speaking to someone who talked in a very strange voice. When she neared the open window to the living room, she crouched down, then slowly rose just enough to get a view of the room. From the other edge of the window, the boys did the same. Amber's heart sank at the sight. Chris knelt on the ground holding Holly's limp figure in his arms while the woman from the asylum stood over them. Her aggressive demeanor seemed to suck the life out of Holly.

"What are you doing? This isn't like you!" exclaimed Chris.

Something else caught Amber's attention, not exactly in what he said, but rather the way he said it. Chris seemed to suddenly adopt a British accent. For the life of her, Amber didn't see how disguising his voice would help. But as Amber listened in more to the conversation, Chris sounded almost natural speaking in this way.

"This is madness! What does violence solve?" he continued.

The figure took a step forward and when she spoke, it sounded like she was speaking into a cold, empty cave. Her words and tone equally cruel, she said, "We are capable of many things. You apparently do not know us as well as you thought. The woman is expendable, she will only be a hindrance."

The next moment remained forever burned into Amber's memory. The woman reached out a white hand toward Holly. Dark purple, snakelike veins crept from her arm and slithered down her wrist. The veins climbed her long, bony fingers, finally reaching their destination. Her once plain nails became a dark purple. Within seconds, Chris pushed his mom aside as a purple beam of light shot from the villain's hand, inching its way toward Holly. With his two hands cupped together, a silvery beam shot from Chris' hands, intercepting the deadly beam. He held his focus for as long as he could, but a faded blue light wrapped around the purple beam, making it too powerful for Chris to handle. He collapsed as the purple beam struck Holly dead.

3

Before they saw what happened next, the brothers fled the scene. Adam grabbed Amber's wrist pulling her away, just as she saw Sphinx race to Holly's side and curl up next to her heart—an unusually loud purr emanated from the cat echoing in Amber's ears as she ran away. Shock paralyzed her. She had just witnessed her mother's murder, and Chris seemed to be involved with her murderers. Her world flipped upside down in a matter of moments, and nothing could reverse it. Silent tears streamed down her cheeks as the two kept running. Neither of them stopped until they reached an empty park where they caught up with the two brothers. All three boys collapsed underneath a tree on the leaf-strewn ground trying to catch their breath. Amber held onto the cold trunk for support. Her body refused to move, even her mind seemed paralyzed—as if her whole world was slowing down to a sickening crawl. Her body felt cold, and she wanted to scream and curl up in a fetal position. Her mind continuously replayed that dreadful scene of her mom's body lit up by a powerful death beam. And how did Chris gain these strange magical powers that he had managed to hide from her all her life?

The boys finally caught their breath and now muttered amongst themselves about what happened. None of them paid attention to Amber; they were too self-absorbed with how terrified they felt. After some time, Amber's senses returned, like a fog slowly sweeping away. She wanted answers, and only Chris had them. While the boys were still distracted, she tried quietly to slip away. Unfortunately, someone noticed her absence.

"Hey, you can't go back! What if that weird ice creature is still there?" called Adam.

Amber stopped and a look of confusion grew on her face as she turned and said, "What ice creature?"

James' voice shook as he exclaimed, wide-eyed, "How could you not see it? It had shards of ice poking out of its body, it floated in mid-air, and aside from its dark blue holes for eyes it had razor sharp teeth that looked like it would eat Chris!"

Amber's body became numb as her mind raced with many thoughts. It seemed quite clear to her that the figure was the one from her dreams, but gained the power to change appearance. A terrible thought suddenly crashed through her mind. *Could this being have more than one power?* She shook her head at the idea and focused on the task at hand. "We all got different looks at the thing."

Completely unconvinced, the boys just stared at her incredulously. They knew she saw something else, which only worried them more. Adam stood up and approached Amber. Unlike his companions, he had always admired Amber for her spunk and intelligence. Secretly, he always thought they could have been good friends if the circumstances were different. "Amber, are you sure you want to go back? You may not like what you find."

Amber heard the sincerity in his voice. She was surprised at his comment, since normally he hardly ever spoke. Of course, James usually spoke for the three of them. This unexpected situation changed all of their perspectives of the world around them. Whether it was permanent or not was an entirely different story—one which Amber didn't have time to read.

"I got a feeling there will be a lot of things I won't like, Adam. But this is reality, and not everyone is going to be happy," she said somberly.

Before Amber gave him a chance to respond, she turned away towards home—terrified the ice beings waited for her return. Despite the fact the park was less than a mile from the house, her walk home felt like an eternity. The fear and dread which blocked her mind just made everything worse. She wanted to ask Chris so many questions, but there was no guarantee he would be honest. As she turned the last corner, her house came into view, along with a police car parked by the sidewalk. An ambulance blocked the driveway. Her heart raced, and she shifted her gaze to the side not wanting to see anything. In fact, she longed to run back to the park and sink deep into her own mind. But soon she would have to face reality. She walked through the grass, avoiding the ambulance, the medics, and police officer who took notes. The medics stared at her—sympathy on their faces while the officer tried to avoid her sorrowful glance. Amber stopped as two paramedics carried a stretcher—a pure white cloth covering Holly's body. Hyperventilation soon set in as the tears started to flow. Another medic noticed Amber's trembling figure and gave her an apologetic look and continued walking toward the back of the ambulance.

Amber heard a sound coming from Chris' truck and turned her tear-stained face. Chris poked his head out of the window, calling to Amber to get in the vehicle. There was a mixture of emotions plastered on his face. His mind flowed with all possible ways of how to handle the situation. To him, Amber wouldn't know how to take the real story, at least not at this point. Amber rushed to the truck and jumped in. As usual, she expected to find comfort in his presence, but the atmosphere just felt tense. She knew what she had seen, and nothing could change that. Gulping down the bile that steadily rose, she asked with a shaky voice, "Chris, what happened?"

Chris backed out of the driveway to follow the ambulance to the hospital. His next words completely took her by surprise, "Mom...mom was murdered."

Honesty. The last thing Amber expected after what she had seen. Seeing an opening for the conversation, she gently pressed further, "I know, I saw. I just don't understand."

Chris briefly looked at Amber and then returned his attention to the ambulance that turned a sharp corner. He remained silent, trying to put his thoughts in order. There was so much he had to say and in such a short amount of time.

"There's more going on than just mom's death, isn't there?" Amber prodded.

"Yes," said Chris in the same British accent she briefly heard before, "yes, unfortunately, there is. And as much as I would love to tell you everything, I can't."

"Wait, freeze. You can't just leave me hanging like that!" Amber replied, becoming angry.

Despite her plea, Chris remained silent as they continued down the road. When they finally reached the hospital he put the truck in park and said, "I'll tell you everything I can. But first, you have to tell me everything about your dreams and anything else that might pertain to them."

It was as if he had a mom's mind, knowing everything Amber did or experienced without her needing to say a thing. She felt a little uncomfortable about spilling her secrets to Chris. Sure, they had a close relationship, but normally she confided in her mom about personal things. Hesitantly, Amber revealed the incident at the asylum and her dreams. With each word, Chris' face grew paler until it appeared no different than a fresh blanket of snow. He stared down at his dashboard as if it held the answers to how their conversation would turn out.

"Okay, I told you what I know, now spill," said Amber crossing her arms.

Chris now moved his attention toward the windshield, his mind seemingly anywhere but in the present. He slowly closed his eyes as he mysteriously said, "The stories are true, you know. Mom's fantasy stories about those worlds."

Although her mind spun with just this little bit of information, Amber continued to listen, remembering only a little of the bedtime fairytales. Chris now had her undivided attention as she replied, "Okay, I'm listening."

"The woman you saw is part of a group known by some as the Sidhe. Now, they are not the Sidhe of Irish folklore. I assume a superstitious Irish person must have seen them and mistaken them, this would have been before the Sidhe closed off the Portal that connected our worlds. That may have been how they got their name. But the ladies reside on a planet called Galaseya. There's three of them. Levendria, the woman you saw, she is in control of the land and waters. Vaeris is turquoise and is over the weather, and Analira is pale pink, and she watches over the animals. The Sidhe are powerful, yet good beings that...only want the best for humanity. They often communicate with me as they have taken a particular interest in our family. In certain cases where I am not with the family to deliver messages, they will do it themselves," Chris began.

"Okay, so they're real. Why would these creatures care about us humans?" Amber pointed out.

"It's complicated to explain right now." Chris said hesitantly. "As for our family, we have been helping them for generations."

"All right. Great—happy, strange aliens. What about the ice or glass creatures I keep seeing in my dreams?" she asked, making sure she had her facts straight.

"Yet another complicated explanation." Chris replied, "Just know that you don't want to mess with them."

"Chris, I heard you just before mom died. You say the Sidhe are good, yet they killed mom. Could those evil creatures have just portrayed themselves as the Sidhe?" Amber asked, reflecting back on what the boys saw.

"That's exactly what I've been thinking," said Chris, shaking his head as he started opening his door.

Feeling even more uncomfortable about bringing their recently deceased mother up, Amber asked carefully, "Speaking of...the incident. There's one more thing I don't get...where...where did your power come from?"

"Ah, that. I hoped you would overlook that slight issue," said Chris, absentmindedly closing the door again. "Of the stories mom told, that happens to be true. Our family has those supernatural powers, and all of us have something, different something we acquire when we turn sixteen."

"Um...*all* of us? You mean there's more than just you, me, and mom?" Amber asked, ignoring the last part of his explanation for the moment.

"Yes, but, that story is far too long to explain. Perhaps another time. Come on, we need to meet up with the coroner and make this look like an ordinary death. Let me do the talking," said Chris nervously.

Chris did the talking all right. In fact, he did more than that. If Amber didn't know any better, she would have instantly bought Chris' lie about his mom having a heart attack, as that's exactly how the coroner diagnosed her death. Amber felt like she was discovering a whole new side to her brother, but she wondered if this was something he grew up with before she was born.

He was only six years older than she was, but maybe he was dealing with this mess with the glass creatures longer than she thought.

Amber tried ignoring the conversations Chris had with the funeral director a few days later. It seemed like a waste of time, not that she didn't want to remember her mother's life, but given how much danger they were in, the funeral seemed almost too risky. She explained her concerns to Chris, who couldn't agree more, and if he had his way, he said, the funeral would be very quick with little effort, very much as Holly would have wanted. But a lot of people knew them and for them to do something callously would raise suspicion. Appearances were important, but to Amber that might soon be their downfall. Fortunately, Holly saved up for situations like this, so they didn't struggle to try to find money for the expenses.

But everything went by so fast that adjusting to the changes felt overwhelming. Amber often found herself sitting with Sphinx on the window seat in her bedroom. Most of the time, this took place at night when the stars hung high overhead. Several times she looked up at the sky, wondering if she could see any signs Galaseya was among the billions of small dots. But then she was reminded of what Chris said. As a child, the Sidhe placed a small block in her mind so she would see nothing of their world. According to him, this allowed Amber to live the normal life he and Holly wanted for her. Only once did Amber look down at her pale hands, wondering if they too, would emit a strange glow like her brother's. He didn't say anything about what her gift was, only because he wasn't sure.

Life finally calmed down a little after the funeral. Amber saw the boys earlier in the day after, but they paid no attention to her. She tried flashing a smile in their direction, but even Adam seemed too nervous to even acknowledge her existence. As far as Amber knew, the boys were still terrified about what they witnessed, as no rumors spread. To her surprise, some of James' bullying stopped. It was almost as if the creatures put his mind in a whole new perspective. Not that Amber wasn't happy about their change in behavior, but the way it happened seemed a bit too sudden. As Amber walked up the steps of her home she heard drawers slamming shut and different doors flying open, crashing against the wall. Either someone had broken into the house, or Chris was in a frenzy.

Hesitantly, Amber opened the door to find suitcases sitting by the door and half-filled boxes of her and Chris' belongings covering the floor. Sphinx already sat in his cat carrier evidently unamused by Chris running around him frantically. Amber blinked a few times, making sure the sight before her was real, then said to her brother, "Going somewhere?"

Chris nearly jumped out of his skin. His attention was so fixed on his task that he didn't hear the door opening. Without stopping he replied, "Yes, we're moving."

"Um, excuse me?" she questioned, unsure if she heard him right.

Chris put a framed picture into a box and turned toward her, "I said that we're moving."

Amber stared at Chris blankly, waiting for him to crack a smile–but no smile came. The seriousness in his expression startled Amber as she replied, "What happened?"

Chris replied grimly, "The Sidhe sent me a message today. Those creatures you've seen in your dream, they're coming for you."

"Why now? I mean they got mom a week ago, they could have gotten us both," she replied trying to sound brave.

"No, they needed to regain their strength. Killing mom took a lot out of them," he replied. "Their power is limited on any planet other than their own."

Amber let out a sigh and said with a hint of hopefulness in her voice, "Well, at least we know they have some kind of weakness."

"True, but the Sidhe have the same weakness. In fact, they have even lesser power on this planet. They cannot constantly protect us here. No, we must rely on our family to help. We have a safe house in a town called Ipswich, Massachusetts. It is a small location, and with enough family members, we just might be able to ward these things off," Chris explained.

"And if we can't?" Amber asked.

"We'll cross that path when we get there," he said, as his eyes nervously shifted back to the boxes.

Amber watched Chris return to the packing, his panic receding to a hastened pace. His mind seemed to be racing at a million miles per hour with worry and fear. He buried something else deep in the recesses of his mind, something he wanted to keep hidden forever. "Chris," she murmured, "They killed mom because she protected me, didn't they? Why? Why do they want me dead so badly? I didn't do anything to them!"

Chris dropped one of Holly's favorite vases and watched it shatter as its blue shape hit the tile floor. He hung his head and slowly turned toward Amber saying, "It's not what you did, Amber, it's what you were born to do."

"If I wanted a fortune cookie answer, I would have ordered Chinese. Be real with me!" she said sarcastically.

"I am, Amber. Their plan has been put into motion since...well for thousands of years. They were very close to completing it as well until you were born. I don't know much about them aside from their name, the Brothers. And according to the Sidhe, these creatures want to destroy humanity. Modern horror films can't even compare with how evil they are," said Chris with a hint of fear in his tone.

Silently, Chris ended the conversation right there as he began ordering Amber around, filling the bed of his truck with the boxes and suitcases. Against Chris' better judgment, Amber took Sphinx out of his carrier and insisted he ride in the front on her lap, as the carrier itself wouldn't fit with the two of them in the cab of the truck. Knowing the trip across the country would be uncomfortable as it was, he grudgingly allowed this exception.

The second the truck was packed, they set off on an unknown adventure. Amber wondered about the boys and if she'd ever see them again. In a way, they acted like a symbol of normalcy in her life. Not even three hours away, she already missed their taunting and to that extent, them, although, given the situation, if she and Chris stayed, James and his crew might be in the line of fire as well.

Then her mind drifted back to the Brothers. As far as she or anyone knew, she had no special ability, so how could she be the one to save humanity and stop their plans? This was the first thing she would ask her family when they got to their new location. She accepted the fact that her brother's secrets only meant to protect her, but those secrets could do more harm than good.

They drove for several more hours, and aside from Sphinx, silence was their only other passenger. This long trip required the occasional bathroom breaks and food stops, but all the while Amber and Chris's minds seemed stuck in their own separate worlds, trying to sort through the results their decisions would inevitably make. In the reflection of the window, Amber often saw Chris glance in her direction, seeming to want to start a casual conversation, but unsure how. Concern outlined his face, but so did fear.

Not able to stand the silence any longer, Amber pulled out her headphones and mp3 player, allowing the music to fill the void in her heart. She fixed her eyes on the side mirror as she watched the sun dip below the horizon—she could relate. Her life had taken an unexpected turn and plummeted as well. A single tear escaped her eye as she contemplated her life right now. Most sixteen-year-olds went through their high school years thinking the world revolved around them and that the weight of the world rested on their shoulders. In Amber's case, maybe that was true.

Soon she began seeing signs for the next state, Illinois. Amber had never left Wisconsin, so she wasn't sure what to expect. But a bright, blinding light was not the first thought on her mind. At first, it appeared as a speck, but as they sped closer, it took on an all too familiar form. Amber stared at the glass-like creatures—terror filling every part of her. Her scream of warning came almost too late. Chris slammed on the brakes as the pickup came screeching to an abrupt stop. Sphinx slid onto the floor and, in the most cat-like way, chewed Chris out for his terrible driving. But not even Amber paid attention to the cat. Her eyes were glued to the creatures who only stood a few feet from them. Their outstretched sharp bodies looked menacing, and their razor-sharp teeth looked ready to sink into their victims.

Amber almost forgot Chris sat next to her as he murmured, "So that's what they look like...That's what you've been seeing?"

She suddenly came out of her daze and stared at Chris, tears falling down her cheeks as she replied, "Yeah, that's them. What do we do? We can't exactly go around them!"

Chris' eyes darted to any possible area of escape, but the Brothers seemed to grow to such an extent that they took up nearly every inch of the road in front of them. He looked down at his dashboard and shook his head while deciding on the best course of action. Then his face lit up as a thought came to him, "I have an idea. Grab the cat and hang on. It's going to be a bumpy ride."

No sooner had he said that then their surrounding area, including the Brothers, disappeared into another ray of light. This time the light engulfed the truck, shaking it while the digital clock rapidly moved forward and the dials on the dashboard waved back and forth as if they were in the middle of the Bermuda Triangle. Amid the strange phenomenon, Amber looked over at Chris, and her jaw dropped. The light originated from him as his hair turned a silvery-white color, and through his half-closed eyelids Amber saw faint traces of opalescent eyes. He appeared strong, but based on his pained expression, Amber knew he was overexerting himself. Fortunately, the light began to fade, as did Chris' energy. She expected to see a clear view of the road ahead but instead found the truck parked in front of a tree. Amber opened her door and let Sphinx explore his new surroundings. But her eyes seemed glued to the sign before her which read, 'Welcome to Indiana!'

It took Amber only a moment to realize what just happened. Chris had somehow teleported them miles away from the danger. But he had also shielded Holly from The Brothers' attack. Did he have more than one power? She turned around with another question at the ready when her heart sank. Chris' body slumped over the steering wheel. She quickly grabbed Sphinx and gently plopped him down on the passenger seat as she slammed the door shut and ran to her brother's aid. Unresponsive, yet alive. That much she determined.

Amber turned the high beams on to get a better view of where they had landed. Tall trees surrounded them, and only a one lane road lay ahead. Amber thought their situation through. Chris was far from reckless and definitely wouldn't have done something that crazy if he thought they'd end up stranded. No. Beyond these woods there must be a town and where there's a town, there might be a hotel. All she needed to do was get behind the wheel and start driving. Fortunately, she recently got her license, so getting pulled over wouldn't be a concern, but the different area would prove to be an obstacle, as she had only driven in her town, mostly to run errands for her mom or brother. But desperate times called for particularly desperate measures.

Amber carefully pulled Chris off the steering wheel and

pushed him over toward the passenger side while Sphinx jumped up on the dashboard, staring curiously at Chris' unconscious figure. With her heart racing, Amber buckled her seatbelt and started the truck. Just as she turned onto the road, Amber caught a quick glimpse of Sphinx, who jumped back down onto the seat, curling up on Chris' chest, and began purring so loudly it nearly shook the truck seat. Amber knitted her brow in confusion. Why would Sphinx think purring would fix the situation?

With every car that passed them, Amber's heart skipped a beat. She didn't notice any signs of police, but with her luck, they'd be out prowling for speeders. Her theory of Chris landing near a town was proven right. Less than a mile from where they arrived sat a rather large town with restaurants, businesses, and to her relief—hotels. Some looked downright sketchy, but a few others appeared relatively decent. Amber chose the least noticable location and parked in front of the building.

Everything seemed laid out for her, but there was a catch. She was way too young to get a hotel room, to say nothing of her dragging her brother into the building looking like he had had too much to drink. She kept telling herself that Chris had a plan for all this. He was super smart and seemed to have dealt with sticky situations like this before. Amber got out of the truck and went around to get Chris out, with Sphinx trotting along beside her. She rolled her eyes and shook her head as she struggled to help her brother along the way. She and Chris might get a room, but Sphinx? Most hotels frowned upon animals.

Embarrassed, Amber stumbled into the hotel lobby as a few staff members came to her help. The man behind the front desk came around, and Amber waited for him to kick them out, but instead, he did the unexpected.

"Miss Oak, I presume?" he said kindly.

Amber blinked a few times, wondering if she heard him right, then out of the corner of her eye, she saw the staff take her brother into the elevator. She tried to play it cool when in reality her heart hammered in her chest. She smiled and said, "Yes, that's me."

"Perfect! We've been expecting you and your brother! Your room has already been paid in full," said the clerk.

"Right," said Amber, "but I'm afraid my cat is a bit attached to us and I know it's probably against policy..."

"Of course not! Don't you worry, your aunt already told me that your brother had a few too many drinks at his birthday party. I completely understand. As for your cat, your uncle also said that he is a service animal for you. Everything is fine, Miss Oak. If you would like, I can have one of my staff take any luggage to your room," said the man a little too enthusiastically.

Amber wanted more than anything to let out a bloodcurdling scream. Sure, she had a family in Ipswich, but they didn't know where they were, what hotel she'd choose or anything like that, to say nothing of the blatant 'No Pets Allowed' sign plastered on the sliding glass doors. She knew of only one explanation. The Sidhe. Their counterparts would only want her and Chris to keep running.

She swallowed back her panic as best she could and reacted as if this situation was routine. When the hotel staff brought up the last of their luggage, Amber waited until they were far enough down the hall before grabbing a pillow and screaming into it. Her screams turned into cries as her tears stained the pillow. She lifted her blotchy face as her brother lay on the bed, still out cold–Sphinx lay curled up by his side, purring loudly and staring at his mistress, slightly annoyed that her screams had disturbed his peace.

For the first time, she ignored her friend and went straight to the bathroom, hoping a long, hot shower might erase the memory of the terrible evening. Well, it did, sort of. Her tight muscles loosened, and the hotel soap made her skin feel smooth. Her soft pajamas made her feel a little more at home–that is, until she opened the door to find her brother sitting upright on the bed, flipping through channels on the TV.

"Chris!" she screamed.

"Shhh! Not so loud, my ears are still sensitive!" he whispered as he waved his hand at her, as if turning down her volume.

Amber nearly jumped halfway across the room and landed on the bed beside her brother, hugging him tightly. He let out a pained sound, and Amber released her grip as she said in a quieter voice, "What...what happened? I thought you were dead!"

"I suppose the Sidhe had other plans," he replied looking around the room, "I knew we were in for it when the Brothers appeared so I sent a telepathic message to the Sidhe in hopes they'd lend a hand. It seems they did far more than that."

"Okay, that answers one of my questions," said Amber, already piecing that mystery together, "what about your teleportation powers? I thought you had a shield ability or something."

"Actually, that was mom's power. Her shield is what kept you safe for the last fifteen years. That's why it took such a long time for the Brothers to find you. And believe me, they've been trying to find a way to get to you for years." Chris said reflectively, "No, my power is...complicated. The Sidhe gifted me with various abilities so that I could use them to protect you. Teleportation is one of them. But, as you can see, I'm not nearly as strong or practiced as I thought."

Noticing an inconsistency in his story, Amber pointed out, "Wait, you didn't know who these creatures were before I mentioned them."

Caught off guard, Chris' eyes shifted nervously away from his little sister as he replied, "To be honest, I have always known of them, although I haven't come face to face with them before. I hoped what you saw in your dreams was only a minor threat, but then the Sidhe confirmed my fears."

Amber knew Chris long enough to tell when he lied. This was one of those times, but from the sounds of it, he just didn't want to tell her the truth. Yes, it could have been handled better, but he only lied to protect her—that she respected. Amber brushed the annoying matter aside and brought the conversation back on track. "Well, no more teleporting. I can't lose you. We'll just have to hope the Sidhe can find a way to protect us the rest of the way. Deal?"

Chris smiled. He always thought it was cute when his little sister told him what to do. In ways, he also admired her stubbornness. He took Amber's hand and squeezed it reassuringly as he said, "Deal."

4

After a few hours of sleep, they left the hotel, grateful that no one batted an eye at their departure. To their relief, the rest of the journey went by smoothly. They didn't even get stopped for Chris' insane speeding. Even though they provided a distraction to the Brothers, the Sidhe were out there doing something to help Amber and Chris. Naturally, Amber wondered what they could be doing since their power was minimal on this planet, but considering nothing else went wrong, why question it?

As she looked out the windshield, the headlights shone on a small oncoming welcome sign—they now entered their new town. She knew that it would take some time to get used to it. She looked out on the area as they drove through quiet streets. The early morning darkness revealed little due to the absence of street lights. This didn't settle right, as she had just come from a city whose population was double in comparison. Once they passed the train station, they were almost immediately in the downtown part of Ipswich. With the morning sun now barely skimming the treetops, she caught glimpses of the shops and restaurants that lined both sides of the streets.

Chris noticed Amber's nervousness at her new surroundings. Trying to be supportive, he said, "It's going to be all right, Amber. The house is fantastic, and you will feel right at home."

Amber remained silent—she wasn't sold on his pitch. This place would never be home, only a constant reminder of the danger she and Chris were in. After driving down a few more roads, they passed the historic district of the town and soon slowed down to a small, well-paved driveway. From what little she saw of the house, it paled in comparison to their Victorian manor. The truck's high beams glared off the light-yellow clapboards. Chris parked the truck and turned it off, leaving his lights on to guide their way. Amber got out of the vehicle and Sphinx followed after her—he seemed satisfied with the new territory. Her brother jumped out of the truck and ran to the front steps. He unlocked the door and turned on the outside light. Amber shook her head at the situation—from here the adventure into the unknown continued.

Chris came out on the small front porch and said, "I know it's not home, but it's better than being constantly on the run, right?"

She just shook her head and replied, "Chris, our family isn't living with us, and who's to say the Brothers won't come and attack in the middle of the night?"

"There's no need to worry about that, there is massive protection around the house and property which will redirect the Brothers," he replied, looking around as the morning sun shone through the surrounding trees.

Her skepticism increased as she replied, "Okay, I may be safe here, but what about school? The town? I can't stay inside the house forever!"

"That's where our family comes in. They'll be with you," said Chris, "In this town, you have our grandfather on Mom's side who has an unusual ability that can be used as a weapon against the Brothers. We also have our grandfather on our dad's side whose ability is only useful in certain situations, but he is very nosy and intelligent. If something strange is going on in the town regarding the Brothers, he will know."

"Our dad? What can you tell me about him?" she asked eagerly, hoping Chris would open up more.

A smile flashed across his face as he replied, almost beaming at the thought, "I only knew our dad for a short period of time, but I can tell you that he is a wonderful man. He always wanted to see you grow up, but...situations rose where that was deemed impossible.

"Oh," she replied, now wondering what made him evade the question.

"Yeah, anyway, you won't have to worry about the family causing disruptions or anything. They agree it would be best for you to try and continue to have a normal life while you can," he said with a smile, avoiding the awkwardness.

"I can't see how that would be a distraction. Besides, I wouldn't mind bonding with my estranged family," she replied, appreciating his consideration.

"Amber, I know how important you are to the Sidhe and their planet, but you are first and foremost my sister. You never asked to be a hero, and I want you to enjoy your life and make decisions on your own without having any other influences on you," said Chris, with a hint of regret in his voice.

"But you said only I could save the Sidhe's planet," she replied confused.

"You are the only one, but you still have a choice, and no one can make it for you," he replied. "Whatever you choose I will always stand by you."

A sense of warmth filled Amber's body, and it had nothing to do with the sun shining on her. She was at a loss for words, as this was a side of Chris she had never seen before. A part of her wondered if he had always felt this way, and maybe their mother's death had given him more of an initiative to show this side of him.

As Amber took some boxes from the truck and brought them into the house, she felt as if she walked through a teleporter. The house, although quite small, had a setup similar to their home in Wisconsin. She poked her head into each room, confusion growing with every pause. She walked back to the entrance and carefully commented, "Why does this look...familiar?"

A ghost of a smile broke through on Chris' face as he said, "Mom knew that it'd be hard for you to move if the situation came up. So, she made it look as similar to our old house as possible."

With that, a thought immediately hit Amber. She ran up the narrow stairs and began looking inside the rooms. Chris followed after her, smiling. He found her standing in an open doorway as light from within a room shone on her emotionless face. Chris tried to understand what went through her mind, but to no avail. Coming up behind her, he looked in on the room. This was almost the exact replica of her old room. Of all the rooms in the house, it appeared the most like the Wisconsin home except for a soft looking window seat.

"Wow, that's...that's really cool!" she exclaimed, staring at her new window seat—the perfect view of the town partly covered by an evergreen tree.

She looked up at her brother and said, "All right, we can make this work."

Chris smiled as relief filled him. He watched Amber walk into her new room and sit down on the window seat. Sphinx ran in between Chris' feet into the room. He jumped up on the seat next to Amber and sat next to her, his bright blue eyes daring Chris to take his spot.

As he turned to leave, Chris mentioned, "I know it's cutting it rather close, but Monday is around the corner and that means so is school. You can start whenever you'd like. The principal is aware that you'll be attending, but I told her that I would call when you want to begin."

"I think Monday will be a good start," she replied with a smile.

Chris backed up to the door and said, "Okay, just take your time!"

Amber stared at him as he walked away. His receding footsteps faded as he went down the stairs. Surprised by his reaction, Amber slowly turned her head to the window. Chris always was a great person who helped anyone he could and respected even the most irrational people. But this behavior was strange even for him. It was one thing to want the best for her, but he was laying the kindness and patience on really thick. That could only mean one thing to her— whatever plans the Brothers had for her and the rest of humanity were beyond anything she could think of.

Chris continued his strange burst of generosity by bringing in the remaining boxes from the truck. By the time he brought up the last of Amber's things, Chris found Amber and Sphinx had transferred to the bed and fell fast asleep. As he looked at Amber, he silently hoped that her new school would be more welcoming to her.

The weekend proved to be quite a reprieve from the chaos of the last few days. For once in weeks, Amber found herself feeling rather peaceful in the hustle and bustle of the small historic town. She smiled as she walked the streets looking at all the shops, some closed for the weekend, while others welcomed the many tourists and locals with open doors. Smells of pizzerias and seafood restaurants hung in the air, beckoning her. Several of the local children wandered around on bikes and other various forms of fun transportation while others played on a rock covered hill in front of the town church, without a care in the world. A few times, she passed some elderly men that could easily pass for grandfathers, and she wondered whether they might just be part of her family. But due to their absent stares as she passed, their minds seemed to be on something other than looking out for a long-lost granddaughter. But if her family was anything like Chris, chances were that their eyes were watching her as she explored the town.

That Monday morning Amber woke up exhausted. She figured her journey throughout the town that weekend was a factor, but she felt mental rather than physical exhaustion, almost like the day before an arduous calculus test. She remained quiet when she went down the stairs so as to not raise concern. It was too early in the morning for any kind of panic.

"Hey, Amber! Ready for school?" asked Chris cheerfully.

Amber smiled faintly as he offered her a bagel. "I guess so?"

"Is something wrong?" Chris asked, hoping her response wouldn't be anything to worry about.

"I think so. I just feel drained, but mentally," Amber replied confusedly, "and before you ask, no, I didn't have any dreams last night."

"Well, I suppose that's a good thing. Your mind just might be wandering too much with everything that's going on. It's natural," Chris replied positively. "You should probably get going, or you might be late for school. If anything goes wrong, the family will be watching out for you. And as for money issues, you don't need to worry. Mom...saved up a lot of money so we should be okay. But I have to start looking for another job today just to keep up pretenses. You'll be okay."

Amber said goodbye to her brother as she walked out of the house with a bagel in her hand, feeling uncomfortable knowing someone would constantly be watching her.

She and Chris had passed the high school on their way to the house a few days prior, so Amber knew what direction to go. Her trek to school was not far or long, and in fact, Amber found it almost relaxing. She saw several old houses with wooden plaques, indicating how old they were and who once lived there. Amber admired the town's interest in maintaining its history. She breathed in a waft of the crisp fall air and along came a hint of something else—the ocean. Amid his many conversations, Chris told Amber that Ipswich sat on the coast of the state. She had never visited the ocean before, but had always wanted to see it and feel the warm sand slip between her toes. *Think I know where I'll be spending most of my time!* she thought with a smile.

Amber soon arrived at the high school and stared at the large complex which looked to be about the size of her old school. It wouldn't be hard for her to turn invisible—that was her only talent. Next to the building, she saw an empty field covered in early morning frost. As she walked toward the building, Amber hoped that no more troublesome boys would cross her path. She opened the heavy metal door of the entrance and walked in.

No one seemed to notice her. They seemed too wrapped up in their own conversations to notice the new girl. As usual, she kept her head down and only occasionally glanced up to see if anyone took notice. *All I have to do is make it to the school offices, and then I'll be in the clear*, she coached herself, her stomach doing flips with nervousness.

Amber glanced up one last time and immediately regretted it as she noticed an attractive young man watching her every move. He appeared to be around her age but was a few inches taller than she was. His short brown hair and ivory complexion made his piercing blue eyes stand out. He wore a black leather jacket and dark blue jeans. He leaned against the locker with his arms folded, trying to pull off a bad-boy look. His expression toward Amber wasn't of mockery or disgust, but more like curiosity—something Amber hardly ever saw in anyone who looked at her. She quickly averted her eyes, knowing the young man still stared at her.

She had almost taken a left down another hall when a creepy feeling came over her. She turned to the right and saw a group of jocks leaning against some lockers. One of them whistled at her, and they all began to check her out. Immediately repulsed by their actions, Amber tried not to say anything but kept going. They weren't going to let her go that easily, though.

One of the boys, who appeared to be the leader, had noticed Amber glancing at the young man leaning against the lockers and laughed. Now he stepped in front of Amber and condescendingly said, "Sweetheart, you want a real man."

Disgusted, Amber retorted, "Well, if I see one, I'll let you know."

The others in his crew mumbled under their breath, surprised the new girl had the audacity to say that to their leader. Amber, on the other hand, didn't care and proceeded to walk around the surprised jock. She quickly glanced at the mystery boy whom she had seen earlier. His position changed as well as his expression. His eyebrows rose in curiosity and a small smile formed on his lips, but no words came. He nodded his head in approval of her comment. Smoothly, he turned around and walked into the classroom right next to him. Somehow, Amber felt they would cross paths again. From her first impression of the students, the mystery boy seemed like the only person worth getting to know.

The rest of the day went by relatively quickly. The classes and teachers were just the same as her last school. But this kind of familiarity she was more than glad to welcome. The strangest part of the day was her classes, because it seemed that the mystery boy was in every single one. At first, she wondered if the boy was part of her family, but he barely looked old enough to be considered a high schooler. Amber merely brushed the idea off as a coincidence, but that didn't stop her heart from skipping a beat each time he glanced at her. However, that coincidental feeling left the minute school let out.

As soon as the last bell rang, Amber quickly shot out the door. She pulled out her headphones and mp3 player, trying to block out the surrounding sounds. While she walked along the sidewalk, a feeling of being followed suddenly overcame her. Instincts. That was the only word that fit her unexplainable feeling. Discreetly, she pulled her earbuds out and listened. She heard the wind whistling through the trees and leaves flittering along the cold ground. But, something else echoed in the wind—something different. At first, it sounded like shuffling behind her which then grew into soft footsteps. Someone really was following her. Adrenaline started pumping through her system as a terrible thought came to her mind. *Great, I'm going to get harassed the first day at a new school. Why did I have to tell that moron off?* She turned, ready to face the inevitable, but was surprised to see the mystery boy standing a few feet away.

Masking her confusion, she said rather coolly, "Can I help you?"

The young man gave a small smile, as if he liked the new girl's spunk. "No, but I may be able to help you."

Amber rolled her eyes and turned away, as she sensed no immediate threat. She couldn't tell if it was some cheesy pick-up line or if he was genuine. Either way, she needed to get home before Chris sent his own protective force after her. The last thing she wanted was for a seemingly innocent kid like him getting caught up in her family drama. She politely smiled and replied, "No offense, but I'm not in the mood for riddles."

The boy ran around Amber and stopped in front of her. "Look, I just wanted to tell you that I was impressed with how you handled Logan. Not many people have the guts to do that."

Amber looked into the boy's eyes and saw something strange. His facial expressions showed compassion and friendliness, but his eyes hid something. She shrugged as she replied, "Yay for me, now can I go?"

He chuckled a little at her stubbornness and said, "I think we got off on the wrong foot. My name's Hunter. What's yours?"

Not even remotely interested in the niceties, Amber thought about running back to the house and cuddling with Sphinx. At the same time, making two enemies in one day was not a record she wanted to break. "Amber."

"That's a great name. It suits you," replied Hunter with a kind smile.

"Um, thanks? I guess," said Amber walking around Hunter.

"For what it's worth, I'm glad you decided to come to Ipswich. This little town could use a bit more excitement," he called after her.

Amber stopped once more. Without turning around, she said solemnly, "It wasn't by choice."

"Things aren't always as they seem, especially in this town. Who knows, you may end up loving it here. If you ever want someone to show you the area, I'm just at the end of the street," said Hunter, his thumb pointing behind him.

Amber whirled around when she realized what he first said. This was the second time she heard that phrase, "Things aren't always as they seem." There was no way it could have been a coincidence. But what was its significance? Sure, she knew that nothing was ever as it appeared, but how could that be applied to almost every part of her life? She watched as Hunter walked farther and farther down the broken sidewalk, wondering whether or not he could be trusted.

The next few school days felt pretty mundane in comparison to what Amber had been through. The excitement of the move seemed to exhaust her from all normal activities. She occasionally greeted Hunter as they passed each other in the halls, but no conversation came from those moments. It made things pretty awkward, as they had every class together. Amber just kept her nose in the textbook or focused her attention on the teacher— whichever seemed more interesting at the time. She sometimes wondered if Hunter was waiting for her to start a conversation, but why? There had never been any need for her to converse with people before unless it involved some kind of argument.

The normality of the days started to grate on Amber's nerves. The reprieve felt wonderful, but then it just started to feel weird. It felt like the Brothers' invisible force loomed over her. Even her sleep remained dreamless, but her mornings left her exhausted—as if she ran a marathon throughout the night. She merely attributed that to all the stress from the last few weeks. Once the weekend finally came again, all those strange events came back to Amber in a massive wave.

Sunday afternoon Amber finally slept in without any interruptions. This came as a relief as the day before, she and Chris had spent most of the day touring the more historic parts of their new town. After getting ready and putting her cell phone in her back pocket, she made her way down the stairs where she heard Chris' muffled voice. Curious, she quieted her steps and listened in carefully. She saw him pacing in the living room with his cellphone to his ear. He seemed worried as his voice sounding pleading.

"We need to go home. It's not safe here anymore, the Brothers will only be held back for so long before they find a way to us," he said as he stopped to pull back the drawn curtain and peer out the window.

Amber heard some muttering coming from the other end of the phone, and the voice sounded male, but she couldn't make out any words. Chris interrupted the person as he said hurriedly, "No, I don't know what they're planning, but I'd rather not stay around to find out. Please, she'd be safer in Galaseya."

The voice on the other end responded, as Chris' pace quickened with every second. His brow furrowed as his expression grew serious. When he spoke, his tone flat, "What do you mean, what's wrong?"

Amber continued watching her brother go from determined to despair in a matter of seconds as he moved away from the window and plopped down on the couch. With his phone to his ear and his other arm resting on his knee cradling his head, he asked "How is this possible? We...I thought we got rid of her years ago!"

Got rid of her? What kind of a family am I in? thought Amber as she adjusted her position. She waited for Chris' back to turn before dashing toward the front door. Hoping to make more sense of the conversation, she stayed a while longer waiting for Chris to speak.

"Well, this changes things," continued Chris, trying to stifle his growing frustration, "Amber will eventually have to return home and probably sooner than we expected. Please, dad, you must do something. I don't want her coming home to a bloodbath."

Amber didn't stay long enough to hear the end of their conversation. Quietly, she opened the front door and slipped out into the cold afternoon. She ran away from the house as fast as she could. By the time Amber reached the end of the road, her mind immediately went to Hunter. He was the only person she knew that seemed normal— whatever that meant.

Amber nervously walked up the driveway of the last house on the street. With no words to say, she started up the narrow walkway. She needed someone to talk to and right now almost anyone would do. But after she knocked on the door, a tall, pencil-thin man opened the door. He appeared to be in his forties, and wisps of his short black hair blew in the mild breeze—small traces of gray hair barely skimmed his ears. But his strange, muddy green eyes made him appear crazy. As the tall man looked at her, she felt his eyes bore into her soul. This created a feeling that sent terrible shivers up her spine. The corners of the man's lips turned up as he called back into the house, "Hunter! Your girlfriend's here!"

Amber's cheeks flushed red as a sound of shattering glass came from within the house. Hunter quickly came to the door and shook his head. "Amber's not my girlfriend, Uncle Mason."

"Ah! So you're the Amber that my nephew hasn't stopped talking about. Well, I can see why," said Uncle Mason, still looking into Amber's eyes.

The redness in Amber's cheeks expanded to her entire face. She looked away from him and towards the ground. This kind of embarrassment never existed in her experience. Hunter noticed the awkwardness and quickly said, "Well, thanks for your input, Uncle Mason. I think I can take it from here!"

Mason glanced from Amber back to Hunter and gave him a knowing look—like a silent inside joke between the two of them. He shrugged his narrow shoulders and replied, turning back into the house, "Okay, don't do anything too crazy without me!"

After he had shut the door, Amber turned to Hunter and said, "Well, he's bold."

"You have no idea," Hunter replied looking slightly embarrassed. "So, what brought you to this end of the street?"

Amber's face returned to normal but gradually became pale. She didn't know how to tell Hunter what she just witnessed. In fact, expecting him to understand, or for that matter believe her, just seemed like too much of a big request. Choosing her words carefully she replied, "It's...just been a rough start. My brother and I are still trying to get our bearings in this new town, and there's just a lot going on in my life that I'm not sure about yet."

"Wait, you're living with just your brother? I was told a full family had moved in," said Hunter seriously.

Amber started walking toward the street as Hunter followed, "We once were...before my mom died about three weeks ago."

"Amber...I'm so sorry! I had no idea. What about your dad?" Hunter asked as he began walking closer to her.

The physical closeness didn't bother Amber as much as did his question. Dad. The name itself sounded so foreign to her, but based on the conversation she overheard, he would be coming up in future topics with Chris. Avoiding eye contact, Amber simply shrugged her shoulders and replied, "I never knew him."

"Oh, I'm sorry to hear that. I never really knew my parents either. I always considered Uncle Mason as a father figure. He was always the one to take care of me. My family's kind of messed up," he replied shyly.

Amber snickered and replied, "Aren't all families to some extent?"

"True," he replied kicking a branch out of their path, "But I've tried not to let my family's history define who I am. That's how I keep on with life. I'm my own person."

"Yeah, that's what I thought at first too, but unfortunately my family got involved in something, and I have to clean up their mess," said Amber, realizing she said more than intended.

Hunter nodded as he shoved his hands in his pockets and said, "Oh, I know that feeling all too well. I've been cleaning up my family's mistakes for years. I don't know what's going on with your family, but just remember, you do have a choice in the matter."

"Funny, that's what my brother says, but it doesn't feel that way," she replied as they neared the main part of town. Suddenly, Amber's phone went off before Hunter could say anymore. Amber took a quick look at her messages and saw that Chris was texting her, wondering where she was. A wry smile crossed her face as she held up her phone saying, "Reality texted, I gotta get home. Thanks for the talk, maybe we can do this again sometime?"

Hunter nodded his head, looking disappointed that their conversation had to end so soon. He watched as Amber started down the sidewalk and said, "That'd be great. I may not understand what you're going through, but just know that I'd like to be friends. If I can help in any way, you know where to find me."

5

Two weeks passed since meeting Hunter and his uncle. Within those weeks, Amber and Hunter's friendship grew. Chris didn't seem to mind too much about their hanging out as he reminded Amber that her invisible bodyguards were always just out of sight. He even occasionally asked about Hunter. But all the conversations she had with Hunter didn't consist of too much. They mostly spent their time studying or just talking about family life, that is, the parts they felt comfortable talking about. The only thing that Amber kept to herself were the energy draining dreams that haunted her every night. Unlike those from a month ago, these current ones held many differences. With beautiful green fields and clean forests with soft, friendly looking animals, these felt pleasant. They were the only elements that resembled her old dreams. Exhaustion wouldn't nearly be an issue if her dreams remained in one location rather than several. But these were just dreams and it confused her as to why they put her mind and body through such physical stress.

She tried brushing the exhaustion off every time she saw Hunter, but he could clearly see through her guise. To Amber's relief, he never pointed it out, but rather spoke about something else. She really enjoyed getting to know this young man. She noticed a lot of similar characteristics between them like in the way they laughed or even said something. To her, it was the mark of close friends. It made her feel warm and comfortable inside knowing that Hunter saw her the exact same way. Although, telling him about the dreams needed to wait a little longer. Their friendship was still young and he was too normal to understand.

A few days before the school held its big Halloween Bash, Amber walked into the school with all intentions of ignoring the signs for the upcoming events. Amber wasn't at all interested in joining in on the festivities despite her brother's complaints. He continuously told her how the Bash provided another way for her to forget the craziness of the family and enjoy life. Large gatherings were never really her thing, but she did enjoy looking at all the decorations. Cobwebs hung from the ceiling with fake hairy spiders glued to them. Some of the classrooms sported fake blood on the windows. Amber reminisced on how her old school set up the same things during this time of the year. As she walked down the hall toward her first class, she smiled at some of the other decorations. When she turned into her history classroom, however, she sensed an immediate change. Normally, her teacher waited to greet her, but no one stood behind the desk. Usually, this time before class gave Amber a chance to talk to the teacher about her passion for history without the other kids scoffing. She sat down in her seat as Hunter came in.

He smiled and slid into a seat next to her, striking up a friendly conversation. "Hey! Ready for the Bash?"

Amber rolled her eyes as a smile escaped her lips. She shyly replied, "I wasn't planning on going to that. I didn't know you were interested."

"Oh yeah! Everyone goes to the Halloween Bash, or they go to the local cemeteries and scare the kids," he replied.

"Sounds like fun?" she replied sounding uninterested. "It wouldn't matter if I went anyway. I don't have a costume."

"Huh! How about, after school, we go downtown and look for one?" he suggested encouragingly.

"That'll definitely make Chris happy. He's been nagging at me to go," she replied, slightly bitter.

"Hey, even more of a reason to go," Hunter said with a smile.

Just as Amber was about to reply, the bell rang. Moments later, a young man came in. He wore a green vest and long-sleeved white shirt—the ensemble accenting his red hair and dark brown eyes. He was about Amber's height, and he seemed to be excited about the subject he was about to teach.

"Hello, everyone! I apologize for being late. Your teacher Mrs. Brown is sick, so I'll be taking over for her until she is better," the teacher said with a surge of enthusiasm. "I'm Mr. Pryce."

Amber stared at the young man, her eyes immediately drawn to the scar going from the top left corner of his lips diagonally to the bottom right. Aside from this prominent mark, he appeared old enough to still be in college, yet his eyes told her a different story. When he began talking and explaining different timelines of history, Amber saw that he really knew his stuff. Although he seemed like a nice person, she felt slightly uncomfortable with him for some reason. Something inside told her that he would be here permanently. When the bell rang, signaling the end of the class, Mr. Pryce was cut off mid-sentence. He told the students that they would pick up the lecture the next day.

Just as Amber and Hunter were about to leave, Mr. Pryce asked for Hunter to stay back for a minute. Amber looked at the teacher and then to Hunter in confusion. With a kind and reassuring smile, Hunter nodded his head toward Amber. She shrugged her shoulders and walked out of the room. Feeling a strange need to hear the conversation, Amber hid behind the lockers.

"Has she said anything to you?" asked Mr. Pryce, his voice breaking into a quiet British accent.

"No, but I know there is something she hasn't told me," replied Hunter, his voice equally changing.

Mr. Pryce breathed a sigh of frustration but said, "Things are not well back home. I am afraid she will return to see much fighting, and I am not referring to the family. Something strange is occurring within the royal court."

"That is what I have heard as well. It is my belief that only Ameliana can resolve that conflict," said Hunter with assurance.

"Kaleya has eyes and ears all over the land. There is not one thing she is not aware of. I fear if a new element were to be added it may cause suspicion. You have been gone for far too long, Huntinylar," said Mr. Pryce, his voice growing colder.

Amber froze as Hunter's footsteps approached the door. Mr. Pryce called to him, "We must discover her power. Only then can we see if she will be of help to Galaseya."

Amber dashed into a girls' restroom across the hall as Hunter came out of the room, obviously agitated by the news. Her heart raced as the conversation left an imprint on her mind. Their familiar accents seemed similar, but Mr. Pryce's sounded more formal. Along with their cryptic words it reminded Amber of Chris' phone call. A connection existed after all. Maybe somehow Hunter and Mr. Pryce were part of the "family" that decided to come here for extra support. Even though a few pieces of the puzzle were finally coming together, the conversation just left her with more questions. After regaining her composure, Amber opened the girls' room door and entered into the eerily empty hall. She ignored the strange, partially lit area and walked down the hall and to her next class, hoping that the bizarre conversation wouldn't repeat.

Fortunately, no conflicts or awkward confrontations developed. Hunter just acted as if nothing even happened. Not wanting to question the break from the weird aspects of her life, she left the matter alone. Looking for a Halloween costume made the afternoon much more enjoyable than sitting at home. It seemed as if they stopped at every single store in town, but no outfit seemed her style. She decided to give up on the whole idea and try to dig through her closet to see what she could throw together. Hunter insisted they still had several more stores to visit, but she rapidly lost interest in the whole idea. Eventually, Hunter gave up on convincing her to stay and walked her back to her house.

When they arrived, Amber said goodbye to Hunter, promising she would still go to the Bash with him. He smiled at that as he walked away, saying he needed to find a costume himself.

"Hey, what's with the long face?" asked Chris as Amber came into the house.

"Believe it or not, Hunter convinced me to go to the Halloween Bash. But I don't have a costume, and I couldn't find one in town. I told him I'd come anyway, but maybe it's a sign that I shouldn't go or something," she replied slightly glum.

"Is that the only reason? Amber, you got loads of clothes. Why not put on that black dress you have collecting dust? With that and maybe a hat or fake blood, you could pull off a witch or vampire," he replied positively.

Amber shrugged, not entirely sold on the idea, but the Bash was in a few days, and if she wanted to look halfway decent she needed to start putting the outfit together now. After dinner that night, she holed up in her room and pulled out every article of clothing she owned. Buried in piles of clothes, Amber looked at her options, none of which seemed all that great. She was never one to be a designer of any kind.

Moments like this made her miss her mom. Holly always had a creative eye and came up with solutions to any fashion disaster. Thinking about her mom gave Amber an idea. She headed out of her room, remembering that Chris had kept many of his mother's possessions, stored them in boxes up in the attic. However, he kept more than just old clothes, which made it much harder for Amber to sift through everything. When she found the right box, one of the first things she pulled out was the most beautiful medieval style gown she had ever seen. A small train spread across the floor in the back of the green floor length dress. Gold thread accented the green, and sparkly, swirled gold embellishments reflected on the ivory undercoat, which showed through a V in the front of the dress. Long sleeves gracefully draped at the wrists. The gown was made of a velvet-like material. Amber held the dress and sized it up to her body. Aside from the sweetheart neckline, Amber really loved the dress. After hastily cleaning up the attic, Amber went down to her room and put the dress on.

Knowing exactly where Chris would be, she walked down the stairs, careful not to trip over the long dress. She turned the corner into the living room and saw him reading the paper. He nearly dropped it when he saw her.

"Where...where did you find that?" he asked in surprise.

"I...I found it in the attic with a bunch of mom's stuff," she replied, nervous that she was in trouble.

"I forgot about that dress. That would be perfect for the Halloween Bash!" he replied, standing up to get a better look at the outfit.

"Why did she have it? Did she go to Renaissance fairs or something?" asked Amber, still confused about the origin of the gorgeous gown.

"Not exactly, we used to live in a place where this type of wardrobe was...predominant," said Chris, careful with his word choice.

"That place wouldn't happen to be Galaseya, would it?" asked Amber hoping he'd be open with her.

Chris let out a sigh and replied, "So you heard?"

Amber nodded feeling slightly awkward and replied, "What's going on, it sounds like our family's in danger. Maybe we can help?"

"Unfortunately, I don't know how we can help. It isn't a familial matter but rather a civil one. We try to stay out of...political issues, we have enough of our own," he explained.

The conversation took a serious turn, more than Amber was comfortable with, so she ended it on a positive note by saying, "Well maybe one day we can return. I for one would like to know where I come from."

"Perhaps, but for now, you have a Bash to get ready for. The dress is all yours!" he replied with a smile.

The next few days dragged on for Amber. Part of this was due to nervousness about the party and the other part came from excitement she had never felt before. Hunter often asked her what her costume looked like, but she kept it a secret. It was a bit of fun on her part, but she also had butterflies in her stomach any time he asked. If he really was from Galaseya as she suspected, he might be part of the problem they were having. After all, Chris never mentioned royalty or anything. Who's to say the conversations she overheard involved the same problem? Naturally, Chris didn't go into detail about the subject of the phone call, but at least he knew she had some knowledge about a problem. When the time came for the costume reveal, Amber knew something would happen at the Bash, whether a conversation or more secrets that would come to light. Chris mistook her nerves for excitement, as he could have sworn she downed a pot of coffee earlier in the day.

"Amber, relax, it's just a party! You'll have plenty more in the future!" he laughed, shaking his head at his bouncy little sister.

"Chris, I'm starting to second guess this whole idea," she said looking in the mirror at her ensemble.

"What's wrong? You'll be safe, I mean the family is always nearby, the Brothers can't get to you," he replied, trying to sort out her words.

"That's what I mean. I've heard weird things lately, other than the call you had with our dad. I heard Hunter talking with a new music teacher about some woman wreaking havoc in Galaseya. I just wasn't sure if that had any connection to what you heard," she replied, as her words came out like a flood.

Chris looked at Amber. The blood drained from his face and his expression reminded Amber of a deer in headlights. The room grew so silent that for a moment Amber thought she heard his heart racing. Chris closed his eyes as if in defeat and replied, "Amber, I promise to tell you everything you want to know. But right now, just please, go and enjoy yourself while you can."

"While I can? What...what's that supposed to mean?" she asked as Chris began ushering her out the door.

Chris didn't respond, since Hunter stood right outside on the front porch. Again, all went silent, aside from the chilly October wind that blew through the trees, creating an eerie rattle as it brushed against the dead hanging leaves. Hunter stared at Amber in amazement. His eyes shifted to a tiara that sat in front of her bun, which was neatly arranged at the top of her head, small green jeweled clips adding a touch of royalty to it. The elegant gold earrings and matching necklace were the perfect touches to her ensemble. Her make-up only accented her true beauty. For his part, Amber noticed Hunter dressed up in a similar style to hers. He looked like a prince that stepped out from a fairytale. It made Amber smile a little, seeing how they both had a similar idea for a costume. The only difference was that his ensemble was a dark royal blue. It accented his eyes, making them brighter than usual.

"You...you look amazing," said Hunter, nearly at a loss for words.

As she walked down the road, she held her head up high, trying to practice her "princess walk." But when she entered through the gym doors, all of that confidence disappeared. Loud music filled the room, and so many unique costumes packed the room. Some appeared handmade, whereas others looked as if they came from high-end businesses. It was the easiest way to spot the rich kids. Regardless of their outfits, they all seemed to be having a great time. Some laughed and danced underneath the cliché disco ball—which threw ominous shadows on the already spooky decorations scattered around the room.

But then others stared at the dancers, completely uninterested in making a fool of themselves on the dance floor. Many people stood on the sides of the gym, busily engrossed in their own conversations. Amber suspected most of those conversations consisted of idle gossip. From the way things looked, it seemed more of a social gathering.

As Amber walked around the outer edges of the room, she noticed a few teachers acting as chaperones. One teacher was dressed up as Abraham Lincoln—hat and all! Amber took a closer look at the person as he greeted her in passing. She almost released a huge laugh when she realized it was Mr. Pryce. *Well, at least he's dedicated!* she thought as she chuckled to herself. The other teachers seemed to be dressed up in the generic Halloween costumes, although not a whole lot of effort went into them.

Once she finished looking at the teachers, her eyes wandered off towards a darker section of the gym where she noticed two figures deep in conversation. She moved closer toward the dessert table, trying to conceal herself. Squinting, she saw Hunter and Mason. *Why is Mason here?* she thought, disregarding the fact she could swear that Hunter stood right beside her this entire time. Seeing them act this way concerned her, as it was the first time Hunter ever publicly displayed any form of secrecy. However, given how many bad things came from eavesdropping on conversations, Amber tried to ignore the situation and move her attention onto something more pleasant.

Mason caught her eye in mid-sentence and quickly put on a front, pretending their conversation consisted of lighthearted talk of the Bash. Hunter immediately noticed his change in demeanor and saw Amber as well. His face seemed to light up. As he jogged over to Amber, dodging groups of chattering people, Mason slowly came out from the shadows. He was dressed up as Dracula. In ways, Amber saw that this costume fit him well. Although she found it difficult seeing Mason as a chaperone, she figured the school needed more seeing how many students showed up.

"So, what do you want to do first?" Hunter asked.

Amber shrugged her shoulders, "I don't know. I usually just watch people at big events. I've never been one to actually get in the middle of things."

"Well, no time like the present, right?" he said urging her into the crowd.

Although the festivities were great and Amber enjoyed many of the games and some dancing, she still watched Mason out of the corner of her eye. Unlike the other chaperones, who fully immersed themselves in the night's events, Mason continuously stayed in the shadows for some reason, just barely in view. He seemed to be taking a leaf from Amber's old book, to get as far from attention as possible. Soon, however, Amber grew tired of all the activities. She walked back to the dessert table, concealing her mildly shaking hands.

Realizing she left, Hunter quickly followed after her. "Are you okay?"

"Absolutely, I'm just a little tired," she replied, brushing off the lightheadedness that was slowly increasing.

Hunter didn't look convinced, but let the matter drop as Amber suddenly wrapped her arms around him in a hug, "You were right! This Bash is really amazing!"

The moment Hunter returned the hug, Amber's lightheadedness dramatically worsened. The room began to spin as something warm and sticky dripped from her nose. She backed away from Hunter while her hands rested on his shoulders for support.

"Amber, your nose..." he said, startled.

She lifted her manicured hand and saw small traces of blood. The room began to spin more when Hunter gently took her forearms to steady her. But, that wasn't enough. Her legs crumpled from underneath her weight and her hands slid down to his arms, trying to grab for more support, but her body resisted. As she fell to the ground, Hunter quickly wrapped an arm around her waist and held her free hand, gently leading her down as if dipping her in a slow waltz.

Within moments, a bright golden light filled her vision. Slowly, it faded away as a beautiful wooded scene replaced it. The area reminded Amber of the land in her dreams. The vision narrowed in on to two people. The first person looked exactly like Hunter and the other a beautiful blond woman who wore the exact same gown as Amber's. Amber peered into the vision closer, only to find that the woman was a younger version of her mom! The next moment sent Amber through a few loops as her mom and Hunter hugged like longtime friends. Their conversation, however, came across far more disturbing to Amber.

"We should not be here. What if they find us?" exclaimed Hunter with that familiar British accent, his eyes darting to every tree.

"The Brothers will not be a problem at the moment," said Holly with a gentle flowing accent. "Besides, I did not want to alarm the others."

"Speak quickly then, I fear they are not far behind," he replied with his eyes returning to the trees.

Holly couldn't speak. She merely began to cry as she looked down at her stomach. Hunter knew immediately what that meant, and his heart sank, "You are with child again?"

Holly lifted her head as tears streamed down her cheeks, "Yes! I am absolutely thrilled to have another child. However, the Sidhe say she is the one who can restore the Balance!"

Hunter's eyes drifted toward Holly's stomach. His initial excitement quickly vanished. "Remember what they did with your last child? Are you not afraid that it may happen again?"

"That is what I wanted to speak with you about. The Sidhe say that Christolar is to be her guardian and lead her to her destiny. I believe they are right but despite the fact they...chose him for this task, the Brothers are far too powerful. Christolar will need help," she said, babbling on.

"Holisiana, you know our family is not entirely happy with the Oaks. I will be there to help you protect your child, but I cannot say the same for the others," he replied taking her shaking hands.

"Perhaps one day they will. I cannot explain my feeling, but I believe this child will bring our families together," she replied.

"You ought to tell the others about your child sooner rather than later. The Sidhe may have a plan as to how to keep her safe from the Brothers until she is ready to fulfill her destiny," said Hunter kindly.

"Do not worry, Father, I intend to tell everyone shortly. However, I needed to have this conversation with you first," said Holly with a smile. "Thank you for listening."

Hunter and her mother hugged one last time before the vision faded out. Amber woke up, lying on a thin piece of cold metal. *Why am I on the playing field?* she asked herself, realizing she lay on the bleachers. As her eyes adjusted to the lighting, she focused in on Hunter's face. The track lights cast harsh shadows on his facial features, making him look more worried. Nothing about him changed from the vision she just witnessed. In fact, his wardrobe looked almost exactly the same. With a heavy head, she slowly rose to a sitting position.

"Amber, are you all right?" asked Hunter, gently helping her up.

Amber stared into his eyes, the eyes she thought she once knew. Somehow one vision managed to turn her world upside down again. How could it not be true? Even with her creative mind, it was impossible to conjure up something so insane. For now, she took the vision at face value until something else came to prove it wrong. Now, if the vision was true, then how could that have possibly happened? Judging by his appearance, Hunter and Amber looked about the same age, and he seemed so normal! These thoughts and so many more came in tsunami-like waves and crashed along the walls of her mind with a mighty force.

Shoving them to the back of her mind, she crafted her words carefully, hoping to get to the heart of the matter: "Grandfather, huh?"

"I told you we had a messed-up family," he replied in his accent.

As Hunter helped Amber off the bleachers, Amber noticed a few other figures on the field. Chris, Mr. Pryce, and Mason stood near the bleachers, all seemingly prepared for this moment. An awkward silence fell over the field as they stared at Amber, waiting for her to say something to explain how she knew about Hunter's true identity.

But instead, she replied, "Okay, someone start talking. And I want the truth—all of it!"

The men exchanged nervous glances before Chris finally spoke up and said, "I really am your brother, and Mr. Pryce here is our grandfather, on our father's side."

"It is a pleasure to finally meet you, Ameliana, my name is Jermiar," Mr. Pryce replied formally.

That was the one thing that Amber noticed about these people. All had the same British accent, but some spoke more formally than others. Amber just assumed the more formal ones had just come to the area.

"Okay, and Hunter is my...grandfather on mom's side. What's your deal?" Amber asked, turning to Mason.

"Well, I'm not your brother, you don't need to worry about that. I'm your great-grandfather; Hunter's grandfather," he replied casually.

"Great, extreme longevity, so far I'm following. Now, what's this about some woman taking over Galaseya? And seriously, don't be surprised I overheard," said Amber noticing their expressions of surprise.

Eyes shifted to Jermiar, who had only recently arrived in Ipswich. He didn't seem excited about revealing everything to Amber, but he knew his back was against a wall. He shook his head and calmly replied, "Galaseya is ruled by a monarchy, and it has been since the beginning. The queen is gravely ill, and her daughter will soon take her place. However, there is much concern growing throughout the land about another woman, Kaleya, whose only desire is to rule Galaseya as she sees fit. Naturally, we have done everything we can to ensure Princess Renalia's safety, but I fear that that may not be enough. Although Kaleya is not related to the royal court, she has a tight grasp on many of the more naïve Galaseyans, who believe she will make their lives easier."

"Wow," said Amber absorbing all the information. "Well, what am I supposed to do? I mean, that is what most of your conversations consist of. Me stopping this Kaleya person."

"She's destroying the Balance or at least part of it. Your destiny is to save the Balance and restore it. Stopping her is only the beginning," said Chris.

"Then why haven't we already gone to Galaseya to fix this?" asked Amber.

"The other members of our family believed they could contain the situation, but as I suspected, Kaleya has grown far too powerful and quicker than we anticipated," said Jermiar.

"But..." started Amber.

Mason interrupted, "I think that's enough questions for now, don't you? Why don't you tell us how you knew Hunter was your grandfather?"

Amber could see that Mason was not one to argue with. He may not be able to read her mind, but he certainly noticed things others passed up. Put on the spot, Amber felt slightly annoyed rather than nervous. Dozens of other questions weighed her down, and here she was having to explain something that was probably not a big deal. Amber shrugged as Mason continued to stare at her and replied, "It was a vision. I saw mom talking to Hunter about me when she just found out she was pregnant with me. But I mean, come on, that's got to be a normal thing in our family."

Again, they all looked at each other, but this time smiles broke out on their faces. Chris looked at Amber and said, "No, none of us has visions. I think you've found your gift!"

"How can seeing visions of the past help restore this Balance?" asked Amber doubtfully.

"Because you will be able to see things that we cannot," said Jermiar.

Amber knew from the start of this craziness that she would eventually have to come to terms with her destiny, but this? This just seemed too much. Overthrowing a woman that even her powerful and older family members couldn't handle? Visions were just that—visions. In her opinion, this woman wasn't even part of the family, so Amber didn't feel it was necessary to intervene. Yet again, hidden within the explanation lay a deeper meaning. Somehow her family involved themselves with the monarchy of this mysterious place, and somehow Amber felt the Sidhe weren't far behind.

"What if I don't want to?" she asked after a few minutes of uncomfortable silence. "After all, you did say I had a choice, and you'd respect it, right, Chris?"

He silently nodded, secretly regretting his previous comment. Jermiar spoke up and replied for him, "I understand your hesitation, but lives are at stake, and this woman must not come into power. I do not believe you realize the danger we are all in."

"You're right, I don't. So why don't you explain to me why some woman is so important to our family—someone who isn't even related to us! What hold does our family really have on some far-off planet that I'm sure no one has ever even heard of?"

Jermiar grew annoyed with the challenge. He didn't know Amber as well as the others and condescendingly thought she would comply with the situation and immediately go back to Galaseya, but her questions had him cornered. He heaved a sigh of frustration and replied sternly, "It is more than just some *planet*. Our family once ruled Galaseya centuries ago, but due to our longevity, we had to remove ourselves from power as we did not wish to arouse the suspicions of the citizens. You must understand. We cannot just leave Galaseya to be ruined by Kaleya."

"Deep roots or not, I'm not helping anyone, let alone a family who have hidden away my entire life all because they were afraid of the Brothers," Amber said, watching as her family members' eyes grew wide with surprise. "Don't get me wrong. I'm glad to find out I have some huge superpower family somewhere out there, but I never signed up for being the hero you claim I am. I've always been normal. And honestly, I prefer to stay that way."

"Please, see reason..." began Jermiar.

Ignoring his plea, Amber turned to Chris and said, "I'm partied out, Chris, I'm going home."

6

After the Bash, Chris stopped asking Amber about going to Galaseya. She had made it quite clear to everyone that night that she had no interest in helping. Of course, he knew he and the others were in part to blame as they kept secrets of the situation from her. The problems in Galaseya grew worse as the weeks went on. Chris brought Jermiar back to Galaseya after realizing Amber wouldn't be persuaded. Guilt briefly swept over Amber at this news, but in her mind, a few psychic visions hardly seemed important enough to save a kingdom. That was something for heroes of the fairy tales she heard as a child.

Hunter and Mason rarely came over. In fact, Hunter stopped going to school, which made Amber realize that he went to school only because of her. Occasionally, when she walked about the town, Amber saw Hunter or Mason running errands, and unlike Jermiar, they acknowledged her presence, but that was the extent of their contact. Amber got what she wanted, a normal life like before her mom's death. Not that she complained or anything, but now she was back to having no friends and some new bullies—her only friend was Sphinx, who seemed more attached to her than before.

Despite her former life returning, her dreams became more frequent and clear. By now it felt as if she traveled to other worlds in her sleep, but the "traveling" still left her exhausted the next morning. However, none of her regular dreams were nearly as tiring as the night when she had a very strange dream. It was similar to the one at the Bash, but not as strong. It happened on a cold late November evening, as Amber drifted off to sleep. A bright golden light shone in her mind as she started to see images of people. This time, however, the beautiful countryside was replaced. The dream brought her back to when her mother lived in Galaseya, but the sight was anything but pleasant.

Chaos erupted around Amber as she took in all the sights and sounds of terror. Two groups of people, who Amber assumed to be her mom and dad's families, with the Sidhe by their side, were using their powers to fight off the attackers. But at the request of Hunter, Holly started running away, holding a four-year-old Amber, with a teenage Chris trotting along beside her. With all the commotion going on, the family failed to see the massive water-like whip strike Holly and Chris from behind, causing Amber to fly through the air. Her high-pitched screams filled the twilight sky. Her cries immediately stopped as everyone turned to see her land only a few inches from where the Brothers now stood—her cheek sporting the only visible wound. Not a soul moved. One group looked terrified, and the other group looked almost curious as to what would happen next. Even the Sidhe stared in confusion, wondering what their enemies would do next. Amber watched her young self, trying to understand why a seemingly powerful memory felt foreign to her. The vision brought her closer to the intense scene as one of the villains, who Amber assumed to be the leader, knelt down and gently brushed the droplets of blood that graced her pale cheek. I know that face! Amber thought, reflecting back on her recent dreams. The woods behind Amber were suddenly lined with huge animals larger than any on earth, and all seemed to be working in unison, despite their diverse species. Out of the group came a rather small cat, walking up to Amber's side—Sphinx. Not a growl escaped nor did he bare any teeth as he stood there with his eyes daring the villain to harm the young girl.

Amber watched as her younger self placed a hand on the cat's back—his presence alone comforting her in this scary moment. She wore a stoic expression, trying her best not to show any fear. Ignoring the glares from the woods and the leader of the animals, the man lifted his blood-stained finger and examined it, then strangely glanced up at the sky as a twisted, almost victorious smile flashed across his face. Suddenly a brave soul spoke up—Holly.

"Martheykos! She will not go into the Abyss like us; she cannot be killed!"

Martheykos stared at Holly as if they were only the two in the whole world, his bright lapis-colored eyes revealing nothing but an evil mind and cold heart. His thin black brows rose as his deep voice menacingly replied, "Oh, I don't plan to kill her. I've got something better in mind."

"Which is?" challenged Holly as she rose to her feet, as Chris slowly returned to her side.

"Something that even the devious minds of you Grunewalds can't comprehend," said Martheykos, as his eyes widened with demented excitement. With his eyes still on Holly, he brought his finger to his lips and licked the drop of blood. "Enjoy your life...while it lasts."

Amber shot up in bed as if lightning struck her. Frantically, she looked around her room and saw that the moon hung lower in the sky. A small meow tickled Amber's ear as she looked down on the floor, seeing all her blankets strewn about the room. Poor Sphinx emerged from underneath a comforter looking frazzled. Amber whispered an apology to the cat as she quickly threw on some clothes and headed downstairs. She needed to leave the house, just go for a walk or something—anything to free her mind of the vision. Quickly, Amber jotted down a note for Chris about her leaving, then headed straight out the door into the brisk early morning air.

Of all the nooks and crannies hidden within this small town, Amber had found one in particular that seemed cut off from the outside world, a place she considered her personal sanctuary, as no one ever crossed her path there. She called it the Bluffs, and she had found it on the second week of her arrival. She often went there to clear her mind and relax. Her favorite spot sat on top of a rather large hill; a line of trees encircled the top, creating a kind of privacy from the town. On her first visit, Amber looked over the edge of the Bluffs and saw that it sloped steeply into the ocean— brambles and sharp rocks catching anything that fell. She always sat far enough away from that danger, though, watching the seagulls soar above and passing boaters enjoying the sun.

That was in the fall. It was now almost winter, and the seagulls still went about their business, but their calls seemed less joyous than when the bright, warm sun shone on their wings. Boats rarely went out, unless they were fishing, but even that seldom happened. Instead, it was just her and the ocean, no noise aside from the waves crashing below. This time, in particular, the setting looked different as the sun peeked over the horizon, casting rays of light on the water. Her mind felt numb as she tried to block out her dream, but nothing seemed to work. Too many questions flooded her mind that even the sound of the roaring waves couldn't dim in comparison. She shook her head as she stood to leave. But a bright turquoise light from the tree line stopped her in midstride.

The light danced between the trees and performed a few spins before finally turning into a beautiful young woman. She casually walked out of the shadows and into the early morning sunlight, the rays making her look almost unreal. She had turquoise eyes, brown hair, and wore ordinary clothing for anyone her age. But despite her normal appearance, Amber already knew who she was. One of the Sidhe. Vaeris, to be exact.

"Hello, Ameliana," she said kindly.

"That's my Galaseyan name, I take it?" Amber asked, remembering that Jermiar had called her that.

"Yes, it is, although your mother preferred an Earthlier name," Vaeris replied.

Amber stared at her, knowing she didn't come here just for a chat. She started off her round of questions with the one at the top of her mind. "What are you?"

The Sidhe smiled as she came to Amber's side and looked out over the ocean. With her eyes still on the horizon, she replied, "I, along with others like me, are not human, although when we are on this planet or near other humans, we do not like to appear in our natural state as it tends to terrify people. We decided to look like the youth of this world, seeing how most adult humans do not pay much attention to them. I came because I know you are very confused. I want to answer your questions if I can."

"What is the Abyss? I heard it mentioned in a vision," Amber asked, not sure if she even wanted to know.

"That is a very dangerous place, one which you cannot go to, fortunately, but your family can. They are neither human nor creature and therefore cannot go to a normal human afterlife, so they end up in the Abyss, a vast empty space that holds their souls. That is one of the many reasons we do our best to keep your family safe. However, as with your mother and your great-grandfather Claemar, whom you never had the chance to meet, we were unable to do so, and I greatly apologize for that," said Vaeris regretfully.

"It seemed like a pointless sacrifice," Amber muttered.

"Ameliana, Galaseya is in grave danger. The Balance that it depends on is in jeopardy from the Brothers," Vaeris said, almost pleadingly.

"So I've been told. If it's such a huge deal, why doesn't the rest of the family come here?" asked Amber, hoping for a simpler resolution.

"If the Balance is destroyed it will affect this world as well. There will be no place to escape to," the Sidhe replied solemnly.

"Oh, I didn't know that part." Amber replied, looking at the cold ground. "But why does it have to fall to me? I'm only a person with weird vision powers. Yes, I suppose the past can help, but I can't stop beings that even my family combined can't stop! Besides, I just don't want to."

Vaeris looked at Amber and said, "Ameliana, your family has sacrificed far too much just for you to let your indecisiveness get in the way. When your mother and brother escaped to this planet, they came with nothing—not even knowledge of the culture. Your mother had to steal and lie just for you to have a life. She was never even a nurse. All those times she went to her job, she merely went to find more ways to allow you to have the life you always wanted. Your mother not only stole for you, but she almost exhausted all her protective power just to shield you from the Brothers. Her shields are the reason they did not come sooner, Ameliana! She knew her death was possible, but she believed in what you could do. Are you really willing to let her die in vain just because you are uncomfortable?"

Amber jumped back from the strange being and exclaimed, "Shut up! You know nothing about my mom. She was a good woman who would never even dream of stealing from people! Just...stay away from me!"

As Amber started for the tree line, Vaeris called out, "April of two thousand and five. What happened to you then?"

Taken back by this sudden comment, Amber abruptly stopped. She turned around, completely shocked. "I was wanting to be an equestrian. I was training with my horse for an upcoming competition and...I fell off. But how did you..."

"And did you sustain any injuries?" pressed Vaeris.

"Yeah...I did," said Amber feeling uncomfortable with where the conversation was leading. "I have a rather large scar on my arm that reminds me. I...I never saw so much blood in my life."

"Did your mother come to your aid?" asked Vaeris, who seemed to know the answer.

Amber closed her eyes in disappointment as a tear fell from her eye. She then looked up at the strange young woman and admitted, "No, Mom...Mom didn't know what to do aside from wrap my arm up. I should have gotten stitches, that's why my scar is so large."

"Galaseyans do not get sick often and rarely get injured. We have little need for healers. I do not know why your mother chose such a foreign occupation. I suppose she felt that being a healer would compensate for the bad deeds she committed."

Vaeris's words seemed to penetrate the very depths of Amber's consciousness. Her mother had lied to her and this Sidhe seemed intent on exposing the truth, no matter how much it hurt. According to Amber, thievery and lying were the exact same things that classified a bully, at least the ones that she knew. But her mom had been the kindest person Amber ever knew. Could there really be a gray area?

Amber couldn't look Vaeris directly in the eyes as the tension clung to the air like thick humidity. An awkward silence fell between them as Vaeris walked back toward the other edge of the Bluffs. But just before she disappeared in a ball of bright turquoise light, she turned back and said, "Ameliana, I know you do not want to be involved. But this fight is just as much yours as it is your family's. If you do not fight back with the others, the Balance will die, and humanity will cease to exist. The choice is yours."

When she disappeared, Amber started for home, this time feeling as if it took twice as long. As she entered the woods she muttered to herself, "Choice, huh? Doesn't seem like I ever had one now."

By the time she reached home, it was well into the morning, and Amber knew that at this point Chris would be wondering where she had run off to. As far as she knew, he may have even sent Vaeris her way. But as she walked into the house, waiting for her brother to barrel around the corner and scold her, the house was silent. She looked around the entryway, allowing her eyes to adjust to the lighting. As she walked into the living room, she saw that Hunter, Mason, and Chris were all waiting for her—all wearing expressions of relief. She then realized Vaeris had come to her of her own accord.

She stared at them, her confidence waning. After a moment, she said, "Let's go. I'm...I'm ready."

Although a wave of relief swept over her family at her sudden change of heart, much needed to be done before they could go anywhere. Amber asked her cat-loving neighbor if she would take care of Sphinx while they left for a family emergency. The lady was all too happy to help, as she always loved seeing the cat sunbathing in the window. To avoid any unnecessary curiosity, Chris called up Amber's school and told the principal the same thing Amber told the neighbor— a family emergency. While Chris was on the phone with her school she ran up to gather things for their journey, starting with slipping on a ring her mother had given her for her Sweet Sixteen—it was the only piece of her that Amber had. As she began packing, Hunter quickly stopped her, reminding her that the wardrobe on Galaseya varied considerably from what she was used to. He suggested she change into her dress from the Bash, but time didn't allow for that, as Chris quickly alerted them that they needed to leave at once, as the Sidhe weren't responding to his telepathic calls.

Amber half expected a portal to open up in her living room, but something more familiar became their mode of transportation—Chris' ability. Naturally, Amber objected to this idea, remembering how a small jump in distance made him feel the last time. However, he told her that like the Sidhe, his power was limited here, but going back to his world was less taxing on him. Avoiding any further questions he knew Amber had, Chris raised his arms as a bright, almost lightning-like light emanated from his arms and danced toward his hands. His appearance changed into the strange, humanoid looking creature Amber had seen in the truck, as the light wrapped around her, Mason, and Hunter. At first, it felt like a small burst of static electricity and then it grew into a warm, comforting feeling. Just as before, their living room disappeared and a different site took its place, something darker than Amber expected. No one needed to tell Amber that something was wrong—she felt it. Instead of the smooth arrival as she remembered, they all fell to the ground, landing in different areas.

Amber slowly rose and allowed her eyes to adjust to the dimly lit area. She stood up and took in her strange surroundings. A barren dock was covered in mold and appeared to be falling apart. Old and broken boats jutted out of the water next to the remains of the dock. It was hard to see the entirety of the port, as the natural light hid behind thick, dark clouds. Small rays of light peaked through the gloomy atmosphere, which cast an ominous glow over the land. Nervously, she turned around, afraid of what everything else might look like.

To her horror, everything looked anything but what she was told it would be! In fact, it could easily pass as the sister to a small Third World village! Closest to her were large houses clustered together and falling apart, their metal roofs holding each other up. Tall weeds grew out of the cracks in the paved roads. The streetlights constantly flickered, making for a perfect horror movie setting. Only a few cars could be seen in the distance, and they looked ready for the junkyard. Most of the trees had been removed to make way for a few large factories, their pollution climbing high into the air, creating an awful stench.

Her eyes wandered away from the village and looked toward a large structure at the top of a hill—a palace, or what was left of it. It was almost entirely ruined, as if an explosion had destroyed half of it. Many of the stones, which Amber assumed were once part of the structure, were now haphazardly scattered around. A real war zone. It was now clear to Amber the urgency of her arrival—she had to fix this. The only question was, how?

7

Covered in sweat, with a trickle of blood escaping his lips, Chris weakly rose to his feet, an expression of horror plastered on his face. As he turned around, he noticed Amber's gaze seemed to be set on the terrible scene. He then shifted his gaze to Mason and Hunter, both of whom were speechless at the sight of their once beautiful land.

"This...this can't be Galaseya?" Amber's voice quaked.

"It is, but it isn't," said Mason grimly.

Chris nodded his head and looked around, a little confused, "Galaseya is known as the planet of light. It becomes dim, similar to that of the twilight you're accustomed to. But never this dark or cloudy. Even the constant warmth of the planet has disappeared!"

"Okay, obviously Kaleya had something to do with this. But I don't get it, how can something this dark happen in a place that seemed so...light? Could the Brothers be part of this?" asked Amber, taking notice of large heaps of trash.

"No, they can't do something of this magnitude on Galaseya. I'm afraid Kaleya may have tapped into something beyond our knowledge," said Chris.

"Maybe the Sidhe can shed some light?" asked Amber.

"No, they're not here...at all! It's as if they disappeared," Chris replied nervously.

"And so have the villagers," said Mason as his brow furrowed.

"If the Brothers aren't the cause, then what could be so powerful that it turned Galaseya into a sister of their planet?" asked Hunter.

Chris opened his mouth to respond with a theory but had no time to speak as a different sound rang in his ears. The other three heard the noise as well and ran off the dock, diving behind nearby barrels. For a moment, Amber couldn't hear anything unusual, except for the sound of doors violently shutting. The few lights within some of the houses were extinguished, and not a soul could be seen on the streets, except for a young teenager who looked to be only fourteen. He wore ripped, faded jeans and a graphic t-shirt. In his hand was a can of blue spray paint and at his feet were a few discarded cans. Amber never condoned vandalism, but the teenager's design was that of a beautiful flower. It was an unusual form of graffiti as most came with a rebellious phrase or foul language. The flower almost seemed like he was trying to add a little beauty to this dark land.

He was just about finished with his artwork when Amber saw movement coming down the street. At first glance, it looked to be a large animal, but as it crossed beneath the streetlights, it became more pronounced. Soldiers. Or rather that's what they seemed to be. It was really a large group of very muscular men all wearing skin tight black t-shirts, olive green cargo pants, and military grade combat boots. But unlike most soldiers Amber had seen in pictures, most of these guys had a malicious look about them. They marched in a synchronized fashion carrying large weapons ready to use on anyone who so much as looked at them strangely. As they came closer, Amber saw a few others who looked as if holding a weapon was foreign to them. But now they seemed to be only looking for trouble—and trouble they found. The second they saw the young graffiti artist a few men in the front line blasted the youth without warning, his blood splattering all over his design. The teen's hole-riddled body lay forgotten as the soldiers left. Some spat and chuckled at the boy's demise.

Amber turned her head to the others who stared at the bloody scene, their brows furrowed. Chris spoke up and said, "I don't understand, those are Galaseyan farmers. Violence isn't even in their vocabulary! What's going on here? How could our family let this happen? This isn't like them to not intervene."

"Better question, why hasn't this curse affected us like the soldiers and the boy?" asked Mason skeptically.

"Maybe this was their way of fighting? What if because of our powers the curse didn't affect us, but the family knew it would affect the villagers so they rescued the ones they could?" suggested Amber, tearing her eyes away from the ghastly sight.

Suddenly, a small movement from the edge of the woods that surrounded the village and palace caught Amber's eyes. The others stared to see what caught her attention but looked back at her in confusion. She blinked, wondering if it was the pollution getting to her head. But then, a faint glimmer of hope flashed across her face as she realized this had nothing to do with the factories. It was a vision.

At first, it started with a tall man with sandy brown hair, waving his arms toward the village. Amber turned her attention to the dystopian village only to find cute houses and vendor stands in their place, much like one would imagine the medieval period to be. Hundreds of villagers swarmed out of their houses as an ensuing darkness crawled over the land. Within the mass of people, Amber noticed other "leaders" much like the man at the tree line, guiding the villagers toward the safe haven of trees. Unfortunately, it didn't appear that all of the villagers made it out before the darkness took them too, transforming the buildings and people into the despair she arrived to see. The vision ended rapidly as Amber stared at the tree line. She had no proof but somehow knew those individuals saving the village were members of her family.

"Amber, what did you see?" asked Chris.

A faint smile grew on her face as she looked back at her brother and said, "I think I know where they went."

Déjà vu overwhelmed Amber as she set off for the woods, her family pelting her with questions just as the boys had done, what felt like years ago. However, this time, she just explained that she had a vision of where they needed to go. When they stepped into the dark forest, Amber had to open her mind more and rely on her instincts—the only source of guidance she seemed to have lately. With small patches of light illuminating their way through the eerie woods, it was challenging to see what dangers lay within the shadows as objects were barely outlined in front of her.

Amber accidentally came across one of these dangers as she tripped over something—falling to the ground while the palm of her hand smacked against a jutting rock. Blood ran from the long gash in her hand as Chris tore a piece of fabric off his shirt. He quickly stopped the blood flow while reducing some of the pain. With her eyes adjusting to the darkness, she saw what it contained—bodies of fellow Galaseyans in similar conditions as the boy in the village.

If she kills too many, she won't have a kingdom! But is that her plan? Does she want her own personal utopia? It doesn't make sense, thought Amber, weaving through the trees, all the while making sure her family kept up. She continued deeper into the woods, noticing on occasion how the many bodies didn't seem to faze any of the others. Either they had been to a number of funerals in their long lifetime, or something far more sinister. Among the corpses they passed, Amber noticed the absence of any wild creatures. Not even birds sang or flitted through the treetops. By now, they had to have crossed paths with at least something of the forest. Then a horrible thought struck her. What if the animals were the first to go?

Daylight broke through her fear, bringing Amber back to reality. All three stopped just before the light touched them. They looked to their left and right, seeing how the light and darkness created a barrier. The contrast was like stepping out from the night and into the day.

What in the world could be so powerful, yet have its limits, she wondered, looking back into the dark woods. Knowing her instincts were leading her directly into the bright part of the forest, she stepped into the warmth leaving the strange and intriguing darkness behind. The others followed behind, and as she walked over the next rise, she came to an extraordinary sight.

A circle of large wolves, each about the size of a grizzly bear, stood guard above a large oval valley. She stood still and silent as the most important of the wolves approached her, its size about that of a polar bear. His gray fur shone in the light, and as he gracefully walked toward her, the ground trembled. The creature nosed Amber as if making sure she wasn't a threat. He lifted his head, and his silvery eyes stared into Amber's green eyes. For a moment it felt as if the world stopped, both wolf and human equally curious about the other. Without thinking, Amber slowly lifted her hand and gently rested it on the canine's snout. The creature closed its eyes as if in understanding. It lowered its head in a bow, then turned toward the valley, stopping only to make sure Amber was following him. Amber nodded her head, then silently gestured for the others to follow her. But as the lead wolf walked over the edge of the embankment and out of sight, Amber's jaw dropped as she saw what the valley contained.

A large refugee camp stood below Amber and judging by the size, these were many of the same people she saw in her vision. In the center of the numerous makeshift shelters sat a large fire pit where several people stood, seeming to strategize their next plan. Helping the other villagers were other kinds of wild animals, each one as massive as the wolves. Aside from their unusual size and kind temperament, something else was different about them. Chris quickly explained that each creature lived three times as long as normal animals and had a special healing talent. He then went on to say that each century an animal from one of the four species was born to be the leader of all. The animal leader had all the powers of each species.

This century, Sphinx was born and became the leader, though due to his size, no one expected him to be in the position. According to Vaeris, Sphinx understood the Balance better than the other animals who were mere followers. He knew that protecting Amber was essential. That's why he had left Galaseya to be with Amber, but he ended up seeing her more as a friend than a job. It bothered Amber a little that her truest friend even held a big secret from her, so she changed the topic by asking about what all the animals did. Chris gladly explained that the wolves' saliva healed any wound no matter how deep and the cats' purr acted as a defibrillator. The bears, which were seldom seen, had fur that reduced any type of pain inside or out, and the sight of the deer removed sadness making one feel at complete peace.

These astounding creatures made Amber think their talents might be put to good use. As she followed the wolf through the crowd, all eyes were on her. Even their quiet murmurs seemed to cease. A few times Amber glanced into the crowd and saw how some of the people had bruises and minor wounds while others appeared to be sick. Somehow Amber didn't find this a typical situation. A lot of them looked frantic, just trying to attend to what sounded like a simple cough.

Amber ran into the wolf's fluffy rear as it abruptly stopped without warning. She quickly backed out of the way to avoid any embarrassment and the canine turned its head, giving her a disapproving look. She looked away, hoping he wasn't too upset. But instead, he stepped out of the way, revealing the people around the fire pit—the leaders of the refugee camp. Her family.

"Ameliana, it is a pleasure to officially make your acquaintance. My name is Stephria," said a young woman as she approached Amber. She looked barely in her early thirties. Her long, strawberry blond hair waved in her wake, and her dark brown eyes seemed to have a shine to them. The energetic young woman seemed overly enthusiastic given the situation, but Amber merely attributed that to nerves. The woman tried to make casual conversation with her, but Amber's eyes were fixed on one man in particular: the green eyes, pale complexion, and a ghost of a smile. He carried himself well despite the fact he leaned heavily on a thin, black metal cane. Amber approached him, her heart pounding in her chest while everyone else stood silent. No one needed to tell her who this man was.

"Dad?" she asked, her tone rising an octave.

"Hello, Ameliana, or do you prefer Amber?" he asked kindly.

Amber's heart fluttered at the kindness in his tone. His compassionate demeanor was one of the many qualities she hoped to find in her estranged father. She smiled, knowing that their relationship was just getting started as she timidly replied, "Whichever works for you."

"Amber, I am so glad you have decided to return home," he replied, taking her hands.

"I wish it were under better circumstances," she replied, bringing the conversation back around to the problem at hand.

"Right," he replied solemnly, "but before we get to that, allow me to introduce the rest of our small family."

He formally introduced himself as Rogalar and then began introducing the rest of the family as well as their power. Stephria was the oldest, whose ability was to identify where an internal injury lay. Considering they were entering an unexpected and unfamiliar war, Amber thought her ability would be quite useful. The next person was Jermiar and with his ability, other powers of the family could be boosted. Then there was Amber's dad whose ability seemed at odds with those of his elders. No matter what weapon he wielded he instantly became an expert at it. As for the Grunewald family, Mason had the power of illusions, and to some extent, he could read minds, but he didn't use that part of his power unless absolutely necessary. Hunter could turn himself into a shadow at will, although he stopped Rogalar from going into too much detail, something Amber determined to find out at a later time. She felt overjoyed to meet the rest of her father's family, but it still left the Grunewalds, her mother's family, most of who were mysteriously absent. Her curiosity itched as she wanted to understand more, but for now, there were more important things.

With her mind so focused on the questions about the darkness, Amber almost didn't see a person nearly curled up in a ball, sitting on a nearby log. She moved away from her family to get a better look at what appeared to be a man. He seemed to almost cower in fear and pain. Amber felt her body gravitate toward the figure, an invisible force compelling her to confront him. She crouched down in front of the person and tilted her head to see his face. His gray eyes were bloodshot from crying. Amber glanced back at her family in hopes of finding some sort of explanation. Only Mason would exchange a glance. He told her the name of the man: Flaedar. But that's all she needed to know. As she turned back to the man, she looked down to his left hand, which he clutched close to his chest. Giving in to her instinctive feeling, Amber held out an open hand, hoping he would understand her silent gesture. Ever so slowly, he began to move his bloody, bandaged hand towards hers, looking slightly confused. He glanced at the other family members, all who remained strangely silent, eager to see what would happen next.

Cautiously, he touched her hand—and then it started. A vision began as a mere pin-drop of light, then slowly grew, revealing a scene as if in an old movie.

It seemed relatively normal. For the first time, Amber saw Princess Renalia, now queen, her blond hair falling past her shoulders, and her soft gray eyes looking full of kindness. She sat upon her throne having a private discussion with Flaedar, who Amber assumed was the queen's advisor. Neither one seemed at all concerned about the topic at hand; it seemed more of a casual conversation. Then the mood of the vision drastically changed as both the queen and her advisor lifted their heads, abruptly stopping their conversation. Confusion, then fear, replaced their calm demeanors.

Amber's viewpoint quickly changed location and she could now see the entirety of the room from the side. She was still unable to see what they were staring at until the doors of the palace flew open. Kaleya barged into the grand room, the tattered edges of her long gown flapping in the breeze. Her long black hair blew wildly about her. She looked exactly as one would imagine a wicked witch to look like, although without the hideous appearance.

Without saying a word, she stormed toward the throne, a manic expression marring her face. The faithful advisor stepped in front of Renalia. With Kaleya nearing the throne, the vision closed in. She gave Flaedar no time to even try negotiating. He had his hands up in a defensive position, but Kaleya was merciless. Within a second, she drew a dagger from her sleeve and cut off most of his left hand—leaving only his thumb as a remembrance. She pushed him to the ground after the follow-through

Renalia sat on her throne like a statue. She fearlessly faced Kaleya and didn't beg for her life. However, Kaleya's ruthless streak was just beginning. With one mighty swipe, she slit the young queen's throat and dragged her body off the throne. Then Kaleya lazily sat down, her icy eyes shooting to the terrified advisor, who cradled his wounded hand and stared horror-stricken at his former queen. Kaleya dangled her dagger over the arm of the throne and playfully swung it, watching the blood of her victims' drip on the ground, permanently staining the gray stones. She switched her focus to the queen's body as a smirk crossed her face. Amber could see words coming from her dark red lips; they came slowly enough for Amber to catch what was said: 'I win!'

Amber expected the vision to stop there, but now it moved to a different time, not long after Renalia's death. It was a fast-paced vision, starting with Flaedar as he raced through the halls in a panic. At his last turn, he ran down the corridor leading to the throne room. He skidded to a halt as he came upon a gruesome scene. Kaleya stood in the center of the room, surrounded by the mutilated bodies of the entire royal court. She cleaned off a blood-drenched blade with her dress, completely disregarding the fact that she was covered in blood. Just by her look, Amber could tell that this was only a warning to Flaedar who, despite Kaleya's sadistic attempts, was still loyal to Renalia.

The vision abruptly ended, bringing Amber back to the present. She clutched her head in pain and sat down on the soft ground. The dramatic scene had taken more out of her than she thought. Tears streamed down her face. But as she dabbed at her cheeks, the consistency of the tears felt odd— it was blood! She turned and met the looks of surprise on her family's faces. Through the sharp pain, her eyes welled up with the crimson tears again as she said, just barely above a whisper, "This...this is all my fault!"

8

Jermiar took a piece of cloth and dipped it in a bucket of cool water. Gingerly, he handed it to Amber and watched with concern as she wiped away the blood.

"It was not your fault, Ameliana," Stephria spoke up. "Kaleya would have still attempted some kind of *coup d'état* even if you did arrive earlier. It might have even been worse."

"How can it possibly be worse? She's massacring everyone!" exclaimed Amber, pointing to the dark woods.

No one had anything to say to this. The family knew Amber was right and it wasn't the only thing Kaleya was going to do. No, she had another plan, but on a much wider scale.

A medium-sized wolf, a bit smaller than the one Amber first met, brushed up against her legs, interrupting the tension. She didn't know anything about the creatures of Galaseya, aside from their obvious size. From what she could tell, this wolf was young. She looked down into the wolf's face, and her eyes were immediately attracted to the creature's bandaged leg—the white cloth spotted with blood. Amber knelt down and greeted the friendly canine. His large tail began to wag, and his ears fell back against his head. He clumsily lay down and put his injured leg on Amber's lap, hoping she could heal him. The whimpering wolf tugged at Amber's heartstrings. It amazed her how anyone could do such terrible things to a seemingly pacifistic group of people, let alone such benign creatures. Amber shook her head as she looked into the poor creature's eyes. She couldn't heal him, but she was determined to prevent any more injuries or death from happening.

Amber looked up and ignored the surprised looks of her family. Judging by their expressions, this behavior was abnormal for the wild creatures of the woods. Suddenly, something else caught her attention. Another wolf, much larger, but not the leader, stood on a mound of dirt, staring out into the woods. It turned its head and nodded to Amber. She could see it meant for her to follow. Silently, she gently lifted the canine's leg off her lap and rose to her feet, the other wolf waiting patiently.

"Amber, you are not going anywhere alone," said Jermiar, grabbing her wrist and pulling her back.

"If she goes, then it would be best if I come as well. You may run into those soldiers," argued Hunter strongly.

To everyone's amazement, the wolf let out a low, guttural growl. These creatures had always been so gentle. Showing any type of anger was unheard-of. Could the curse on the land be affecting them also or was it something deeper than that? Amber held up a calming hand to the irritated wolf. Although she felt equally frustrated with her grandfather's insistence she said to the wolf, "No, it's okay, both of them can come." The wolf relaxed a little and continued waiting for Amber, but it still eyed Hunter suspiciously.

"Fascinating! In all my years I have never seen a wild creature obey a human!" exclaimed Mason, looking from the wolf to Amber with curiosity.

"Don't know what to say, but maybe they understand how dangerous things are?" suggested Amber as she turned toward the wolf.

The wolf grunted impatiently, signaling for the group to follow. Amber didn't really want to leave her family; she was more interested in finding the secrets they held. But at the same time, she was mildly afraid of testing the wolf's patience. Silently, she followed the canine deeper into the woods, with Jermiar and Hunter following closely behind. The wolf jumped over logs with ease and occasionally stopped so the humans could catch up. It didn't seem to mind too much. However, with its keen sense of hearing, it caught the irritating chatter of the people behind him. All Hunter and Jermiar did was talk, mostly arguing about how to end the war. Even Amber was getting rather annoyed, and when the wolf turned its head, it seemed to agree with her. She turned toward the others, not caring why they started up this argument, but only told them to cut down on the arguing. Suddenly, she almost ran into the wolf again as he stopped in front of a large stone building.

The wolf trotted off into the woods, leaving Amber with only one question. She asked, "Why would the wolf leave us here? How is this going to help us fight the war?"

"This is Grunewald Manor. Why the creature led us here is beyond me," said Hunter quietly.

"Well, can we go in?" asked Amber hesitantly.

"Definitely, but just be prepared for anything. I don't know if any of my family is in there right now," he replied.

"Huntinylar, this is a bad idea. She should not meet them like this, it is the wrong time," said Jermiar insistently.

"Clearly the creatures think otherwise. Amber will find out eventually," he replied, heading toward the house.

Amber looked to Jermiar for some kind of explanation. But he just stood there pale-faced, regret masking his once happy demeanor. She knew her mother had a slightly dark side, based on what Vaeris told her. Maybe the other Grunewalds were the same? She walked toward the structure, feeling awe and intrigue. It seemed rather empty, but Amber just hoped they wouldn't find an ambush of some kind once they entered. Before she even reached the door, Amber caught a glimpse of the surrounding area and noticed the woods in the back were oddly darkened. These people were living on the fringe of the curse!

Amber didn't know exactly what she would see inside. Perhaps gaudy décor or maybe even garish furniture. But, there was none of that. In fact, most of the rooms she looked into held furniture which seemed as if it didn't fit with the eerie building. Every room looked as if it hadn't been used in years—thick layers of dust coated everything and cobwebs dangled everywhere. In front of her was a grand staircase that led to the upper floors, with a hallway on either side.

She went upstairs and discovered five bedrooms, each with a king-sized bed. Aside from that one particular element, every bedroom had its own personality, reflecting its owner. Three of the rooms screamed masculinity, clean and Spartan. The fourth room was much more modern than the rest, and the bed looked as if it had been slept in, but not for a long time. Clothes hung out of the closed dresser drawers, as if the owner of the room had been in a rush to get out the door. Amber meandered about the room, trying to figure out who slept in here.

Before she looked much further, Hunter quickly told her that it was his room. Amber looked back to the two men who were standing in the large doorway. Hunter seemed uneasy, but Jermiar continued to give Hunter a strange sideways glare. Amber disregarded it for now, reminding herself it was probably due to his nervousness. Satisfied with her search, she was just about to walk out of the room when a small sketch laying on the dresser caught her attention. She picked up the drawing and walked over to the window. With the outside light shining on the small piece of parchment, Amber was amazed at the beauty of the drawing. It was an image of a stunning woman. She smiled and asked Hunter who it was, but he quickly snatched the piece of parchment from her hand and crumpled it up, saying it was no one special. Given the exact details of the picture and the way it was portrayed, Amber highly doubted that it wasn't someone special. Sensing Hunter didn't want to continue the conversation, she walked out of the room, continuing her tour of the house.

Her journey soon brought her back to the staircase, but she stopped abruptly at the top of the stairs, causing the others to almost run into her. It was the fifth room that changed her course of direction, but this one wasn't like the others. In fact, it was entirely different from the other four rooms partly because it looked the most kept. Almost immediately, Amber could tell that this room belonged to her mom.

The room was flooded with bright light due to the large window that covered almost the entire length of a wall and had a huge window seat. Although the walls were made of stone, they were whitewashed, making the room ten times brighter. The furniture was made of a lighter type of wood, and there were beautiful designs carefully carved into it, adding an almost innocent, childlike touch. There wasn't much else in the way of furniture aside from a dresser similar in style to Hunter's and a writing desk of sorts off in the corner.

Amber's lips curved into a slight smile as she walked toward the window seat, thinking how alike she and her mom were—for one, their love for window seats to comfortably look out into the world. She sat down on the soft cushions, which were just moss-like grass stuffed between a few sheets of fabric. Then her gaze came across a small handmade journal. It wasn't even a bound book. The small pieces of parchment were sewn together, and the cover was cleverly made of a type of thin bark from a tree like that of white birch.

Gently, Amber took the journal and opened the pages carefully, reading the words her mom had penned. She spoke mostly of her life as a child and how different she felt from her family. She regretted having to steal, among other things, but it was the only way to be accepted by the rest of her family. Holly mentioned how close she was to Hunter and that he was an excellent father figure. From her perspective, Hunter understood her desire to be good. He was the only person she could truly confide in. Amber's heart soared as she put the book carefully back in its place. Holly's words merely solidified what she already knew of Hunter.

Suddenly, a vision interrupted her exploration as she looked out the window and to the ground below. The time appeared to be early morning. Her mother came out of the woods in hopes of finding someone. Out of the corner of her eye, she noticed a small spark coming from behind a nearby tree. A figure leaned against the trunk and bounced little sparks of electricity between its fingers.

"What are you doing here? You know Dugon has disowned you," came the man's voice.

"I am not interested in what Dugon thinks. I only came here to say goodbye to my father, Davylar," said Holly.

"Goodbye? I think it is a bit late for that, Holisiana," he replied, intrigued by her response.

Holly sighed and glanced around the area before saying, "You do not understand. My children and I are leaving Galaseya. The Brothers are after my daughter. They know she can stop their plans."

Already aware of the situation, Davylar sighed in frustration as he replied, "You should never have gotten involved with those Oaks! They are in over their heads with this Balance."

"At least they are fighting for a cause!" she exclaimed trying to keep her voice hushed, *"Besides, I never wanted you or any of our family involved. I just came to say goodbye and to warn you about the Brothers."*

"Why should they care about us? We want nothing to do with them or the Oaks," he replied nervously.

"That does not matter to them. You know of my daughter, you have even seen her yourself. That will be enough for the Brothers to interrogate you. We have already lost one of our own to them. Claemar, Stephria's father. I do not want any more deaths. Please, just be safe!" she begged.

Davylar stepped into a faintly lit area, the light from the house casting vague shadows across his face. He brought Holly in toward him in a hug as he replied, "I am truly sorry to hear that. Fortunately, we already are a reclusive family so maybe remaining in relative hiding will help. Do what you must, and I will tell your father for you."

Amber rose from the seat after the vision ended and looked at Hunter, knowing the man in her vision kept to his word. She felt sad that her mom never got to properly say goodbye, but at least her family was still alive, for the most part. Quietly, Amber left the room, avoiding the curious gazes from the others.

She made her way down the staircase and found another feminine looking room on the bottom floor, also unlike the others, in that it had various types of clothes scattered all over the floor.

A typical teenage girl's room, mused Amber, moving on to the other rooms on the ground floor. She saw a large kitchen, which was the only room in the whole manor that was actually filthy. Dirty dishes and cookware were piled high on the table, and the massive fireplace had piles of old ashes spilling out onto the floor. Amber turned away in disgust and walked toward another room, which seemed to have been a living room at one time, but was now completely empty except for a single luxurious chair in the corner of the room.

"With the amount of noise you have made, one would think you are trying to alert those pathetic soldiers," came a soft, yet dangerous voice.

Amber nearly jumped as the voice broke the dead silence. She didn't even hear Hunter or Jermiar move behind her, let alone a woman enter the room. Amber looked at Jermiar, who seemed repulsed by the sight of her, whereas Hunter looked almost embarrassed.

"What a pleasant surprise—Galaseya's lady of the night," Jermiar spat.

"How wonderful it is to see you too, Jermiar!" she replied in a highly sarcastic tone.

Amber watched as the woman settled near the window, casually inspecting her nails. Her style of wardrobe was definitely Galaseyan, but as Jermiar mentioned, her clothing appeared relatively risqué. It didn't bother Amber much, as some girls she went to school with dressed in tight tank tops and miniskirts. However, unlike the high school girls, this woman had a sense of unapproachableness about her as well as danger.

"That is Joyra," said Hunter quietly pointing her out. "Joyra is my eldest daughter."

Hunter's daughter. The whole longevity thing Amber had gotten used to, but the relations were an entirely different story. She looked at Joyra, who looked nothing like her father. With long, sandy brown hair, sea green eyes, and tall, plump figure, she could have passed for an Oak. However, there was something immensely dark in those eyes, something so dangerous it could send Kaleya running.

"Joyra! How many times must I tell you?" exclaimed a man as he stormed into the room, carrying a limp figure over his shoulder. The blond-haired man heaved the body onto the ground and looked up at Joyra with irritation.

Joyra looked at the farmer, who seemed to have been caught in the curse, as his clothes were more modern. "What do you wish for me to say?" she replied. "He bothered me."

"But that is no reason to use your power on him! Wake him up immediately!" he replied angrily.

Annoyed that only she found the situation reasonable, Joyra stared at her relative in disgust and then looked to her father, who gave her a reprimanding look. With a snap of her fingers, the young man began to awake. Though groggy, he seemed terrified of the woman and left the room, yelling obscenities at her.

For her insolence, the blond man pointed his finger at Joyra's rear and a spark of electricity shot out. It was quite entertaining to see Joyra's reaction, although Amber dared not let her amusement show. Inwardly she felt relieved that he had a sense of humor about him.

"How dare you, Davylar!" shrieked Joyra, covering her rear. "I will tell Dugon what you have done."

"Tell me what?" came an older voice, coming into the room.

The man slowly came into full view and hobbled over to the dusty armchair in the corner. He looked quite different from his descendants, aside from his older appearance—he was somewhat short, with tan skin and jet-black hair. His chocolate brown eyes scanned the room and came to rest on Amber. His eyes squinted in curiosity—as if he were trying to figure out who she was.

"Nothing, Dugon, we were just having a disagreement, is that not correct, Joyra?" asked Davylar, hoping to avoid any unnecessary conflict.

"Would this have anything to do with the strange young woman standing in our presence?" asked the old man, eyes still locked on Amber.

The group looked at Amber, surprised that they hadn't seen her standing between Hunter and Jermiar. Davylar appeared slightly confused. Joyra casually looked Amber up and down, a look of disgust evident on her face.

"What is *that*?" Joyra hissed.

Heat rushed to Amber's cheeks as she calmly replied, "My name is Amber Oak. I am the daughter of Holisiana and Rogalar."

"She had another one?" exclaimed Joyra irritably.

"I would have thought she learned her lesson from the first," said Davylar.

Why does everyone refer to Chris' birth so negatively? Mom never mentioned physical complications, Amber thought as the heat spread across her entire face. She turned to Hunter, who shook his head at his family's behavior. A part of him seemed to hope they'd be kinder. Jermiar, however, held in so much frustration and annoyance at the Grunewalds that Amber was convinced he was just as red as she felt.

The corners of her lips turned up as she decided to stir things up a bit, hoping for some kind of response, "Davylar, I thought you knew who I was. I mean, you spoke to my mom before she left Galaseya with Chris and me. She even said you met me when I was little. Isn't that right?"

Hunter smirked, knowing Amber had a vision only a little while ago, but Jermiar stared at Amber in horror. The only way to get through to these twisted people was to talk their talk. Dugon's gaze moved toward Davylar, who seemed unsettled by Amber's words, "Is this true?"

"Holisiana came to see Huntinylar. She warned me that the Brothers were not only after the Oaks but specifically her daughter. I...I knew about Ameliana, but only for a short time. All Holisiana wanted was to say goodbye to Huntinylar and asked that we be careful, as we might be in danger as well," said Davylar nervously.

Amber didn't expect him to be honest about his encounter with Holly, but behind the behavior he exhibited, she saw that he knew the situation was getting worse, and avoiding the disaster surrounding them was a bad idea.

Then it happened again. Another vision, but not just a normal one.

This one was quick, almost like a brief daydream. A beautiful young woman who looked exactly like Stephria but a few years younger came into view. Her strawberry blond hair blew in the wind, and her equally dark brown eyes seemed to shine, as if she was in love. And she was, with none other than Davylar. The vision showed the couple walking through the woods and nearby fields, but a darkness seemed to rapidly overcome them. All Amber saw before the vision abruptly ended was the darkness coming from Dugon, who didn't approve at all of Davylar being involved with someone who represented so much light. Naturally, Davylar put up a fight for his love, but somehow a sneaky plot to separate the two permanently was concocted. Amber didn't see who it involved and how, but it wasn't necessary. She now understood why her great-grandfather was more lenient toward her mother's plea. He knew her pain of having to leave her family and the one she loved.

As the brief vision ended, Amber now understood her mother's exile. Yes, she joined the Oak and Grunewald families, but at least the one she married had a dangerous power. Dugon might have been the only one unhappy about her "betrayal," but it seemed that the others of the Grunewald family approved of Holly's lover. She had a feeling that Davylar's romance split them all apart—something the majority of them never wanted to happen again.

"Ameliana, I asked you a question!" said the elder firmly.

Hunter and Jermiar knew Amber well enough to know she had a vision, but they dared not ask in front of the family. In their mind, the less they knew, the better.

"I'm sorry, what was the question?" she asked, acting as if she really did have a daydream.

The old man sighed and rolled his eyes. "How did you know this?"

She looked at her new family members and realized that beating around the bush or even lightening the truth would only make them more suspicious of her. She took a deep breath and said, "Much like you, I have an ability as well. I can see the past of a place or person. The degree of my visions depends on the event that took place."

"So you know everything about us right now?" asked Joyra nervously.

"No, I'm only shown what I need to see. I also don't exactly know how to control it yet," Amber replied, feeling slightly embarrassed at the last bit.

"That is fascinating," said Davylar with a faint smile, wondering how her ability may be used as a weapon.

"Yeah, well I didn't really come here to talk about what I can do. I'm here for help," Amber said, finally realizing why the wolf led them here. "You're probably well aware of the darkness that has taken over most of Galaseya. I know you've all stayed here most of the time and that's fine, but you also weren't as involved as the Oaks. Have you noticed anything out of the ordinary on the outside?"

"What do you mean, 'out of the ordinary?'" asked Joyra, who started to become interested.

"This curse was Kaleya's doing. Now, unless she's a long-lost member of one of our families, which I seriously doubt, then she must have gotten her hands on some kind of weapon of the Brothers or maybe they're indirectly involved," she replied.

Suddenly Dugon's brown eyes seemed to light up, accenting his short black hair. But then his tan skin grew a few shades paler as he whispered, "The Alchemist."

He leaned forward in his chair as the room filled with silence. All eyes were now on him, hoping he'd continue. He stared at the floor in serious thought, searching his brain for even a smidge of memory. Then he stood up slowly and walked toward the window. Joyra quickly moved out of the way. Dugon lifted his eyes and looked toward the dark forest, hoping it held some answers.

Nervously, Amber stepped closer to her elder and quietly asked, "Dugon, who exactly is the Alchemist?"

He turned his head and said, "I have not thought of him for the last one thousand years. From what I remember of him, he was a scientist and often conducted experiments in the mountain. Many nights I would sit here in this room watching strange lights rise into the sky. Of course, the forest was much younger then."

"Thank you for your help, Dugon. I'm sorry, but we have to go," said Amber, rushing toward the door.

Dugon called Amber back. She stopped halfway out the door, with Hunter and Jermiar nearly running into her again. Amber looked at Dugon. His hands were clasped behind his back and he still faced the window as he replied, "There is also rumor that this Alchemist is the reason for our families' gifts. Tread carefully."

Not entirely sure what to think of this new development, Amber thanked the man again and rushed out of the manor. She ran around the house and into the partial darkness toward the direction Dugon had been looking, hoping this mountain wasn't too far in the distance. Jermiar repeatedly asked Amber to slow down, but she was on a mission. The only way to stop Kaleya was to find the Alchemist.

But something quickly stopped her after she jumped over a small stream. It was a run-down house, the roof caved in. The forest was claiming the building as its own. The building itself didn't seem strange, as it reminded Amber of the old asylum in Wisconsin. But there was something dark about it, as if a terrible event had taken place.

"Amber, come, we must keep moving!" said Hunter, hastily grabbing her wrist.

The force of his pull inadvertently twirled Amber in towards him. She stared into his blue eyes and almost immediately saw the horror they beheld. Nothing about this vision seemed normal, aside from how it actually began.

Hunter stood with a beautiful young woman with thick, long, light brown hair, fair skin, and hazel eyes. She was incredibly attractive, and Hunter seemed to adore this young lady. They were laughing, and he occasionally stole a kiss. Amber heard words being spoken. "Maelia." That was the woman's name. Hunter mumbled the name often— as if it was the most beautiful thing he had ever heard. However, this warm feeling of love and romance drastically changed as another vision took its place.

The happy couple stood on the edge of the woods just outside the Grunewald manor. At first, Amber didn't understand the significance of the vision. Then she heard their muffled words.

"My love, where are you off to? Did we forget to get something in the village?" asked Hunter lovingly.

The young woman looked at Hunter and innocently replied, "Yes, I...I am making dessert for after dinner, I forgot an ingredient."

"Oh, well, then I shall join you," he replied joyfully.

"Darling, that will not be necessary. The girls should be looked after, do you not agree?" replied Maelia.

Hunter hesitated for a moment, trying to see what his wife was concealing, but to no avail. He shrugged his shoulders and silently agreed to her request. After a few hours, Maelia didn't return, so Hunter took it upon himself to make sure she hadn't fallen on her way back or run into trouble in the village. But by the time he reached the vendors and shops, his eyes grazed the crowd only to find that his true love was kissing another man. Hunter stood close enough to hear them, yet far enough away out of sight. And what he heard tore him apart.

"I am finished with Huntinylar Grunewald. He and his odd family have no social standing and are reclusive. Besides, I have seen what he is capable of. He and his family are nothing but monsters," she said to her lover.

Hunter walked away—completely crushed by his wife's words. He went home and for a while spoke to no one, until his grandfather came in, somehow seeming to know of Maelia's immoral behavior.

"If you would like for me to make her disappear, I would be glad to," said Mason with acid in his tone.

Hunter looked down at the yard and saw his daughters happily playing, his youngest practicing her shield power against soft objects that Joyra threw. His daughters deserved a better mother than Maelia or none at all. He turned to Mason and replied darkly, "No, Maelia is mine!"

Within seconds, the next and last part of the vision showed just how furious Hunter really was. Amber was in the rundown house, which she assumed belonged to Maelia or her family at one point. She looked at her reflection in a pail of fresh water and saw that she had taken on the appearance of the woman. It was strange; Amber could feel everything the woman felt and even remembered things that belonged to her past.

What could be so important that I see the past in this way? she thought, as her body moved toward the bed as if getting ready to sleep.

Just as she peeled back the rough covers, everything went dark. But not the darkness Amber saw in the cursed village. She whirled around and watched as shadows entered the house from every cavity—swarming in a tornado like fashion around her, paralyzing her body. Amber opened her mouth and spoke, but it was Maelia's voice that came out: "I am sorry! I should have never deceived you! You will never hear or see me again, I promise! Please do not harm me!"

Hunter came out of the swirling tornado and walked slowly toward Amber. Their noses nearly touching, he stopped, his once friendly blue eyes filled with hatred and vengeance, rage such as Amber had never seen before.

He stared at Amber silently for what seemed like an eternity, contemplating what he was to do. He nodded, his decision made and her fate sealed. In a quiet voice, much like his grandfather's, he said, "Let me show you what this monster can really do."

He raised his hands and all the shadows in the room come to his beckoning call. Holding them, he slowly guided them into Maelia's ears, nose, mouth, and eyes. She was literally burning from the inside out. It was excruciating pain, unlike anything Amber had ever felt. The closest she could imagine was the feeling of acid eating away at her flesh. She collapsed into his arms. He lifted her face to his to see the agony etched into her face. A malignant smile formed. He was enjoying every moment of the young woman's death as he said sinisterly, "Do not worry, you will never betray anyone again."

What Maelia did was wrong, but Hunter was no better! Amber thought as she felt the world permanently go black.

Exiting the vision was probably the hardest thing for Amber. She found herself in the exact same position she had been in at the end of the vision. This time, however, Hunter was pale with fear and concern. Her body ached, and lungs burned just as they did in the vision. It made her wonder how she looked during the vision. With all the energy she could muster, she tore away from Hunter's hold and in a hoarse voice yelled, "Get away from me!"

Jermiar ran to Amber's aid and held her in his arms as any good grandfather would. "I warned you this would happen, Huntinylar."

Amber disregarded the fact Jermiar knew. She had a feeling he knew about a lot of the Grunewalds' secrets, probably for leverage at times like this. Hunter straightened up, genuine guilt written all over his face. "I never wanted you to know."

"What? That you happened to kill the love of your life just because she cheated on you? You don't think I should have known that?" exclaimed Amber, while Jermiar held her back.

"The woman didn't just betray me, she abandoned your mother," he replied, his guilt quickly vanishing.

"So the ends justify the means?" she shot back, Jermiar's grip tightening.

"Yes, death was a proper punishment," he replied without any feeling.

Now she could see the darkness that hid so deep behind Hunter's blue eyes. His heart was filled with the same poison embedded within his shadow. This was his true form. But why? Why would he conceal his identity from Amber if he felt no shame? Did he see her as Holisiana, another daughter he could take under his wing? But even she wouldn't have approved of what he did, unless, like the kind woman Amber always saw her as, she looked past his mistake. Did he hope Amber would do the same?

With Jermiar's help, Amber rose to her feet, the burning sensation now a mere tickle. She looked toward their destination, then to Hunter, who, surprisingly, seemed hopeful. She shook her head and said, "Maelia was wrong...the only monster I see is you.

9

Amber continued toward the mountain, leaving Hunter behind, thoroughly embarrassed and guilt-ridden from being caught. Eventually, he caught up with her and Jermiar but made no attempts to apologize. She wouldn't do him any favors. She had already made her decision about where their relationship stood. That didn't mean he was going to give up repairing what could be fixed.

Jermiar, too, ignored Hunter's pouting presence. Just like Amber, he was mildly annoyed with Hunter's desperate attempts at fixing the situation. In truth, he never wanted this to happen either, but it really was only a matter of time before Amber would find out. All of these things Amber could see within the two men. Although Jermiar mentioned she had officially mastered her ability, she didn't feel so confident about that. She still didn't know how to control her gifts, but that would have to wait. Amid her thoughts of the recent events, something quickly distracted her.

After a few hours, they arrived at the mountain. It stood almost as high as Mount Washington, but this mountain seemed to be more pointed and steep. There was little foliage, just rocky terrain, but the rocks appeared to sparkle in the dim light. Amber stepped into the open and heard the roaring sounds of distant ocean waves thundering against treacherous rocks. She gazed up at the top of the mountain and saw patches of what appeared to be snow, but the longer she stared, the more the wintry substance began to take on texture. It was merely just a unique type of ground covering, almost moss-like.

"I am so sorry that you had to see it in this condition," said Jermiar solemnly. "It really is a beautiful place."

Amber looked at Jermiar, confused, and turned back to the large land formation, but then jumped back in disgust. The once beautiful mountain was now layered in human filth and garbage. It piled so high at the base that the ocean created a moat around the mountain. Amber looked down at her feet and realized they were soaked in dirty water. Tears filled her eyes as she saw rotting garbage float by. But then, something strange happened—another vision, but one unlike any Amber had ever had.

She flashed back to what the mountain had looked like, but Hunter and Jermiar had completely disappeared. Frantically, she looked around again, expecting it was some trick her vision was playing on her.

"Ameliana, what is wrong?" came Jermiar's disembodied voice beside her.

Amber let out a small shriek and jumped away from where the voice originated. "Where did you guys go?"

"We're still here, Amber," said Hunter suddenly, his voice full of concern and confusion. Despite her anger towards him, his voice was quite calming, given the circumstance.

"Ameliana, tell us what you see and feel," said Jermiar, putting an invisible hand on her shoulder, assuring her it was all real.

"I...I'm not sure, but I think there's a way to get into the mountain. If I didn't know any better I'd saying I'm seeing the Alchemist's past!" she said with a hint of hope.

"This is a good thing?" he asked uncertainly.

"Yes, we can find out for sure if he's part of Kaleya's plan," she replied, walking toward the mountain.

Jermiar tried to tell Amber something, but she was already well ahead. She scanned the mountain wall with her eyes and found several openings that looked like tunnel entrances, but were only large crevices. Rather than struggle to decide where to go, she let the memory of the Alchemist guide her. She could hear the footsteps of Jermiar and Hunter race up to her, their heavy breathing a sign that they didn't realize she had already left. They were probably in deep conversation or argument.

"Amber, there is nothing here. You are only seeing a memory," said Hunter, trying to help.

Ignoring his comment, Amber followed the Alchemist's memory and raised her hands to a bare section of the mountain wall. Before anyone could utter a word, part of the wall began to dissolve, revealing a hidden entrance. Judging by the shocked gasps of the men, Amber knew they could see it too.

"How remarkable! Did you see him do that?" exclaimed Jermiar in awe, still trying to understand how her ability worked.

"No, I'm literally following what he did when he came to the mountain. It's like I am taking his place," replied Amber, still confused as she entered the dark tunnel.

To her relief, it was lit with some kind of fluorescent rocks. For some strange reason, they grew brighter as she continued walking down the tunnel, as if their intent was to guide her in the right direction. She was grateful for the rocks, as several tunnel offshoots appeared to have barricades. Years of disuse would make any tunnel cave in. However, some tunnels that branched off looked as if someone had just recently walked down them. If this Alchemist was as powerful as the curse over the majority of the planet, Amber wondered if he was somehow still here. This thought lingered on in Amber's mind as she neared the memory's destination.

Suddenly, dark images began to play in her mind, as if they were the Alchemist's thoughts while walking this exact path. They were difficult to see at first, but then a dead forest with disturbingly scary looking creatures arose. Could this be something his twisted mind conjured up or was this a real place in which he once lived? Amber shook the dark imagery from her head, thinking it was probably a random location of the cursed part of Galaseya. She didn't bother telling the men, as it would only cause unnecessary panic. She pushed on, letting the main memory control her every move.

The path eventually led the trio to a rounded-out, small cave deep within the center of the mountain. Just like the other cavern Amber had seen, this one was filled with bottles containing various colored liquids and crudely built tables lining the walls, with beakers piled high on top. The liquid in them had evaporated, leaving behind stained containers, as if the Alchemist had been forced to leave the equipment.

The vision suddenly changed, and Amber no longer saw through his eyes. Instead, she became an observer as a new scene began to unfold. A lamp stood in the corner and shone on the equipment and a familiar young woman. The beakers were now filled with bluish-green liquid, and it flowed through the swirling tubes and oddly shaped funnels. The liquid came out onto the table as solid, glowing, rock-like material.

That explains a lot! thought Amber, who had wondered about the origin of these luminous stones. Her attention moved on to the small feminine hands that lifted the glowing rocks carefully, afraid breaking them would be catastrophic.

"Rydan, I still do not see how these can be useful," said a young Kaleya, her eyes fixed on the rocks.

A deep chuckle sounded from a dark corner. "Child, this wonderful invention will light our way through the tunnels."

A tall, thin man with salt-and-pepper hair emerged from the corner. His eyes reflected off the light just as a cat's would, only his shone a silver color rather than gold.

At first, Amber thought it to be the glow of the rocks playing tricks on her vision, but as she moved toward Kaleya, the shine dimmed, and the Alchemist's eyes became a dull silver color, like two new dimes.

Could this have something to do with an experiment gone wrong or is it some genetic defect? she wondered, watching the man pick up a test tube and swirl its contents around.

Kaleya put the last rock into a wagon and turned around, her face the picture of innocence. "Rydan, do tell me again why you left the palace."

Amber could hear the slimy truth behind her words: she was trying to drill more information out of the Alchemist and probably uncover negative feelings. Unfortunately, she succeeded. The man put the tube into a stone holder. He blinked, ridding his eyes of the ensuing tears. "My services weren't required anymore."

Kaleya, in her curious and wicked ways, wouldn't let the conversation go. She walked around her teacher and faced him, so he was forced to look at her. "But that cannot be all. You have always been the best court physician the palace ever had."

Rydan quickly turned away and whispered, "Kaleya, we've already discussed this. The royal court didn't approve of the theories I proposed to them."

"You do not need their approval, Rydan. Is it not enough that I believe you?" said Kaleya, sounding almost hurt.

"Of course it is, Young One, but we alone can't do anything to convince them of the truth," he replied, sitting down on a wood stool.

A devious look grew on Kaleya's face as she leaned against the wall next to her teacher. "Perhaps we can show them the danger of their ignorance."

Rydan looked at the young woman in shock. He quickly rose from his seat and walked over to his equipment, pretending to busy himself with a forgotten experiment on another table.

Amber moved the vision to face him and saw how uncomfortable the suggestion made him. In a frustrated tone, he replied, "You're mad! It's not possible for them to see Darmentraea. Even if it were, none would survive the encounter."

"You and I would. Perhaps we can change Galaseya and bring about some Darmentraean influence. Those who live could abide by our rule," suggested Kaleya, her true intentions slowly being revealed.

"You're speaking treason, Kaleya. I may be an outcast among my people. However, I'm not a traitor. This conversation is over. Now, back to work," he replied in a dangerously quiet tone.

The vision immediately ended, revealing the present condition of the lab. Some empty beakers and tubes sat on a table, while other types of equipment were scattered on the ground either in sharp fragments or partially broken. No one had to guess that a struggle had taken place. It didn't seem right. Rydan seemed upset by Kaleya's suggestion, but how could that have led to a fight?

Amber's mind wandered back to the word "Darmentraea." Given what she knew of the planets, it wasn't a hard stretch to figure out that Kaleya referred to the Brothers' world. Kaleya wanted to change Galaseya, and so she did. Fortunately, Rydan seemed to have nothing to do with it, although Jermiar and Hunter weren't entirely convinced. The question still remained: How did Kaleya pull it off?

Amber briefly explained the vision, and as she expected, the men grew even more worried. They didn't have to say anything; their facial expressions said it all. Rydan taught

Kaleya everything he knew in hopes his teachings would keep her out of trouble. He didn't see she had an ulterior motive from the start.

Amber could no longer see through the Alchemist's eyes, as the vision had brought her only to the specific lab. Instead, she did her best to remember which direction they came. Amber got them lost a few times, but she was able to find more secret labs. Each one she came across was the same as the first. She saw quick vision glimpses of what they contained and like the first lab, they were once full of experiments and papers but were now empty. After a few more wrong turns, Amber finally led them back outside, vowing never to go back in there again without a better light source and some trail markers.

With still no knowledge of how to stop Kaleya, Amber started for the woods to find her family and the other Galaseyans. If anyone knew why Rydan may have been kicked out of the palace, it would be Flaedar. As they made their way around the trees, the sudden urge to turn around overwhelmed Amber, almost as if someone stood right behind her. Without raising concern, she calmly stopped and turned her head to see a figure leaning against a tree— the light from the non-cursed land casting a faded light on the individual. Rydan.

Like her family, he looked no older than when he had mentored the young Kaleya. He glanced at Jermiar and Hunter, both of whom were well ahead into the light, in deep conversation or argument. Rydan shook his head and returned his gaze to Amber. He held up an index finger over his lips, silently asking her to not reveal his position. She nodded in agreement, hoping that one day he might explain more of himself. As the man turned back toward his large laboratory, another vision came into place, one that would remove all suspicion from him. From her perspective, it was evident this memory belonged to Kaleya.

Rydan had fallen asleep in a chair, waiting for one of his experiments to complete. Kaleya quietly walked over to the alchemist, a knife gleaming at her side. Amber was immediately surprised at how recent this memory was. Kaleya wore the same gown she had when she slaughtered the royal court. In fact, in the dim glow of the candlelight, Amber could see large blood stains scattered all over the dress. Some blood spatters marred Kaleya's beautiful face. Creeping up to Rydan, she raised the blade and quickly sliced his arm. Strange silvery-red blood flowed from the wound, just as he was waking up.

He shrank back in confusion and pain from his young apprentice as she brought the bloody dagger into the dim candlelight. A wicked smile spread across her face as she pulled out a necklace—a beautiful, black filigree pendant on a thin chain. The inner part of the pendant was transparent but seemed to be full of an orange liquid. Kaleya took the bloody knife and let Rydan's blood drip onto the piece of jewelry, making the pendant glow brighter.

"What are you doing?" asked Rydan in horror, tending to his wound.

"I am only doing what should have been done years ago. Introducing this disgustingly peaceful planet to the glory of Darmentraea," she replied, the pendant's glow making her appear even more unpleasant.

"You think you can do that by stealing my experiments? I'm not a fool, Kaleya. I know you are the reason for my missing inventions and equipment," said the man, as he rose from his seat.

"But of course! You have taught me everything you know—for which I am eternally grateful. In a matter of hours, this little weapon will bring about a new Darmentraea, and no one can stop it, not even the elusive

Sidhe," replied Kaleya, fastening the necklace around her thin neck.

Amber saw the panic written on Rydan's face. He knew Kaleya wasn't lying, and that's what scared him the most. She had wiped out every lab in the mountain and somehow made a beautiful piece of jewelry into a terrible weapon. He hung his head in near defeat. "You have what you wanted; now leave!"

"Oh, my dear Master. I do not believe you understand. You see, this trinket will do what I ask of it, but it will only affect a small portion of the planet, enough for me to take over the important parts. I need you to complete it! Join me!" she said in an innocent tone.

He raised his face, utterly disgusted by her actions and guilt-ridden that his inventions were used for such evil. "Never."

"Shame, I was actually rather fond of you," she replied, raising the dagger.

A brilliant flash of light nearly blinded everyone in the room, giving Amber a mild headache. The light slowly dimmed, taking Rydan away with it. The vision faded away as Kaleya's screams of anger echoed in Amber's mind, bringing her back to reality. Now she understood why Rydan asked for his presence to remain a secret. She looked off in the distance in hopes of seeing his fleeting figure, but not a soul was in sight aside from Jermiar and Hunter, who had finally noticed she had stopped.

Jermiar urged her to leave the cursed area, as they needed to return to the family to explain what they found. However, she had found more than she had bargained for. Another player was in the game, one who could make or even break the curse. And he wanted nothing more than to remain in the shadows, leaving the rest of the world in harm's way.

10

Later that afternoon, they returned to the camp only to find that the other Grunewalds had shown up. Naturally, this came as a surprise to Amber, as they didn't seem all too interested in getting involved, but Dugon explained that her arrival put things in perspective for them. Holly was dead, and as much as he didn't agree with her life choices, he couldn't let her die in vain.

After the initial shock of their arrival, Amber explained her visions to the family, including Flaedar, who in his process of grief had gotten to the stage of revenge. Although she was glad he wasn't a complete wreck anymore, his drastic change could only prove to be a hindrance to their overall plan. When she told them of the last vision, everyone felt a little more comfortable with this new character. However, Amber kept her word and didn't tell them about his appearing just before they left. She needed answers from him, and if all it took was a small secret, she was willing to take that risk. With this new information coming to light, they now had a better idea of what they were dealing with. Unfortunately, neither of them knew how to get close enough to Kaleya to take the weapon, let alone destroy it.

As night fell, Amber found herself drifting off to sleep under the protection of a shelter. One of the wolf cubs crawled up to her sometime during the evening. She suddenly woke up to find it fast asleep, resting its head on her chest. She smiled, but then wondered what caused her to wake up. That's when she saw him at the top of the valley, partially hidden within the shadows where only she could see him.

Rydan gave her a short nod once he was certain she noticed him, and turned into the woods. Without waking the sleeping pup, Amber slowly moved out of its way, placing a balled- up piece of material she used as a pillow underneath its head. Silently, she stood up and checked her surroundings to be sure no one else was around. Then she climbed up the embankment, hoping the sound of crunching leaves wouldn't alert anyone. She strained her eyes, scanning the trees, but found only a few wolf guards in the distance, none of whom paid any attention to her. Taking a deep breath, she took a step into the night, only to trip over a small root. Two strong arms caught her before she made any noise from the fall. Amber looked up into the face of Rydan, who merely flashed a small smile as he balanced her.

"It's great to meet you, Amber Oak. Take a walk with me, we have a lot to talk about," Rydan said in an accent that sounded like a blend of German and Russian.

"Rydan? I don't understand. What are you? How do you know about my family and me? Are you really hiding from Kaleya?" asked Amber, the questions flowing out like a dam breaking.

"One question at a time, Amber. I came here from Darmentraea a little over a thousand years ago, although it was not by choice. The Brothers saw me as a threat because I was smarter than most and was born with an ability to create serums from little material—serums that could give one special abilities. Surprisingly, the Sidhe did not see me as a threat and saw good in me. They allowed me to live here. Very much like Dugon. He, too, is a native of Darmentraea. But his story is much different from mine," said the mysterious man as he started walking through the darkness. He held one of his glowing stones to light the way.

"How...how do you know this?" asked Amber staring at the man incredulously.

"I have made it my business to know. When you live as long as I have, you tend to know who your allies and enemies are," he replied cryptically.

"And who are we to you?" asked Amber, probing the man for further information.

"You are certainly no Kaleya, so I think that question should be rather obvious," he replied with a smile that seemed abnormally wide in the glow of the rock.

Amber smiled back, appreciating his humor amid the serious conversation. She brought the conversation back around and said, "Okay, so you and Dugon are from Darmentraea. Both with different stories of why you came here. Does that mean Kaleya is, too?"

"Yes and no. Kaleya should be on that planet, but the Sidhe are unreasonably merciful, even to their enemies. Kaleya was influenced by the wrong...people. She is just another example of the Balance deteriorating," he replied somberly.

"Well, as you know, she has a weapon. No one knows how to disarm her but you. We need your help, Rydan," Amber replied, trying not to sound as if she was begging.

He closed his eyes in defeat and shook his head, saying, "I can't do anything. I would only make it worse. The device she has will only grow stronger if I so much as touch it. I fear the only one who is powerful enough to disarm it is my descendant."

"But all of your descendants share the same blood, though," Amber replied, trying to understand the biology behind the weapon.

"True, but they do not share the same DNA as I do, which is what powers that weapon. Not my blood," he explained.

"Great, another manhunt," said Amber sarcastically.

"My descendants are closer than you think, find them,

and you will win this war. Find them, and you will know the truth about me," he replied calmly.

There was a soft sound as a wolf approached them. Amber turned her attention back toward the camp as the light started to show through the trees. Another question came to her mind, but as she turned back to Rydan, he had mysteriously disappeared.

Amber debated whether to tell her family what Rydan told her and their secret meeting in the middle of the night, but keeping secrets seemed to be her family's downfall. They needed to work together to stop Kaleya. However, most of the family didn't have a lot to say about Rydan, or if they did, they preferred to keep it confidential. Dugon, on the other hand, said he never heard any mention of Rydan having children or even family, so the idea of a descendant felt further away than before. But when the conversation ceased, and everyone slipped into his own thoughts, Amber had an idea. She might not be a descendant of Rydan, but if what everyone said about her was true about her restoring the Balance, then maybe she could disarm the weapon. It was the only option they had at the moment, and time was running out quickly.

Amber brought this idea to their attention, and most agreed, despite the fact it was a massive risk. She quickly formulated a battle strategy and said, "To get into the palace where Kaleya is no doubt hiding, that will require a distraction."

A faint, devious smile grew on Dugon's face as he said, "Perhaps I may be of help. I can suppress other abilities. If this Alchemist, Rydan, has put his DNA in his invention, I may be able to break through the weapon's effects."

"Dugon, I had no idea you were so powerful!" Joyra exclaimed, sarcasm souring her voice.

Embarrassed, the elder lowered his eyes and quietly replied, "I am not. My plan would require Jermiar's aid."

"Mine? My power cannot amplify your ability to all of the affected areas," replied Jermiar firmly.

"I speak not of suppressing the weapon itself. You are correct, our powers combined would not nearly be strong enough. I speak of the Galaseyan refugees. They could become a suppression shield."

"That is not possible, the only one with a shield ability is no longer with us," said Rogalar sadly.

Chris shook his head and smiled, "Actually, that's not entirely accurate. Amber, do you still have that ring that mom gave you?"

"It's right here," she replied looking down at the silver ring, now seeing how the white stone in the center swirled behind the glass that protected it. "Wow!" Without hesitation, Amber slid the ring off and placed it in Dugon's hands, now understanding that her mom never intended the ring to be used as jewelry but as a shield for a moment like this.

Despite having been around for a long time, the family was unfamiliar with how to combine powers or even if it was possible. Neither the Oaks nor the Grunewalds ever found interest in experimenting with their powers, as some seemed almost too dangerous to even use. But for this theory to work, they knew Jermiar's ability had to be involved, regardless. Several members offered to practice combining powers just to see how it worked. They set the shield ring aside carefully as it was the only one they had—without it, their plan would fail. Amber had to smile a little as Hunter's and Davylar's abilities created a weird shadow storm. Jermiar was astounded at this new aspect of his ability, although these small tests tired him some. It all was really an amazing sight. Not that their plan was working, but they were finally working together.

As Amber looked at her family, a floodgate of information burst wide open with a vision. Joyra was much more than a lady of the night, killing her husband just because she was bored with him. But judging by her usual behavior, she didn't need to have a logical reason at all. Dugon killed his love as well, but for an entirely different reason. She had somehow accidentally injured their son, Mason. Dugon couldn't trust her anymore, so he felt the only option was to kill her. At least that's all Amber actually saw. Davylar's past with Stephria finally became clearer. It was a complete mess on both sides, and no one seemed to have the courage to let bygones be bygones and move on. Fortunately, the two former lovebirds were the only ones who appeared to put things to the side. They had rekindled their love and worked things out over the last few hundred years.

Looking over at all the Oaks, Amber could sum them all up to be nearly saint-like. Just like any other person, they had their own issues, but none seemed to be a red flag to Amber—at least that she could see. There was always the chance one of them had some impenetrable wall built up. But she was starting to realize that wall would eventually come down.

But looking at both families as a whole, she finally saw them all exactly for who they were: a family of murderers and a family of saints, each member holding centuries of secrets from the others. But nothing surprised Amber more than when her eyes came to rest on Mason. Just like his family, he killed his love. After their child was born, he found no need for her. But the truly disturbing thing about him was that he seemed to be the cause of the family feud. He used his illusions against Davylar and Stephria just to make sure they'd never fall in love. She married another man because the illusions made her think Davylar didn't love her. And all it took was for Davylar to see Stephria at the wrong time. All this was done because Mason followed Dugon's order, and not happily, either. Mason wasn't fond of the Oaks, but interfering with them like that seemed like a waste of his time. Although Mason's dark secret seemed straightforward, something seemed strange about the whole ordeal. It felt as if he intentionally blocked this part of his past from curious minds.

Amber looked away from Mason, determined to find out the truth at a later time. Just as she was trying to sort everything through her mind, a firm hand rested on her shoulder. She turned around and looked into Chris' eyes, expecting to see some of his secrets, too. But there was nothing, not even a wall for her to break down. The harder she focused, the more her head began to ache. She quickly stopped as a trickle of blood seeped from her nose.

"Are you all right?" asked Chris.

As she loosened her focus on him, Amber's piercing headache faded, and the bleeding stopped. She brushed off his question by asking another one. "I don't get it. I can see the bad things mom's family did. Why didn't the Sidhe stop them?"

"The Sidhe are much like gods, in a sense. They don't involve themselves in the affairs of man unless man is doing something to harm Galaseya or the Balance. The Grunewald family has a very different opinion of the value of life," Chris said. Carefully choosing his words, he continued: "Dugon, the head of the Grunewald family, came from a...harsh background and was raised to believe that blood was more important than anything. Anyone who married into the family or even became friends was expendable. They see marriage as a necessity rather than romantic, unlike the Oaks."

Amber looked at Chris with curiosity and asked, "And what about you?"

"All life, not matter how great or small should be preserved," he replied with dignity.

"No, I mean, what do you think about the Grunewalds?" she asked, returning her attention to her family.

Chris sighed, feeling slightly uncomfortable with the conversation. He didn't exactly know what she saw, but given how suddenly distant Amber acted toward Hunter, he could only guess she discovered his dark secret. Chris shook his head and replied, "I'm not going to sugarcoat it. They've certainly made many mistakes. But that doesn't make them bad people. When you were born, the two families started coming together. Yes, we still disagree from time to time. But just like the Oaks, the Grunewalds love you too, Sis. Anyway, I came over here to tell you that we are ready to try out the plan."

Eager to see the results, Amber watched as the other Galaseyans who volunteered for the mission gathered in a group. With his left hand, Jermiar broke the glass ring the shield emerged shooting up his left arm while his right hand charged Dugon's ability. It was quite a remarkable sight as simultaneously the shield and Dugon's power reached their full capacity, both changing into a shimmery, opaque haze that engulfed one of Dugon's forearms while a dull purple haze climbed up the other. Being careful not to suppress the shield itself, Jermiar released his hold on the shield as Dugon then brought his glowing hands together, fingertips pointing at the Galaseyan volunteers. They rustled nervously, some second-guessing the idea. But no one had the chance to move—the beam of power wrapped around the crowd.

Although the beam almost knocked Dugon out, he rested a few minutes while Jermiar instructed the group never to leave the shield and only move as one body. It would only last for about three hours, which would give them enough time to break through the darkness and reach the outside of the palace. From there they would have just enough time for Amber to slip in while the soldiers were distracted. The group would then return to the natural part of Galaseya, hoping to bring the soldiers with them and possibly reverse the effects of the weapon.

It was a nice thought, but a part of Amber started secondguessing the plan, thinking it might only end up as a suicide mission. But if Jermiar was convinced the plan was foolproof, Amber had to show him a little trust. The rest of the family decided to stay behind and wait for their return. As the group made their way into the dark part of the woods, the shield held up well. It looked as if they were in the bubble of the normal Galaseya.

If given a choice, Amber would have liked to see it all play out. But she soon broke away, Hunter and Jermiar following closely behind. She was so focused on her thoughts and the mission she didn't hear them tagging along until she reached the palace. Stopping at the tree line in perfect view of the oncoming distraction, Amber waited for them to come from the opposite side of the palace. But just as she made a beeline for the front doors, gunfire echoed in Amber's ears. Occasionally, she got a glimpse of the Galaseyans, who seemed to be completely unharmed by the shower of bullets. The shield seemed to be working, but it just made the clueless soldiers more aggravated. Once they had the soldiers' attention, the Galaseyans returned to the woods, hoping they'd reach safety in time.

As the glow of their shield faded away into the darkness, Amber threw open the door and bolted inside. For a moment, she paused. The inside seemed almost worse than the outside. Amber didn't know the layout of this palace at all. Suddenly, her mind gave way to fear. There was no way of knowing where Kaleya was, or for that matter if she was even in there.

You have the power. Get inside her head! Think, where would a person like her be? she told herself.

Entering the woman's memory was probably the vilest thing Amber possibly ever did, but it certainly wasn't the hardest. Kaleya had flooded the vicinity with her memories, all of which were horrific. Her arrogant nature and one-track mind allowed Amber to read her past like an open book. Sorting through some of her more gruesome acts, Amber finally found the one she was looking for.

Of all the terrible things Kaleya did, this memory had to be at the bottom of the list. Shortly after her reign of terror began, she trashed Renalia's bedroom, turning it into her own throne room. Amber raced down the halls at high speed, anger fueling her drive. Hunter and Jermiar did their best to keep up. Neither asked what was wrong or how she knew to maneuver through the dimly lit, crumbling building. They knew her facial expressions well enough to know she had a vision.

The doors to the nursery were wide open, and to Amber's surprise, it was unguarded. The distraction had drawn out every mindless guard. Upon entering the room, the trio had to watch their footing as all the furniture looked to have been disassembled by a tornado. Blue curtains covering a large window appeared to have been shredded by a pack of particularly angry cats, and only fragments of material dangled at various lengths over the window. There was Kaleya, clutching the window sill with a vice-like grip. Her knuckles were white as ivory.

"What sorcery is this?" she demanded.

"Not exactly sorcery, still trying to figure it out myself, though," said Amber nonchalantly, wanting to keep Kaleya off-balance.

Kaleya defiantly faced Amber. With her hair in disarray, a crown sat haphazardly on her head, seeming only to be held up by a few strands of flyaway hair. Dark bags hung low under her piercing brown eyes.

Amber's heart raced as she bravely approached the wild woman. Her eyes glanced to Kaleya's neck and saw the weapon radiate the same orange glow. Kaleya's eyes widened in fear as she exclaimed, "How did you do that outside?"

"I didn't. My family and several of the villagers did. You underestimated the strength and will of the people!" Amber replied.

"The only person I know who has that kind of power is hiding like a coward!" Kaleya yelled into the empty air, as if she thought Rydan might somehow overhear.

An epiphany. All it took was the words of a lunatic to make Amber realize exactly what Rydan meant about his descendants. Amber smiled as she replied, "That *coward* is my ancestor!"

Amber reached out and wrenched the weapon from Kaleya's neck. Forgetting she had injured her dominant hand on a rock, she absentmindedly squeezed the locket, reopening her tender wound, and a trickle of blood fell to the floor. Suddenly, light began to appear outside as if dawn slowly approached. All four people peered outside and saw an amazing sight. The darkness was slowly melting away, just like paint dripping down an artist's canvas. People soon emerged from the woods dressed in their usual Galaseyan attire. Off to the side, Amber saw a teenaged boy walking around with a sort of dazed expression on his face. It was the same boy she saw shot when she first arrived in Galaseya. Even the soldiers' guns were part of the large weapon!

Amber looked at Kaleya, whose face was nearly completely drained of blood, "My...my world! You...you destroyed it!"

Amber glanced down at the necklace, which was now empty of its orange glow. The blood from her hand had permeated through the makeshift bandage and smeared the top of the pendant. Amber looked at Kaleya, who appeared almost pitiful. Amber would have felt sorry for her, but then remembered everything she had done and just said, "No, Kaleya, you did."

A fiery rage fumed within the insane woman. Lifting her hands, Kaleya reached for Amber's throat. Immediately, Amber raised her arms in a defensive position just as a brown glow encased her hands. Just as quickly as the light came, it vanished. Afraid Kaleya would still attack, Amber stepped farther back; Jermiar and Hunter came to her side.

Kaleya looked around at the massive room, confusion masking her usual manic expression. Amber carefully asked her if she was okay, but the woman only replied, "Who is Kaleya?" Amber exchanged nervous glances with the others. All wondering if this was a strange last attempt at regaining power.

"You don't remember anything?" asked Hunter.

Kaleya looked around the room again, hoping the mess would jog her memory. But it was completely erased, "No, should I?"

This was it! Kaleya could have a fresh new start at life! There would be no need for exile or worse. Amber began having all these great ideas, when golden flecks slowly rose from the ground and morphed into a cloud formation behind Kaleya. Within them, Amber could see the three figures of the Sidhe. Fully formed, they approached the confused and new Kaleya and guided her away. The pink Sidhe, Analira, whose dress was the same as the others aside from two straps that crossed in the front, replied, "Do not worry, we shall take you home." She nodded her head as her circlet made of deer antlers, that Amber assumed the deer shed, moved around on her pale pink hair.

Vaeris approached Amber in her natural form similar to that of the others, but instead wore a long, flowy blue dress with one shoulder strap. A mini tornado on its side wrapped around her head, creating a circlet. She put a comforting hand on her shoulder and said, "We will take care of her. She will never remember her wicked deeds, though I fear the people of the village will not soon forgive her. We have selected another, safer location for her."

"How did I do that?" asked Amber nervously.

"Along with seeing memories, you can also remove them from someone," she replied watching her sisters disappear with Kaleya.

Vaeris started for the door, but Amber stopped her and said, "Why? Why am I so different from my family? I just...I just don't get it."

"Do not worry, Ameliana. You will see soon enough," she replied just as she disappeared.

Confused by her cryptic response, Amber left the room, feeling a tingle in the spot Vaeris had touched, but thought nothing of it at the moment. As the trio reached the old throne room, light from the open door cast shadows on the bloodstained ground—a permanent reminder of the horrendous massacre which took place only a week ago. Suddenly, the light began to shift, revealing the real beauty of the place. The stones in its walls aligned perfectly and several rows of columns lined the room, making a direct path from the front door to the throne, its large seat in desperate need of repair.

Amber stepped outside into the early morning light and looked out on the village. She noticed how the ocean seemed to glisten. As she briefly took in her surroundings, she saw something in the sky—a sight that only she seemed surprised by. A planet the size of Neptune hung over them like an oncoming storm. The massive world was so close that Amber noticed pieces of the dark land that peeked through the thick, light blue clouds that wrapped around the planet. Darmentraea. Vaeris' touch had removed the blockade in Amber's mind. The dark world stood as another reminder that Vaeris was right. Defeating Kaleya was only the beginning to restoring the Balance.

11

Weeks went by, and so did the months, but there was no word from Rydan. Amber knew he was still around, as he would often appear at random times just out of view of the others. With the battle over and Kaleya no longer a threat, Amber told her family that she had spoken with Rydan and he had explained a few things to her, things that she willingly told them. Most of the family, including some close friends that they made in the camp, were very open to meeting Rydan—except Dugon. Amber didn't need a vision to see that the two had a past of some kind, one which the elder silently refused to delve into, at least for now.

As for the village and other parts of the land, Kaleya did a number on them before the curse began. The people tried to go about their daily routine, although they found it difficult as they had to balance that with fixing their homes and remaking their lives. Fortunately, the palace remained intact, proudly standing on the hill like a miniature, stone Buckingham Palace. The furniture within the great building was another story. They surmised that through her many rampages, Kaleya took her anger out on anything that was wood. The only irreplaceable thing in the palace was the floor of the royal court, which still remained bloodstained.

However, the new owner of the palace thought it would be a perfect reminder of the consequences of war. To Amber's surprise, Flaedar wasn't just the former queen's advisor, he was of the lowest position of nobility. Amber never went to his coronation, mostly because there wasn't much to go to. Were there other members of the court, the situation would be considerably different. To be deemed a ruler, the creatures of the woods needed to see the individual as their leader first. The deer of the land came out of the forest willingly and proceeded to bow to their king. Although this new title seemed to scare him, he took on his own advisor, a cheerful young man by the name of Iethreor who acted the polar opposite of his king.

Flaedar offered for Amber and her family to stay in the palace, mostly because he didn't like the loneliness the stone walls now invited. The Grunewalds took him up on the generous offer only because their home sat far away. The Oaks seemed more inclined to use their large manor that sat nestled in the tree line hidden, from the outside world.

From the manor's position, the village, palace, and ocean were in view—a perfect place to spy on everyone. At first glance, the house appeared to be just like those in the village, but the low-hanging branches concealed an additional floor. The setting was perfect for a fairytale. The interior of the house appeared rather stylish, as much as medieval-style society allowed. Every piece of furniture was made of some kind of finished wood that resembled oak, which Amber found to be slightly comical.

On her first visit to the house, Jermiar introduced her to his favorite room of the entire manor—a library, but not just any library. This one was massive and specifically built for someone with the love of learning. Amber stood at the top of a grand marble-like staircase that led down to the rest of the library. Windows lined the stone walls, alternating with floor to ceiling bookshelves. Each section seemed to be filled with books on one particular topic.

As she walked down the staircase, Amber caught a closer glimpse of some of the books. Jermiar seemed fascinated with books from all over Amber's world, and some he seemed to have written himself. Most of the genres consisted of various sciences and history. The last few steps were large and semi-circular, wrapping around the staircase. Amber hopped off the last step and instantly came in contact with what looked to be a large red and orange rug, which covered most of the dark wood flooring. In the center of the rug stood a large wooden table. On each side sat a large comfortable chair. At one point it looked to have been a dining table that could easily seat seven people. As she neared the table, Amber looked beyond and saw a large loveseat with thick cushions sitting underneath a window, a blanket splayed haphazardly over the edge and a small pillow resting in the corner. Amber smiled at Jermiar's dedication to discovery. Despite the library's beauty and shelves full of knowledge, the only thing that caught Amber's attention was the ceiling, which was not made of stone. This was due to the large mural which spread over the whole ceiling.

At first glance, the mural looked like a strange star chart, but then Amber noticed how among all the stars there were three main planets and a fourth one off to the side. Each one had its own personality about it. One planet looked as bright as the sun; another was dark and creepy, and aside from its thick, light blue colored clouds, it could easily pass for a moon. The third planet looked exactly like earth, but the fourth planet was hard to identify. It was farther away, but from what Amber saw, it was completely green. She asked Jermiar about it, and he said that that was the way the Sidhe described the solar system to them. He wanted to always remember how it looked in case he needed to use it as a reference. Drawing it out didn't seem to do it justice.

Amber often found herself spending time with Jermiar in his library, her eyes always shifting back toward the mural, wondering what the earth-like planet and green planet were. When he wasn't with his animal family, Sphinx would be in the library, distracting Amber from her reading by bumping the forgotten book out of her hand. As soon as Amber and Chris were situated in their new home, Chris went back to gather their things, collect the cat, and sell their house, all of which he did promptly. Amber wasn't too surprised, seeing how he always had things planned far in advance, something he learned while growing up.

The only uncomfortable thing Amber experienced was the queen's funeral. Although her death wasn't Amber's fault, she still felt a twinge of guilt at not arriving to Galaseya sooner. It happened to be the most beautiful thing Amber ever saw. The procession and ritual captured the very essence of the peace and light that the world represented. The parade began in the throne room. Typically, all the royals and nobles would start dressed in white clothing, but since none were left, Amber and her family were put in their place. The servants that had survived the war stopped their duties and joined the procession; their outfits were all as close to white as possible.

The queen's body lay on a type of stretcher set on top of a stone table. She had a peaceful look about her, as if she were asleep, completely without a care in the world—her gruesome wound was covered by a high collar. Her body was dressed in a brilliant white gown with shiny silver embroidery. The crown she had worn in life was carefully placed on her head. Her hands were placed together over her abdomen and held unique flowers. They looked like red tulips, but Amber knew from observation that they were leaves from a tree which only grew in the royal garden in the front of the palace. According to Flaedar, the tree symbolized life. Every year, during the month of April, the offspring of the wild creatures came to the gardens and played around the tree. The older animals stayed by the tree line, keeping a watchful eye on their young. No one knew what attracted the newborns to the tree, but it was a great opportunity for the village children to play with the animals.

The procession soon left the palace. Amber stood in front with her family, right behind the queen's stretcher, which was carried by pallbearers. The palace servants were dressed in the whitest garments Amber had seen them wear. They followed the path past the gardens and joined the villagers. Silence was soon broken by various forms of crying. Some women wailed at the loss of their beloved queen. The pallbearers took a sudden turn across the lawn and headed toward the woods—almost in the exact direction of the mountain. Amber glanced back and saw the villagers fall in line behind the family—each one carrying some kind of flower as did Amber's family and the palace servants. The village looked barren as not a soul remained.

Just before they reached the end of the woods, the pallbearers gently placed the stretcher on the ground. Amber thought it disrespectful but remembered what Flaedar had said a few days prior. Putting the queen on the ground was another symbol of the Galaseyan culture. It showed that the people were giving their queen back to nature. In doing so, one kind of the wild creatures would come out of the woods, and they would carry the stretcher taking the lead of the procession. Depending on which animal and its pack participated in the funeral depended on the ruler's personality.

Amber looked toward the woods as four large cats emerged, their clan following closely behind. The full-grown cats weren't as large as the wolves, but they stood a little bigger than a grizzly bear, and the kittens were about the size of leopards. Their black and brown stripes were the only thing distinguishing them from their African counterparts. Amber thought back to the symbolism of the cats, remembering that meant the queen was intelligent and fierce. Amber opened her mouth in wonderment at the creatures but quickly regained her composure. The large cats took the bars of the stretcher in their mouths and started walking toward the woods. The kittens fell in line after them.

A short way into the woods, the procession entered a large grove of trees. The ground was covered in a vibrant green grass which had a moss-like texture. Scattered around the grove were mounds, rock formations, all in the shape of enclosed caskets. Coarsely designed tombstones were carefully placed at the head of the graves. The larger the stones, the higher the rank. The queen's stone looked more like the size of a boulder. An epitaph was chiseled into the gray stone, but some of it wasn't legible. Either the person was inexperienced or shook with sadness. From what little Amber could read, it stated the queen's name, her birth and death, and below it was inscribed, "Our Beloved Queen."

The cats carrying the queen gently lowered the stretcher to the ground. They then proceeded to push the stretcher into an opening at the end of the stone casket—the rods of the stretcher breaking with the pressure against the rocks. Yet another symbolism. This time, nature was releasing the queen to the afterlife. Although Amber wasn't exactly sure what that was for the Galaseyans, she assumed some type of Native American belief in that the corpse became part of nature. Once the queen was finally laid to rest, two kittens, who looked like Sphinx's siblings, approached the casket, nudging a rather large stone and sealing the opening.

The crying and wails of the funeral goers grew louder as each individual approached the stone tomb placing a flower on the top. The cats backed away from the grave and all bowed, their eyes closed as they all harmoniously let out a low purr. Not in a manner of happiness, but one that resonated the sadness all felt. Some of the kittens even looked pitiful. It surprised Amber a little to see tears began to trickle from their eyes. *Wow, they really do think like humans!*

The crowd began to thin, and the animals returned to the depths of the woods. After that day, Amber often found Flaedar returning to the cemetery where only a few of his relatives were laid to rest. The funeral for the other members of the court was more of a mass cremation, as there was little left of them. Their ashes were scattered around the tombstones upon request of the new king. That way they were buried in the proper place, in a sense.

The Sidhe appeared on occasion, giving advice to the new king and restoring the village and other damaged areas to their original state. However, when Rydan decided to come out of the shadows and introduce himself to the family, the Sidhe seemed to disappear. This wasn't a surprise to Amber, as the Sidhe seemed to stay out of the matters of her family unless it directly involved the planet. Besides, they probably already knew everything about Rydan. But Rydan had a message to deliver, or rather an explanation. He confirmed what Amber already knew, that he was related to the family, but not in the usual sense.

"So, you're the famous Rydan we've all been dying to meet!" said Mason with a hint of sarcasm.

Amber and her family stood in Jermiar's library as they watched this mysterious Alchemist descend the stairs, looking a bit uncomfortable at being on display like this. Gathering his courage, he replied, "Yes, I'm sorry it's taken me this long to approach you. I needed to be sure Kaleya was no longer a threat."

"That is fine, we completely understand," said Rogalar, hoping to ease the tension in the air.

"Thank you, but I did not come here for a simple visit, unfortunately. I came here to warn you that the threat that affects the Balance is growing stronger. I have reason to believe the Brothers are planning an attack," Rydan replied as he reached the bottom of the staircase.

"What is the source of this information?" asked Dugon, surprising everyone that he spoke up.

Rydan's silver eyes darted toward Dugon, and a sly smile crossed his face as his eyes stared the elder down, as if in a challenge, as he replied, "Come now, Dugon. You ought to know, after all, you and I have been friends for a long time."

"Father?" asked Mason who for the first time appeared taken back.

Ignoring his son's confusion, Dugon replied, "How could I forget? You were the one who took me in when I came here."

Annoyed with being out of the loop, Joyra spoke up and said, "Will someone explain what is going on?"

Dugon and Rydan stared at each other for a moment as a feeling of nostalgia overcame them both. At a time that seemed much simpler than now. Rydan then replied, "Gladly."

While he explained his story, Amber found herself slipping into the very vision of the past he described. *Rydan stood outside of a house, larger than the village homes but smaller than the Oak and Grunewald manors. He tended to a rather small, scraggly tree that could easily pass for a large shrub. Amber looked closer at the tree and saw it bore the most unusual fruit she had ever seen. It looked almost like a giant purple grape, except the skin revealed small red bumps. Considering this tree was found nowhere else on Galaseya, she assumed this plant was yet another one of Rydan's inventions. But the purpose of it remained a mystery until the next part of the vision showed Rydan cutting the fruit open and squeezing the juice into the small mouth of a sickly little girl, whom he called Saraleast. Within moments of the juice touching her lips, a strange silvery glow encompassed her little body. The magical fruit lifted the sickness from the girl as she reached her hands up toward Rydan, a single phrase escaping her: "Thank you, Papa."*

In the future scenes, the little girl's mom seemed to be absent, making Amber think she either left the family when the girl got sick, or she passed away during childbirth. But it didn't seem to bother the small family. Rydan continued with various experiments to help make their lives easier. But that exotic plant still grew out in front of their house, the contents of its makeup only known to its creator. The vision fast-forwarded only a little, to when the little girl was a young woman around the age of sixteen, and she discovered something new about herself. She had an ability, something that had never showed when she was younger. Through practice, she realized that her body transformed in a ghost-like fashion, passing through solid objects and even controlling them. On more than one occasion she startled her father, but it never angered him. He thought it to be rather comical. Both father and daughter thought this new development came from his invention that healed her. Rydan went on to explain to her that he boosted the power of the healing fruit by adding his blood to it in hopes his power might make her stronger. Giving her power was far from what he intended. He then explained that when he turned sixteen, he too developed powers and a long lifespan in which he aged one year every thirty years. Because of the content of the fruit, the girl had these traits as well. Although this seemed fascinating to her, she begged her father to destroy the plant in fear that others might accidentally eat it.

Rydan almost did, except the Sidhe came to him explaining that the Balance of Galaseya was in grave danger and someone of his line would eventually not only be the restorer of the Balance but the Protector of Galaseya. At this time, only one person held this position on another planet near them called Diraetus—Amber assumed this to be one of the unknown planets in the mural of the library. But for the solar system to be balanced out the other planets needed a Protector, too. The Sidhe emphasized to Rydan that if something major happens on one planet, then it must happen to the others. However, they refused to tell him how Diraetus came about finding its Protector.

With this wave of new information flooding every part of her mind, Amber almost didn't see the vision change as a young boy was thrown from Darmentraea, landing near Rydan's home. The little boy, whom Amber assumed to be Dugon, made his way through the unfamiliar woods. As he neared Rydan's home he saw the fruit tree. His stomach had growled even before he left his home planet, and seeing the fruit made it worse. Making sure the owner of the house wasn't in the vicinity, he yanked the fruit from the tree and proceeded to devour it all.

Rydan and his daughter ran outside after she alerted her father that someone had eaten the fruit. Both stared at the child in shock, neither one understanding how he had come so far from the village, as their house was farther away than even the Grunewalds' manor. Then Rydan saw the child's clothing and realized the Brothers had done the exact same thing to this child as they had done to him all those years ago. It was pointless to try and figure out how to reverse the process. Besides, if he showed any signs of power like his daughter, then the village would never accept this boy even if he acted properly and wore the right things.

Amber thought it was great of Rydan to adopt Dugon. Both the children got along famously, and to Rydan's relief, Dugon's power was invisible. All he could do was minimize another's power. It seemed harmless enough, and Dugon had no interest in using his power anyway. Life seemed fine for this small family and over time, Rydan forgot his promise to Saraleast and neglected to destroy the tree, which seemed perfectly capable of sustaining itself. Although his daughter often reminded her father to destroy the tree, Rydan simply gave her empty promises, not revealing the truth as to why he lied.

The next vision came as Amber watched through the eyes of Rydan, who stared out the window at his tree, watching as two couples picked its fruit. Amber sensed tension and concern in Rydan at this memory. He followed the Sidhe's plan to a T and never questioned it, but he also knew how painful living forever was to the outside world. And depending on their body makeup and personality, there was no way of knowing now what their power would consist of. The couples below were his daughter and her husband and Dugon and his wife.

A brief vision showed Amber that earlier Rydan finally confessed to Saraleast and Dugon about the Sidhe and what they had told him. Naturally, neither were pleased to hear this news so suddenly. Saraleast was incredibly hesitant about introducing her husband to the fruit that gave her an unusual power, with near immortality to match. But Saraleast had a heart of compassion for people and a great respect for her father, so she agreed to his request in allowing her husband to eat the fruit. Dugon even suggested having his wife eat it too, so as to not make Saraleast's husband suspicious or uncomfortable.

Moments later, Amber found herself standing in front of the tree, watching it become engulfed in flames. From the memory, it seemed the Sidhe only wanted her family to get the powers. Because he was hesitant about destroying his precious invention, the Sidhe took it upon themselves to relieve him of that burden. As Amber watched the flames reach into the sky the vision began to fade, and a black, charred spot on the ground appeared—her entire family still had eyes on Rydan, who had just finished speaking.

As Amber stared dumbfounded at the scene before her, she glanced off to the side and saw the crumbling structure of Rydan's forgotten home. Her visions sometimes lasted a while, but they never made her travel anywhere.

Noticing her perplexed look, Stephria said, "Ameliana, is everything all right? You look quite pale."

"How did we get here?" she asked, not even masking her concern.

The others turned to Amber, and some looked around to make sure they hadn't missed anything while listening to Rydan's story. Rogalar spoke up and said, "Sweetheart, we have been here this entire time. Rydan led us here from the palace and explained his story."

"That's not possible. I had a vision, and I swear, before that we were in the library. Jermiar...you were trying to show us something you discovered that might help with restoring the Balance," said Amber insistently.

"Ameliana, I did that early this morning. It is well near supper time now. Perhaps that vision exhausted you too much," said Jermiar hiding the worry in his tone.

Her heart raced so fast she feared the sound of it gave way to the panic that she felt. Instead of arguing her case, she nodded her head and shrugged her shoulders as she replied, "You know what? You're probably right. It was an intense vision. I'm just going to head back home."

"I'll walk with you," Mason announced. "I'm getting tired myself."

Although she wanted to walk alone, there was something in Mason's voice that made the comment sound less of a kind gesture and more of a statement. She smiled and started for the woods with Mason quietly walking beside her. When they were well out of hearing range, Mason faced Amber and quickly grabbed her shoulders, shaking her slightly. His eyes widened in fear and his voice nearly shook with the same panic that Amber felt. "Amber, you have to get out of here!"

"Whoa, hold it," said Amber trying to reason with him, "Jermiar's probably right, the vision tired me out."

"You know that's far from the truth. You were in the library when Rydan began explaining his story. You have to leave this place!" he exclaimed.

"What? Mason, you're scaring me," said Amber, releasing herself from his grip, "Wait, when *I* was in the library? We all were in the library."

Mason backed away from her, and he looked almost wild with his expression of absolute terror as he shook his head saying, "No Amber, it was only you!"

Only her. Those words rang through Amber's mind that night. Sphinx even seemed uneasy as he continuously repositioned himself on her bed that night. How could it have been only her? Everyone was in the library! A part of her wondered if Mason's odd behavior was something of the norm for him. After all, she didn't know him too well. But he seemed genuinely afraid—a feeling she never thought a man like him ever felt. Besides, where would she go? It's not as if there was an easy way to get off the planet. Despite the millions of questions floating in her brain, Amber resolved to get at least some sleep that night in hopes that in the morning things would make more sense. Unfortunately, that didn't happen. In fact, the mysterious events of the evening before seemed to melt into the next day.

Her family went about their daily routine just as the people in the village did; however, Jermiar seemed uninterested in his research. Instead, he went for a long walk in the woods, something he never liked doing to begin with. When Amber approached him casually, asking what new things he discovered in his research, he gave her a quizzical look before quickly replying, "I have looked through every single book I own. I cannot make any sense of this Balance or how to restore it. I decided that a stroll through the forest might clear my head."

"But you hate senseless walking. You told me yourself. And since when do you give up on anything?" asked Amber, hoping this was some kind of sick joke.

"I do apologize, Amber, but since the Sidhe have not spoken to us in months, perhaps the Balance has already been restored, and all it took was for someone to remove Kaleya from her tyranny!" he suggested, before continuing his walk.

Between Mason's strange words of warning the night before and Jermiar's sudden change in interest, something was definitely wrong, but she had no idea what was causing these bizarre occurrences. Instead of attempting to reason with her grandfather, she ran back to the palace, hoping to find Mason in his usual spot in the gardens. With any luck, he'd be more open to talking to her. She wove in between the trees and across the grassy field toward the large flower garden in front. She slowed her pace as she approached her great-great grandfather, who was kneeling down next to a beautiful rose shrub, examining its greenery.

"Mason!" she exclaimed, "I need to talk to you about yesterday!"

"Morning to you too, Amber," he replied with a smile as he handed her a rose.

Amber looked down at the red petals with slight confusion, but took the unusually kind gesture anyway and replied, "Um, thanks...Yesterday, when you said I needed to leave and I was the only one in the library...what were you talking about?"

His thick brows knitted together as he gave her a small smile and replied, "I don't remember saying anything about that. We were all in the library yesterday morning, of course, Jermiar rambled on about some innocuous theory so I can't remember what he said for the life of me. But I never told you that you needed to leave. This is your home, Ameliana, you have no reason to leave!"

Amber started backing away, absentmindedly allowing the rose to slip through her fingers. She ignored Mason's look of concern as she replied, "You just called me, 'Ameliana.' You've never called me that."

"That is your given name. I can't see what else I would call you. Besides, my name is Marsacor, you've never referred to me as Mason," he replied.

Immediately, Amber ran out of the garden, ignoring Mason's calls. She started for the village where things at least appeared normal. The villagers cast curious glances her way, but she was used to that, as her family was now considered upper class or noble in their eyes. Tears flowed down her cheeks as she made her way through the crowd to a nearby rock wall that bordered a garden. As she sorted through the problems at hand, allowing the soft sounds of the waves and soaring birds fill her with as much peace as possible, a strange sound interrupted her moment of silence.

"Marsacor is right, you know," came an unfamiliar voice.

Amber nearly jumped out of her skin at the sight of him. The blue highlights were absent from his black hair, his skin was as pale as hers, and his once bright blue eyes were now the color of the ocean. The boy from the abandoned asylum looked at her with a calming smile stretching across his face as he continued, "My name is Ambrose, and you need to get out!"

12

"Get out of Galaseya?" asked Amber, confused that some stranger told her the same thing that Mason did, let alone know him by name. "I don't understand. I just came from talking to him, and he's going back on what he said. He doesn't even remember. So why do you?"

Ambrose looked toward the palace and nodded, seeming to agree with something he was thinking about as he replied, "I know a lot about you and your family and this whole Balance thing. I've been doing research myself, just like your grandfather, trying to find a way to resolve the situation."

"Wait, the villagers know nothing about the Balance or about my family," Amber said, whispering as a few local fishermen walked by, "You're not from here, are you?"

Ambrose chuckled and said, with a hint of lightheartedness in his tone, "No, what gave it away?"

For the first time in a while, Amber smiled. She missed the feeling of joking around and relaxing with someone. But it seemed that no matter how much peace this planet offered, it was never enough. Ambrose seemed relaxed too, as if catching up with an old friend, as he continued to explain. "I'm much like you in so many ways, and at the same time we are complete opposites. I am Darmentraea's Protector."

"How did you get here, then?" asked Amber, wondering if there truly was a way to escape to her home planet even for a short time.

"That's where it gets complicated. See, we technically aren't fully the Protectors yet. We are half mortal and half immortal, we're at the halfway point to becoming the Protectors. Although we have our primary abilities, we can also create minor shields of protection and repel any threat. We just can't do it on our other planets, at least not yet. On the other hand, we do have one advantage, and that is we have a telepathic connection which can be accessed from any planet. The people of our worlds will be able to travel to the other planets through the Portal with a single thought directing them to the planet of their choice, but not now, not until the Balance is restored. The only ones who can travel now are the planets in human form, Chris, who has some Sidhe-like powers, and the Protectors," Ambrose replied, hoping the flood of words made sense.

"Well, if you can come here, then why didn't you sooner? We could have totally used you in the fight against Kaleya," said Amber, feeling slightly annoyed.

Ambrose turned his entire body toward Amber and leaned in close enough that she could see the faint flecks of green in his blue eyes, reminding her that she had flecks of blue in her green eyes. He took her hand and whispered, "Because I am not really here, I'm in your mind! Just like everything else!"

A fearful tear escaped Amber's eye as the blood drained from her face. Ambrose looked so realistic it was impossible for him not to be. Was this one big dream? If so, when did she fall asleep? Amber felt her mind tearing apart at the seams when she stuttered back, "Help...help me figure out what's going on!"

Something from the bustling crowd scared the words out of Ambrose. His eyes narrowed on something only he could see. His eyes still glued to the spot, Ambrose replied to Amber almost as if challenging the invisible entity. "I will, you have my word." Still holding her hand, Ambrose rose to leave and said to her, his voice full of severity as if that would save her life, "Whatever you do, don't forget me."

"I won't, I promise," she replied, wondering what the hidden meaning was that lay behind his words.

"Don't forget me," he repeated, as his hand slipped out of hers and he disappeared into thin air.

Amber looked towards the crowd in hopes of finding the person or thing that had scared Ambrose off. All appeared normal, but then again nothing felt normal to her—not anymore. Trying to avoid the inevitable claustrophobia from the noonday rush of the village, Amber turned around, intending to escape the mass by taking a small, rarely used path behind the main houses. But her eyes widened in fear as she found herself back in the gardens of the palace—Mason holding a rose out to her as if their conversation had just begun.

"What about yesterday did you want to talk about?" asked Mason, a little concerned by the intense look of shock on Amber's face.

Any response at this point would place her under some kind of insanity watch—something time didn't allow for. Rather than risk the chance, she merely shrugged her shoulders and shook her head casually, saying, "Just that I'm glad we got more information from Rydan about his past."

"I couldn't agree more. Having Rydan as a family member will make everything complete," he replied, his tone and demeanor sounding joyful.

Amber accepted his rose and turned away, walking out of the gardens and feeling his gaze on her. She grew aggravated, not completely understanding which was real—her family's sudden indifference to the Balance or this strange foreigner who at first sight scared her half to death. Her last shot at getting answers lay in the thousands of books Jermiar kept in his library. There had to be at least one book that spoke about something like this happening. Unfortunately, Jermiar was still on his unexpected walk through the woods as Amber struggled to find the right book. But despite her best efforts to understand it all without his help, nothing Jermiar wrote about the family added up to the things she experienced. With her mind nearly made up on forgetting Ambrose and continuing on with this peaceful life, Amber put the last book away, when Jermiar came bursting through the door, running down the stairs and almost tumbling into her.

"Ameliana, why are you still here? You must leave!" he exclaimed, tugging on her arm and dragging her towards the door.

She removed herself from his grip and stopped him, saying, "You too? What's going on? Mason told me the same thing, and so did Ambrose!"

"Ambrose? He is...he is here?" asked Jermiar, confused and nervous.

"Yeah...wait, how do you know him?" asked Amber, starting to doubt her sanity.

Jermiar looked as if he had accidentally revealed some big secret. He ignored her question and continued his train of thought. "Ambrose's presence can only mean one thing: that the Brothers are behind this illusion."

"Illusion? How can they create an illusion on Galaseya? I thought their powers were restricted here," she replied, looking all around, expecting to see an abnormality in this believable scene.

"You are part Galaseyan and Darmentraean, they can reach into that part of your mind that belongs to them and morph it into whatever they like!" he hastily pressed on. "*Now, what did Ambrose tell you*?"

Amber explained to him their conversation, but then paused as she realized how intensely he emphasized that last phrase. She expressed her confusion about it, saying how it made no sense and questioning why the Brothers would even bother to put her in an illusion. After all, what good would that profit them?

"This illusion will do wonders for them if they succeed. They know you cannot be killed, but they can put your mind in such a state where it will feel impossible to escape," he replied.

"That's not bleak at all," she replied bitterly. "So if I can't escape this impenetrable prison, why are you here to even warn me?"

For the first time in this entire conversation, Jermiar cracked a smile as he said, "You misheard me. I said it will *feel* impossible to escape, not that it is. You and only you can break free of this. We have exhausted all our options, but nothing has helped. Now go, find the weakest part of the illusion and show those fools that you are a force to be reckoned with!"

Amber ran up the stairs as Jermiar's last words bounced off the walls in the library. She ran down the halls of the manor, only to come to an abrupt halt at her bedroom door. A strange pale blue light emanated from the cracks. Curious, she poked her head into the room and saw the most unusual sight. Her entire family, including the king, some of his servants, and the Sidhe, were all crowded into the room. Jermiar and Mason stood on either side of her bed—Jermiar using nearly all his strength to charge Mason, who held a wilted hand tightly.

Amber squinted her eyes to see the figure lying in her bed. It was really herself, with a faded blue haze wrapped around her body, which lay still in a comatose state—one that not even Joyra herself could perform. *Is that really me? What's the illusion and what's reality? When did that even happen?* she wondered as she pried herself away from the awful scene.

Her first idea was to find a way to call the Sidhe. Generally, anytime they were needed, anyone could call on them, though she never remembered their true names. She only knew one personally. Vaeris. When she reached the woods behind the Oak Manor, she yelled for her name until her voice became hoarse, but nothing moved, not even the wild creatures of the woods or the birds that lived in the treetops.

"Will you please stop shouting, you'll wake the dead," came a familiar voice.

Amber spun around to see Ambrose leaning up against a tree examining his nails. He lifted his head and smirked at her. Something in his voice sent shivers up her spine, but she couldn't put a finger on it. Trying to make light of the situation she replied, "Yeah, well, maybe if I did that my mom would be alive."

"I don't know about that. Your mom always came across as a person who would die prematurely regardless," he replied, pulling away from the tree and crossing his arms.

Ignoring his impolite response, she changed the subject, "What are you doing here, Ambrose? I thought..."

"You thought what?" he interrupted. "I was in danger and had to leave you? Please, I wanted to leave. You were annoying me with your constant complaining that nothing made sense. Have you ever thought that the world didn't revolve around you? Some of us actually have a life and don't feel like dealing with your problems."

There it was. The boy in the asylum that terrified her. Was this really how Ambrose acted? Was that even really his name? Did that mean the girl in the mirror with fiery eyes was her, too? Her heart hammered in her chest as she forced the waterworks back. She tried being brave and said calmly, "What are you, bipolar? You acted really nice not too long ago. It was like we were becoming friends."

Ambrose walked dangerously close to Amber, her heart hammering faster with each step he took, so that by the time they stood nose to nose she swore her heart stopped. His eyes narrowed as the corner of his lip curled upward. "Who's to say that this isn't really how I am. You don't even know me, Amber."

She stared into his eyes when suddenly the words of his kinder self, repeated in her mind: *Don't forget me!* Ambrose's eyes searched Amber's face for any sign of weakness, but then the blood drained from her face when she saw black flecks in his blue eyes, "You're right, I don't know you. But I know who you aren't, Martheykos."

Ambrose's face morphed into something almost otherworldly as the young man started turning into the being she had seen in the vision of her mother and Chris escaping the planet. He shook his head and with a crazed expression on his face said, "You just had to ruin my fun."

Swiftly, he raised a strong hand and grabbed Amber by the throat, drew her back and threw her with a violent force through an opening in the trees.

If I live through this madness, maybe I should take up flying lessons, thought Amber morbidly. A tree quickly snuffed out this thought and many others when Amber's back met the coarse bark—her body momentarily wrapped backward around the tree before crumpling to the ground.

I'm dead, it's official. How can I not be? I felt my body break in half! So...then why am I still thinking? she thought as she slowly moved her body, afraid to open her eyes. Her eyebrows knitted as a metallic-smelling warm breeze brushed her face. But this wasn't from the wind but rather someone's breath. Nervously, Amber opened one eye and saw the strangest, yet cutest little monkey she had ever seen.

It stood over her, about two and a half feet tall. Its huge gray eyes, which took up most of its face, leaving no room for a nose or mouth, glowed against its jet black long fur. That left a few questions running through her mind. When did Galaseya get monkeys and where did that warm breeze come from? The once cute little monkey cocked its head to the right as it casually lifted its large, flat tail. The six-foot long beaver-like tail didn't bother Amber so much as did the razor-sharp teeth protruding from underneath it. This was the creature's mouth—this was how it fed. The clicking of the teeth, which started with a small hum, now grew to a near roar as Amber quickly crawled out of the creature's way.

Her heart continued to race as her back bumped into something cold and stiff. Afraid it was yet another monstrous creature, she slowly turned around, not wanting to give it any reason to attack. No...not a creature, something far more disturbing—a hanging corpse. She jumped to her feet as an unearthly scream escaped her lips. Chris' body hung from a dead tree. Judging by the color of his skin, he had been there for a while. Amber turned in a circle around the dismal foggy clearing she had landed in and noticed several more bodies hanging from other dead trees—each corpse, a member of her family. Amber's hand flew to her mouth as bile rose in her throat.

A silhouette emerged from the dense, dead woods and casually leaned against the tree that held Hunter. "Is the décor too much? My apologies, how about this?"

His quiet, deep voice echoed around as he snapped his fingers, causing the horrid scene to disappear. Amber looked at the mysterious person as he came out of the shadows and into the light. His lean figure gracefully walked toward her and stared at her with a manic expression. Behind him draped a long cloak made of what appeared to be black and purple fur. As she watched it dance in the slight breeze, a chill crawled up her spine. It wasn't really fur but flattened porcupine-type quills that reached at least six inches in length. The sadistic-looking garment was securely fastened to the man's tight vest, which was made of a thick leather material and had strange, almost computer-like designs carved into the front. His skinny black leather pants blended in with his boots. The man now stood only a foot from her. He stood about six feet tall, but he was just tall enough that Amber could see into his hard, black eyes. His short black hair spiked up in the front, while the rest stayed in position. The only difference about this man, aside from his strangely large biceps and triceps, was that his skin tone matched the glow that had encompassed Amber's body in her room. The man stared at Amber and asked, almost challenging her to even speak, "How did you know it was me and not my dear brother?"

Movement came from the corner of her eye as Amber's gaze shifted, watching another man appear from the woods. He wore similar clothing to Martheykos, although he had no cape. Instead, this strange man's wardrobe was decked out with bones and skulls of various creatures. Draped across his vest in chain-like fashion were dozens of little bones which Amber assumed belonged to the strange monkey creatures she first saw. The skulls of these monkeys sat on the man's broad shoulders. Masking his face, he wore what appeared to be a partial cat skull. Just as graceful as Martheykos, the mysterious man took a perfectly manicured hand and casually removed the mask, revealing his round, yet perfect face. He bowed his head to Amber silently, waiting for his entertainment to begin.

"I didn't," said Amber more annoyed than disturbed, "but no offense to your brother, he doesn't seem like the type who likes to play with his victims."

Martheykos started following the outline of the clearing as his brother slunk into the center, eyeing Amber as if she was his next meal. "Look at that, Petraylin, we have an intelligent one here."

The silent man shook his head, his eyes refusing to leave Amber. He smiled as he replied in a much higher voice than Martheykos, "Do you know what we do with intelligent humans, Amber?"

"Gee, let me guess. You kick them off your planet because you're afraid they'll challenge you," she spat.

"Well, well, is that feistiness just part of your personality or is it stupidity? I can't really tell," said Petraylin, cocking his head to the side as a faint smile formed at the corners of his mouth.

"I'd go with stupid, Brother. After all, she didn't even recognize her own twin," said Martheykos with a wicked smile.

Amber knew these men fed on confusion and fear. She relaxed her mind and asked calmly, "What are you talking about?"

"Wow, you mean to tell me that your loyal family never told you about your twin brother, Ambrose?" asked Martheykos, who already knew the answer.

Amber's mind froze as her heart raced. *Ambrose is my...brother? How many more family members are there that I don't know about?*

As if reading her mind, Martheykos patronizingly said, "Oh, don't worry, dear. He's the only other family member you need to worry about, at least for now."

"I wonder what other things her family kept from her," said Petraylin with a sly smile.

"Well, they weren't exactly honest about her home planet Diraetus. Can you believe they let her think she was on planet Earth?" said Martheykos mockingly.

Great, I'm not even from Earth. Where is Earth then? Is it even real? she thought, realizing that although she wanted answers, the location and history of Earth wasn't a necessary answer at this point. Sick of their constant jabs at her family and their close connection they all had, Amber's bravery took her to a new level as she felt her body move involuntarily closer to Martheykos. They stood mere inches from each other as she raised her eyes, staring into his hate-filled eyes. "My family may have made poor decisions in the past, but that doesn't mean I love or trust them any less. I believe in them, and nothing you will ever say will persuade me otherwise."

At that moment, Amber knew she said the wrong thing, as a malicious expression with a matching smile swept across their faces. Slowly, the Brothers simultaneously backed away, and Martheykos gave a last sly remark, "We'll see about that." Upon his final word, Martheykos and Petraylin were swept up in a whirlwind of water, but as Amber watched them leave, Martheykos quickly snapped his fingers yet again. Her vision went black.

13

Amber sat bolt upright in her Galaseyan bed, letting out a blood-curdling scream of fear.

Her family stared at her with concern. Sphinx sat at the foot of the bed, afraid his mistress would return to her strange sleep state. Mason stood at the side of her bed, his arms crossed and eyebrow raised, waiting for her to say something. Jermiar stood on the other side of the bed, a bit surprised by her suddenly awakening. Hunter and Chris stood at the base of her bed, exchanging looks as if her waking interrupted a conversation.

The rest of the family was scattered around the room, some huddled in groups still quietly conversing amongst each other. Amber could see the king and his advisor in one of the groups, occasionally nodding to the low whispers of his faithful servant, but still looking at her with sorrowful eyes.

The scene before her was almost exactly like the one in the illusion. With shaky hands, Amber reached out toward Sphinx, hoping this was all real, and the whole room went deathly silent. She picked up the cat, who at first seemed a bit uneasy about the whole thing. Absentmindedly, she slipped out of bed just as a vision began forming.

As Amber slipped into her vision of Rydan's past, things seemed to be going as normal. But then, when he finished telling his story to the others, his eyes widened in horror as that strange glow started wrapping around Amber's now comatose body. They had brought her back to her room in hopes of resolving this strange phenomenon, but even the Sidhe couldn't do anything.

"Do you think they're behind this?" asked Mason, cautiously approaching the bed.

Rydan came to the other side of the bed and waved his hand through the haze. "Has to be. No one else has this power."

"How do you know? What if Jermiar can combine abilities and pull her out?" suggested Mason.

Rydan nodded, considering Mason's words, and then replied, "We can try, but I'm working on a backup plan right now."

Rogalar stared at the new family member with suspicion and said, "Backup plan? What backup plan?"

"Ambrose. He's her only chance. He has powers we don't know anything about yet. If we can't get to her I know he can," said Rydan assuredly.

"You better be right," said Jermiar, as the vision faded.

Amber walked all the way to the window and opened up the shades. Darmentraea hung low in the sky, looking as if it was going to consume her planet. She let Sphinx jump from her arms and continued to stare at the planet in awe. Her gaze then searched the land, falling to rest on the port, which now revealed a large, glowing Portal at the edge of the dock where she had first arrived. Somehow the Brothers' illusion managed to show her more than just lies. Mason came up beside her and stared up at the massive planet. She turned to her great-great-grandfather and saw the planet reflected in his muddy green eyes. "Is it true?"

With his eyes glued to the massive planet he replied, "Is what true?"

"No more secrets, right?" she asked, as his attention turned towards her.

"No more secrets," he replied, defeated. "Yes, Ambrose is your twin brother."

Twin brother. Those two words relentlessly hammered against the walls of Amber's already overwhelmed mind. For days the thought of sleeping terrified her, and instead she aimlessly walked about almost as if in a daze that no one could free her from. Over the next few days after the incident, most of her family slowly gave up the idea of trying to help her.

Rydan explained to her that when she and her twin were born, the Sidhe knew Amber and Ambrose would be the Protectors between Galaseya and Darmentraea. The Sidhe sent him over to the dark planet shortly after his birth. Rydan was already well aware of the twins and communicated with his daughter, who went over to the planet to find the right person to raise the baby. She first found a relatively gentle couple, well as gentle as a Darmentraean could get, but around Ambrose's tenth birthday, they were killed, leaving him to fend for himself. Saraleast kept close tabs on him, always out of his line of sight. He didn't hear much from her during this time, but he was safe and ended up finding someone to confide in. Amber didn't find this at all fair, but since the Ambrose in her vision didn't seem too upset about the betrayal, he must have understood his importance long before she did.

Rydan then explained to her that no one was out of the woods yet and danger still lurked around the corner. A few times he even tried to pull Amber from the recesses of her mind by saying something had happened to Ambrose, but that only made her sink further into her shell. She didn't really even know her twin and Darmentraea always seemed to have problems—why should this time be any different? Despite their lies and twisted speech, the Brothers were right about a few things—who's to say they were wrong? Besides, even if she were able to zoom over there, where would she go and how would she find out if everything was okay?

On the other hand, a few other family members took this new information much differently than Rydan or Mason did. Jermiar locked himself away in his library and only came out for food. With the knowledge of her twin's return, he studied the mural he had painted years ago and also began rewriting some of his history books. During one of her walks, Amber peeked in a window of the library and noticed papers and books scattered haphazardly around the room— not an inch of the once clean floor appeared.

As for Rogalar, Amber always found him outside on the grounds, training those who were interested in various fighting forms. Rogalar saw this step as only logical, as they didn't know if or when the Brothers would return. Amber's heart sank every time she saw this. Already people were beginning to lose hope before the real battle even began. But what was this so-called "real battle?" They had all gone through so much as it was.

Even the Sidhe remained strangely quiet, occasionally appearing for only moral support. She knew Vaeris wanted to tell her everything about Ambrose, but something stopped him, and it had nothing to do with the other Sidhe. It made Amber wonder how connected the planets were, and if revealing the truth behind their silence would only put her and the family in more danger. It was as if they were waiting for her to take the next step, whatever that was. But what she really wanted was nothing more than to enjoy the normalcy that graced her chaotic life, even if it only lasted for a short time.

As for the other members of the family, they understood the importance of keeping the people at peace and continuing on with life. Nothing could be done unless and until the next wave of chaos hit. While life moved on for the palace and the people, Amber often found herself sitting on a hill off to the side of the village with the forest in the background. From her position, she looked out and could see everything, from the village to the palace and to the sea of green. Watching the people below continue about their daily duties brought a sense of comfort to her, but not the deep comfort Amber really needed.

The animals of the woods often came to visit her and bring her food from the forest, as the deep-seated depression she felt left her without the desire to eat. Most often, the deer found their way to her and stayed with her during the times of her solitude. Although their powers of aiding depression helped some, soon it only became a mental bandage. She stroked the soft fawns that curled up in her lap and only responded with a weak smile to the large doe or buck that gently nudged her to eat the food they brought. Despite their efforts to help, these gentle creatures were powerless against the truth that weighed Amber's heart down every time she looked around her.

Amber often found her mind getting lost as she stared into the swirling Portal that led to the other planets, the villagers completely unaware of its presence. She wondered what the planet really looked like and if it really was similar to Earth. Did Earth even exist? If so, why did the people of Diraetus have memories of it? Darmentraea was much harder to ignore as it loomed over Galaseya as the light from the planet dwindled down— Galaseya's light reflecting off the massive dark planet, illuminating its blue clouds and black surface.

Every night and morning, Amber always greeted Iethreor at the front door to the palace. He always came out of his own accord and sometimes took time away from his new duties just to see if she was safe. He gave her his usual friendly smile as she silently passed him every day. But as each day progressed, his smile became laced with pity for her. Amber knew there was something on his mind, something he felt the need to say, but if the deer couldn't console her, what words did he have that could possibly have a stronger impact on her?

One evening in particular revealed to Amber how much this young man had wisdom beyond his years. She neared him, expecting to receive yet another sad look, but instead, Iethreor stared up at the massive dark planet that threateningly hung over Galaseya. A faint smile appeared on his face, as if the sight of Darmentraea brought some strange comfort. Amber slowed her pace and stopped beside the advisor, looking up to see what made him appear so at peace. Nothing changed. The planet looked as dark and foreboding as ever. She turned her attention back to Iethreor, whose face remained in the same position.

"What are you looking at?" she asked, curiosity overpowering her.

"Darmentraea is actually quite a beautiful world," he replied, dodging her question.

Amber shook her head in confusion. "Beautiful? How can you say that? You've never been there!"

"Well, neither have you, Ameliana," Iethreor pointed out.

"I'd say Kaleya's device was a good judgment of how Darmentraea is supposed to be. She even said she wanted to bring its influence to Galaseya," said Amber.

"You are correct. However, her effect on our world should tell you something," said the advisor, now looking at Amber. "A wicked woman lived on Galaseya. Who is to say that there is not a kind-hearted soul living on Darmentraea?"

Amber looked back up at the menacing-looking planet with wonder. For once, the planet appeared to her in a new light. Iethreor was right: neither of them had ever visited the planet, so why judge the whole world based on a very vague experience? The wonder she felt soon disappeared as she realized what Iethreor hinted at.

"Are you referring to my...twin?" she asked, as the conversation took an awkward turn.

"Ameliana, I have known of your family's abilities for some time now. I have done my best to understand them too. However, it is still difficult to wrap my mind around how it all works," he replied, carefully forming his words. "I suppose what I am trying to convey to you is that...just because something is hard to comprehend, does not make it wicked."

Amber paused for a moment while the walls she had placed around in her mind came crashing down. This young advisor saw things from a different perspective than most, which is probably the reason she admired him so much. Everything he ever said to her was only meant to help her through the situations that came her way. She had seen a lot of growth in him from when they first met, and she believed that in many ways, he helped her grow some, too. "You're right, I don't understand anything about Darmentraea or even Ambrose, but that doesn't necessarily mean either one of them are completely evil."

As Iethreor smiled and silently nodded his head in approval, Amber felt a strange, mild pain in her stomach. At first, it felt like a little muscle cramp, but then it quickly spread to her sides and grew more painful, causing her to double over. Whatever Iethreor said was drowned out by the pain that crawled up her spinal cord, flooding her head. She fell as the pain nearly paralyzed every part of her body—a strange force pulling her away.

Iethreor quickly caught Amber. He asked her what was wrong, hoping to get information out of her aside from cries of pain. Suddenly, he let go of her. Through tear-filled eyes Amber saw her body glow a golden color. Beyond the strange phenomenon, Iethreor fled inside the palace to get help. The pain grew too much to bear as the bright golden light radiated around Amber, nearly blinding her. She closed her eyes and awaited whatever was to come next.

It felt like minutes, maybe only seconds, before Amber

opened her eyes again. But the world was shrouded in darkness, a darkness she hadn't seen since living on Diraetus. As her eyes adjusted to the strange environment, her surroundings became clearer and even more peculiar. She lay on the cold floor of a rather large circular cave whose walls were comprised of coarse rocks, nothing like those she ever saw on Galaseya. In the center of this dome-shaped area sat a massive fire, its flames climbing toward the ceiling, where a black spot marred the rocks. Off to the side, she noticed a rack of what looked to be meat and various animal skins—none of which looked like anything Amber had ever seen before.

Moving her focus past the rack, Amber noticed a narrow passageway that led deeper into a different part of the cave system, and along the wall by the entryway stood various types of technology that even the brilliant minds of Diraetus couldn't even think of. Most had screens, all of which reported different statistics. However, a few of these seemed to show images, as in cameras pointed in different areas. From her position, Amber couldn't identify what these images were.

Slowly she lifted herself from her position, wondering why she felt absolutely no pain. A rough blanket slid off her body as she stopped and noticed a wadded-up piece of material sitting where her head had been. *Someone went through a lot of trouble to make sure I was warm,* she thought, as suspicion seeped into her mind.

Almost in answer to her next thought of who this person was, something small moved at the corner of her eye. She turned her head and through the flames, saw a man maybe a few inches taller than her, leaning against the wall with his arms crossed and one foot against the wall. His black, slightly curly hair remained in place as his head tilted slightly. His skin appeared pale in the reflection of the bright fire. His dark brown eyes looked Amber over in a concerned way. He wore skinny black pants with a few tears in various places, and a dark blue vest, which was frayed around the arms. The loose material fell down his arms, showing off his well-defined muscles. He had a black circle earring in his right ear, and from a distance it appeared like a small gauge. On his left eyebrow, there was a small hoop piercing. Faded scars ran down his arms, across his left hand, and one prominent one along the side of his neck.

To Amber, this guy seemed to have jumped out of some weird band from the 90s, but from what she remembered, she hadn't teleported back a few decades—no, she was in a far worse situation. The man silently came toward her. Amber shrank away until her back hit the nearest wall. He never hesitated or tried to comfort her. He continued moving forward until he was mere inches away. His scar-riddled body looked even more terrifying against the harsh shadows from the firelight.

"If I were going to hurt you, you wouldn't be alive right now. So relax," said the mysterious young man sitting down in front of her.

Well, you could certainly work on your bedside manner, thought Amber, surprised by the man's abruptness.

The man continued trying to form a kind smile. "My name is Kylis. I'm a friend of Ambrose."

"Oh," was all Amber could muster in her confusion.

Kylis let out a chortle and shook his head, "Yeah, this is going to be harder than I thought."

"What's going to be?" asked Amber, feeling as if she was missing out on a huge conversation.

Kylis shook his head in annoyance and said, "Does the name Rydan ring a bell? Well, yeah, your brother and I have been in contact with him. We've been pretty much kept in the loop about all your abilities and stuff."

"Hold on, Rydan hinted at knowing Ambrose...does that mean I'm..." said Amber, trailing off.

"On Darmentraea," finished Kylis with a hint of sarcasm. "Congrats, you figured it out. Now seriously, keep up or neither of us will survive."

"Survive? What are you talking about? Why am I here and *how* did I get here?" asked Amber, her heart nearly pounding in her ears.

Kylis stared at Amber completely dumbfounded, fear masking his dark eyes. "You mean to tell me that you just randomly teleported here a few days ago and had no idea about Ambrose? What kind of a twin are you if you can't even sense your other half in danger?"

"Of course I knew something was going on, but there was nothing I could do to help!" exclaimed Amber in defense.

"Lies. There was something you could do, but you were too busy wallowing in self-pity to pay even a speck of attention. And now, Ambrose is in the hands of the Brothers, who are doing who knows what to him!" said Kylis, his voice raised in frustration.

"Kylis, everyone has a choice. I don't even know you or if I can even trust anyone right now!" said Amber suddenly, realizing how selfish her statement sounded.

Silently, the young man held out his scarred hand and said, "Fine, then read my past and tell me if I'm lying."

Hesitantly, Amber reached out her hand. With their fingertips nearly touching, Amber immediately got a wave of memories—some good but many bad. *The journey began with what Amber assumed to be Kylis's younger years before he met Ambrose. None of what she saw looked good; in fact, some aspects of his life were downright terrifying. He never committed any atrocities, but based on a number of things he stole over his life, he was definitely an expert thief. None suspected him of this crime, or if they did, they* were too afraid to say anything. Every person Kylis came in contact with seemed terrified of him, although he didn't appear to revel in their panic, as most Darmentraeans probably would. However, he put up an excellent front and had everyone convinced he was some terrible human, not to be trifled with. In a way, that facade proved to be very useful when he met Ambrose.

The next scene showed Kylis around the age of eighteen. He stood over a small figure, who glowed a strange, pale blue color. At first, Amber thought it was something the Brothers conjured up to deceive the young man. This, however, was no trick. It was Ambrose, covered in bloody rags—hanging on to what little life he had left. Kylis was not at all confused by this sight; in fact, he looked more concerned than anything. Without a word, he effortlessly scooped the young boy up in his arms and carried him off into the distance, the boy's glow illuminating them while casting eerie shadows across the dark, barren land.

The years seemed to pass by in flashes, each one similar to the last. The two young men grew close as brothers and spent all their days watching the screens that Amber assumed Kylis stole from somewhere. He seemed to be explaining things to Ambrose, showing him the ropes of whatever plan he had been working on. Soon, Ambrose was looking into the research more than his mentor did.

Amber's journey abruptly ended at a memory that happened recently. Kylis leaned one hand against the wall of the cave while his other hand rested caringly on Ambrose's hunched over figure. Ambrose looked in immense pain as his body silently shook. Amber looked closer into the vision, at what Ambrose was so fixed on. It was a screen which was attached to a camera of sorts, but the image reflecting back to them was of Amber in the comatose state, which the Brothers put her in. Before she *could mentally react to this shock, Ambrose's body jolted back as if something or someone threw a bolt of lightning at him.*

The memories ended and Amber found herself still holding Kylis's hand, staring into his now watery eyes. Beyond the sadness lay honesty, which threatened to escape. This young man cared for Ambrose more than any Darmentraean should. It made Amber wonder why he wasn't born a Galaseyan. Then again, Iethreor's words about good existing on Darmentraea echoed in her mind.

Amber heaved a weary sigh and shook her head, saying, "Well, if we're going to rescue Ambrose then we are going to need help from my family. Maybe I can go back and talk to Rydan?"

"Amber, there isn't any going back," said Kylis rather delicately. "You shouldn't have even been able to come through here, because the Brothers monitor the other planets like hawks. I've been communicating with your family through the technology I have here, but even they don't have a clue as to how you got here. Rydan's only guess is that the power the Protectors had with one another is stronger than we all thought."

Amber's attention turned toward another part of the cave which she hadn't seen before—the exit into a dangerous unknown. She stared at the narrow exit and replied gravely, "Ambrose called for me. He brought me here. I don't know how; but he did. He's in more danger than you can imagine. Come on, let's go find him."

Kylis reached out and grabbed Amber's forearm, tugging her back, "If you go out there now, you'll die."

"Kylis, I'm the Protector of Galaseya, I have certain powers, remember?" she replied.

He shook his head, mildly frustrated with the unexpected situation. He calmed down enough to kindly explain, "Amber, the transportation did something neither of us expected. And I believe the Brothers had something to do with it. What I'm saying is that...somehow they temporarily took away your Protector abilities to weaken you. You can still see memories, as that's a family ability, but you can't do anything more than that. The only way for you to see your family again is to find your brother and hope that he still has his Protector powers. Maybe he can somehow charge you or something. I don't really know, but we are in uncharted waters right now...we're winging it."

Amber closed her eyes as her heart sank at this news. Kylis wasn't lying, and quite frankly she couldn't handle hearing any more bad news. "Just the average day in the life of Amber Oak, huh?"

Kylis shrugged his shoulders, not entirely sure if he should respond to that. He tried revealing a hopeful smile, but that feeling was rather foreign to him. Both he and Amber had the same thought. They needed to learn more about each other's world to work together. Their lives were changing rapidly and time was proving to be another formidable enemy.

14

"Come on, Amber, fight back!" ordered Kylis during one of their many sparring sessions.

Amber tripped over herself as she stumbled away from Kylis. She spat out a mouthful of blood as he yet again beat her in another match. Of the twenty-three sessions, she remembered, she had won not one of them. This happened to be her least favorite activity during her short stay on Darmentraea, although according to Kylis, she had progressed far since her arrival a month ago.

But Amber wasn't convinced. It took her weeks to get adjusted to the Darmentraean style of clothing, and the knowledge she gained about the civilization of the dark planet, or rather the lack thereof, was almost too gruesome to stomach. But its history was shrouded in mystery and death, just like the present. According to Kylis, life wasn't always as horrific and dismal. Centuries before, Darmentraea was relatively habitable. However, over the years the Brothers grew more powerful, and the Balance that held the solar system together started falling apart, putting the planet in the same condition as the others. The animals became more dangerous and the people more wicked. Due to the changes in their civilization, the people started killing each other over simple disagreements. The citizens of the dark land began spreading out over the planet so as to avoid other people. However, they were still at risk from the other predators such as the animals and even the atmosphere.

Aside from terribly cold temperatures, which the people learned to adjust to, they endured the terrible rainstorms that came without warning. For most people, a rainstorm was welcomed, but on Darmentraea, the rain was lethal. If a single raindrop fell on human flesh, it immediately created a deep laceration, something Amber discovered the hard way as she attempted to venture out of the cave the second day. After quickly pulling her back, Kylis explained that the rain was consumable, but had to be severely filtered through a long and arduous process. Although he explained a lot of Darmentraean life to Amber, there was much more she knew he kept back and probably for a good reason. Despite the fact she had to learn how to fit into their society, this planet was not her idea of a good vacation spot from her life on Galaseya.

After contemplating what she learned, Amber finally got her bearings. "I'm trying, Kylis. I'm not cut out for Darmentraean life. I'm a Galaseyan!"

He quickly jumped in front of her and covered her mouth, saying, "Want to say that a bit louder? I don't think everyone heard you!"

Amber forgot that anything she said could be overheard by anyone, even in the Dead Wood, which remarkably resembled the clearing at the end of her illusion. Kylis said he and Ambrose lived in the caves within these woods, as most people never stepped a foot near the tree line for fear of being killed by the creatures that resided there. From what he told her, the Dead Wood seemed to spread over most of the planet. This made it easier to hide from people and animals, although some did take up residence in the trees, but only those brave and strong enough. Kylis mentioned a few individuals he came across, although he never explained how their encounter ended.

With one last warning look, Kylis slowly removed his hand from her mouth. Amber's eyes darted from tree to tree, looking for any signs of danger. All to be found were only the thin, spindly branches of nearby trees, waiting to strangle any unsuspecting passersby. She rolled her eyes and whispered, "What I mean is that we've been practicing for far too long. We need to start looking for Ambrose."

Kylis brushed a hand through his thick black hair as he said in annoyance, "Amber, you're not ready to go out on a search party. If you leave these woods, you'll be killed. If not by the animals, then the people."

"It's not my life I'm worried about anymore, Kylis. Ambrose is the one in danger and the longer we hide here, the harder it will be to find him. You and I both know the Brothers are aware I am here. They're not stupid and we have to act soon!" exclaimed Amber forcefully.

"Amber, you don't even know where he is," said Kylis, his tone giving way to defeat. "what makes you think you can find him?"

Amber stared off into the dark depths of the foggy Dead Wood, the dangers that lay beyond haunting her. She fought back the frustrated tears that threatened to fall and said, in as loud a voice as she could muster, "You're right, I don't know where he is or even if I can find him..." She paused and looked at Kylis with determination in her eyes. "But that doesn't mean we should stop. He's all we have."

Kylis stared at Amber, a mix of confusion and amazement masking his usually stoic expression. He knew her opinion of Ambrose had changed since coming to Darmentraea and finding out the truth of her twin, but her loyalty to someone she hadn't technically met never ceased to surprise Kylis. All her personal problems and vendettas against the Brothers faded away as Ambrose's need for help took over. Just as he was about to get into a deeper conversation with Amber, Kylis fell silent. Something was coming.

Amber noticed his face turning paler. She listened intently as the surrounding woods quickly filled with the horrific sounds of the deadly monkeys which she had seen in her illusion. The clicking of their razor sharp, teeth-filled tails echoed around them as they dove back into their nearby cave. The haunting racket of the monkeys disappeared as quickly as it came, leaving Amber and Kylis staring out into the Dead Wood. Silently they exchanged looks of concern. Kylis was the first to speak up. "This is all wrong."

Amber watched him as he dashed over to the stolen technology, turning dials and pressing buttons on the large panel at the base of the screens. She knew that it was definitely uncharacteristic of the monkeys to behave that way, but found no real reason for alarm. Hesitantly, she replied, "Kylis, what's wrong? Isn't it a good thing they didn't attack?"

"Far from it," he replied, still focused on the computers and other gadgets, "They never give a warning like that. Besides, for one to hear them means certain death, and I don't know about you, but I didn't hear blood-curdling screams. This isn't the first time something out of the ordinary happened."

"So, what are you saying, Darmentraea has become milder in its darkness?" she asked, slightly confused.

With the screens ready to receive a signal, Kylis looked at Amber with fear-filled eyes and said, "I don't know. Some of the people who I have seen periodically in the woods are even acting nicer. Amber, all of this began when your brother went missing. The Brothers are up to something terrible, and I'm worried that this change will affect the other planets."

Amber walked over to Kylis and put a hand on his shoulder. He turned his head toward her as his dark brown eyes met hers. He was holding something back from her, something crucial, but he put up too many walls for her to be able to gather anything from him.

In a quiet, yet commanding voice, Amber asked, "Kylis, what aren't you telling me?"

Their conversation was quickly cut off as Hunter's face appeared on the screen, calling for their attention. He looked as if he hadn't slept in weeks, regularly sitting by Amber's laptop just waiting for their next conversation. This technology that Kylis stole did not have the capabilities of communicating across worlds. However, someone else did. Shortly after arriving, Kylis explained to Amber that Saraleast, Rydan's daughter, had found a way for him and Ambrose to watch over the family on both Galaseya and Diraetus. With her spirit-like ability, she permanently put herself into the technology, creating a way for them to keep tabs on each other.

For a while, the communication was only one way, but when Amber arrived on Darmentraea, the family on Galaseya had no way of knowing when she would return—if ever. Rydan came up with the idea of using Amber's laptop, which she kept with her as a reminder of her old life, and through many games of charades to explain his idea, Saraleast strained herself to connect to the laptop, creating a video chat of sorts. Because it required more energy, Saraleast could only do this form of communication for a short time, so Amber and Kylis decided to make a call only if an emergency came up.

"Amber, it's so good to see you," said Hunter wearily.

"Yeah, looks like you can barely see me. When was the last time you slept?" Amber asked trying to not sound so concerned—though less angry now, Amber wasn't sure how she felt about her grandfather.

"My sleep or the lack thereof is not of anyone's concern. I will sleep when you return home," said Hunter in a groggy voice, "speaking of which, do you have any idea when that will be?"

"No, we still have to find Ambrose. He's probably the only one that can help," said Amber, trying not to hint at what she and Kylis had been doing.

"What is the dilemma? Have you not had any leads as to his whereabouts?" asked Hunter, becoming more alert.

"Yeah, something like that," said Kylis quickly. "The reason we called is because we were wondering if something unusual was happening on Galaseya."

Hunter rolled his eyes and replied, sarcasm lacing his voice, "Define unusual. In case you have not noticed, my whole family is unusual."

"Look, that's not...never mind. Unusual as in, the Balance. Are the animals acting strange, anything about Galaseya different?"

"Not that I have seen. It must be something affecting only your world. That being said, your world, your problem. Just get Amber home," said Hunter, just as he closed the connection.

Frustrated, Kylis walked toward the exit and leaned an arm against the wall, staring out into the bleak unknown. In a dangerously quiet voice he said, "Well, I see your family is warming up to me."

"Can you blame them?" asked Amber, coming up to Kylis's side.

"I haven't given them a reason to distrust me," he said in defense.

"True, but you also haven't given them a reason to trust you," said Amber crossing her arms. "Hunter knows you're hiding something, and I can guarantee others do too. Keeping secrets in my family is about as bad as committing a crime against them."

Kylis tore his attention away from the woods and stared at Amber for a few minutes. Her expression remained the same—unwavering determination for saving their solar system. Going against everything his Darmentraean mind screamed at him, Kylis nodded silently, then replied, "Then let me give them a reason. Let's go find your brother!"

15

Leaving the Dead Wood was no easy feat. Not only did Kylis and Amber have to be alert for the animals and people lurking in the woods, but many of trees and jutting roots made their journey far more treacherous. Fortunately, Kylis knew his way well around the eerie woods. He effortlessly jumped over the roots and played limbo with a few deadly low hanging branches that just waited to decapitate someone. Amber followed his every move to the best of her ability, although she couldn't dodge the dangers nearly as smoothly as Kylis could. The farther away from the cave they traveled, the more creatures and the occasional human remains they found.

Kylis once mentioned to her that the death rate on Darmentraea was astronomically high due to the dangers of the land. According to what little history they knew, the ancestors eventually stopped burying the dead and just left them to rot. Even when explaining this, Kylis didn't seem to be okay with this idea. He might be Darmentraean born, but he definitely had Galaseyan qualities—proving to her yet again that not all Darmentraeans were evil. Maybe, just maybe, her twin would be the same.

Before they found their way out of the tangled woods, the two ran into every wild creature on Darmentraea—each one nearly worse than the last. Many of the monkeys sat high in the trees, not very much interested in Amber or Kylis; of course, this concerned the two, as these animals were considered the most fearsome and dangerous of all the creatures. Kylis explained that they fed through their tails. They would sit in the trees waiting for humans to pass by.

Silently their tails would drop and wrap around their victim's neck, sucking them dry of blood. The meat of these creatures was definitely edible, provided one could catch them. But their speed through the trees made it nearly impossible to capture, let alone kill.

However, the monkeys seemed to be the only creatures acting out of character. The next species Amber met happened to be what Kylis called Reaper Cats—although, they didn't actually meet this feline, but heard it. Fortunately, the screams of the cat were far enough away that they caused only minor ringing in their ears. Any closer and the creature would have deafened them. Kylis had described these creatures to her not too long ago. He had only seen them once or twice in his twenty-four years of living. They stood about as tall as a lion, but they naturally looked anorexic. Instead of fur, their wax-like black skin stretched tightly over their bones. And like most of the creatures on the planet, their claws were razor sharp, and they usually only let out their ear-piercing cry when they attacked.

As the pair traveled farther away from the deathly screams, another animal crossed their path, this one looking more terrifying than the description of the Reaper Cats. It didn't help that the creature was in the middle of tearing apart an unfortunate passerby. Amber swallowed back the bile rising in her throat as a large canine lifted its head—its glowing eyes seemed to burrow into her soul. Kylis gently pushed Amber forward, urging her to keep moving, but she would never forget the image of the creature. This was what Kylis called a Dagger Wolf. Its name matched perfectly, as the animal's fur resembled porcupine quills, but thicker. Its fur was what Martheykos had worn as a cape when she first met him. The wolf quickly returned to its meal as they passed. From what she learned of this creature, it never went after humans as the other animals of Darmentraea did.

In fact, it stayed as far from humans as possible and only fed on other creatures. But, if it were cornered by a person, it would strike.

Amber expected to soon see a Silent Bear. However, none were in sight. These creatures stood a bit larger than the average grizzly bear and, like many of the other animals on the planet, it had dark, coarse black fur. The only thing that separated it from an average bear was its massive paws with claws so sharp they could effortlessly cut a full-grown man in half with one swipe. In a way, Amber was glad to not run into this beast—the others she met were bad enough.

After hours of traipsing through the woods, Amber and Kylis finally reached the end of this leg of their journey. Haunting screams filled the night air as Amber placed a hand on a nearby tree and looked out on a massive, crowded city that spanned hundreds of square miles. A crudely built wall stretched around the city, warding off anyone daring to trespass. A tall, muscular man stood guard at the entrance. In the middle of this ghetto-like city stood an ominous building that resembled a combination of a Gothic-techno castle, its spires glowing an electric blue color.

"That's the Dark City, and the Brothers' home is in the center," said Kylis, coming up to Amber's side.

"Why do they need a home?" asked Amber, staring at the foreboding structure.

Kylis sighed and shook his head. "They don't. It's just a way for them to show off what they can do. They hold all the technology on the planet...well except for what I snatched. It's believed that centuries ago, our ancestors built most of the technology. The Brothers hated the thought of anyone being stronger than them. The place we need to go is within the city but on the other side."

Amber stared at Kylis, her eyebrows furrowed as she replied, "I was right. You do know where my brother is!"

"Not exactly," said Kylis, still looking out on the plains.

"But I do know of people who can help us rescue him."

"Who?" asked Amber, with a demanding tone.

Kylis glanced around him into the bare woods and quietly said, "They are known as the Elders. They are among the oldest people of Darmentraea—a group so secret that I don't even think the Brothers are aware of them."

Feeling a sense of anger, Amber surprised Kylis by whirling around and pinning him by the throat to a nearby tree, putting everything he taught her into practice. She stared into his eyes and nearly growled, "You mean to tell me that everything we did over the last month could have been avoided? We could have rescued Ambrose and restored the Balance if you hadn't wasted your time trying to make me into something I'm not!"

Kylis smirked, his Darmentraean personality seeping through as he whispered in a cocky manner, "I don't think it was wasted. Look at you, Amber. Your reaction to my secrecy is exactly what will get you through that city!"

Amber jumped back away from Kylis, utterly appalled by her behavior. A lump grew in her throat as tears threatened to fall. This whole thing felt weird. Not only was this not her planet, it just wasn't *her*. How in the world did Kylis expect her to act like someone she wasn't? If the people of the city were as bad as he made it sound, she wouldn't make it within feet of the gate.

Kylis moved away from the tree after making sure Amber wasn't going to attack again and said kindly, "Amber, I know you don't like this, and I'm not asking you to. The thing is we all have a little bit of Darmentraea *and* Galaseya in us. Some have more of one than the other, it's true. But you of all people should know that we aren't defined by how we grew up or where, for that matter. It's all about our attitude and how we handle every situation given to us. That's what most of the people of my world forgot. They let the Brothers affect their way of life—we weren't always this dark."

Amber blinked away the confusion that consumed her mind and said, "So, this darkness, this world, won't change me?"

Kylis shook his head and smiled. "Not unless you let it."

His wise words played on repeat in Amber's mind as they walked toward the gates of the city. Without warning, Kylis grabbed Amber's arm tightly and whispered to her, "Do you trust me?"

Trying to act casual, Amber replied, "Do I have a choice?"

From the corner of her eye, Amber noticed a smirk flash across Kylis's face. "That's the spirit!"

The man guarding the entrance stopped and crossed his massive arms, glaring at the two. "What's your business here?" he demanded.

"Just looking to trade," said Kylis, his voice so dark it sent chills up Amber's spine.

The guard's dark eyes traveled up and down Amber's body, her clothing convincingly that of the Darmentraean women. A wicked smile appeared on the man's face as he disgustedly said, "What are you asking for her?"

Kylis rolled his eyes and shook his head as he let out a short laugh and replied, "She's way out of your price range. Now, let us through, or my bidder is going to tear you apart."

Without waiting for the guard to move out of the way, Kylis pushed past him, still holding onto Amber's arm. Amber felt her stomach churn as the guard called back, "If your deal falls through, I'm still willing to negotiate!"

"What a pig!" whispered Amber.

"Get used to it. The people who live within these walls are the worst of all Darmentraeans. Stay alert and blend in," said Kylis, as they walked into the city.

Amber stared in awe at the massive structures in front of her. The city looked to be made mostly of scrap metal and any debris the people of the city found. Although, where the debris came from was another question. The buildings were all cramped together, and some seemed to have been stacked on top of each other—each structure supported only by the other. If she had to guess, the people probably intentionally set the city up in a foreboding manner. Those tough enough to live within the walls probably found the buildings a welcoming challenge to face every day, not knowing if they would crumble into a heap.

Ropes connected building to building, with various pieces of clothes drying. The stench of death hung in the air as Amber noticed bodies in different stages of decomposition lying in the streets. Some even dangled above her, next to the clothing. Based on what Amber saw of inhabitants of the city, it wouldn't have surprised her if these hanging corpses resembled trophies of those who won some fight. However, the disturbing decorations and the nauseating smell were nothing in comparison to the horrible sounds which seemed to emanate from every corner of the city. Screams of terror rang through the crowded streets as the metallic sounds of clashing weapons met their targets.

Amber shook her head as she stood frozen in place. She brushed away tears of fear as she said, "Kylis, I don't think I can do this."

No response. Amber turned to look at her only friend on this wicked planet and found, to her horror, he had disappeared. Frantically, she turned her head to look in all directions, not concerned about the whiplash she was giving herself. Kylis was nowhere in sight. He had left her alone to be eaten alive by the city and its inhabitants. This was it. This was her chance to prove to herself she had what it took to be a Darmentraean. She tried coaxing herself into this mindset, all the while thinking of all the ways she'd get back at Kylis, should he appear. But there was no telling when or if that would happen.

This massive city seemed more like a maze the farther she walked in. The only way of knowing which direction she was going was the great castle in the distance—the only abnormality among the trash-like buildings—but she had no idea where she was really going. She attempted to look like just an average citizen of the Dark City; however, this façade would only last so long. Unlike the Galaseyan women, who sold their homemade goods, these women were only interested in selling themselves to any wandering man who gave them the time of day.

Amber tried to avoid eye contact with these women, which wasn't difficult. The crimes that occurred nearly around every corner, on the other hand, were another story. Every wicked deed one could possibly commit happened just within the few minutes of Kylis's sudden departure. No one batted an eye. Amber's disgust for this land grew even more as her foot splashed in a pool of some unfortunate person's blood. No matter where she turned, each street contained puddles of scarlet; it was as common as seeing water after a rainstorm. The smell of blood hit her like a tsunami. Despite the fact that the smell was revolting, breathing through her nose was the only feasible option. Any time she opened her mouth the metallic taste of the residue made her gag.

When she wasn't trying to hold down her stomach, Amber took a closer look at some of the buildings and the scrap metal from which they were made. One word continuously popped up in blocky yellow letters: "Beacon." Knowing the Darmentraeans of this city, the name was probably used for either a derogatory term or held some kind of importance long forgotten.

Completely lost in the layers of scrap metal and blood-coated roads, Amber turned down a narrow alley, hoping to take a break and gather her bearings. She wouldn't catch a break that easily though, as a tall attractive man, clad almost entirely in leather, grabbed her wrist and violently spun her around until she was trapped in the corner. His greasy, slick black hair flattened against his head and his strikingly electric green eyes trailed her body, like a wild animal sizing her up for his next meal.

"What's a pretty thing like you doing alone in this part of the city?" he asked in a slight Russian accent.

Think, Amber! You only get one shot at this! she thought, remembering the women she had seen who weren't busy entertaining men, but rather fought them. Amber looked at her attacker and spat, "I'm looking for the idiot kid who decided it was a smart idea to steal my last bit of food from me. Now, unless you want to be the next meal on my list, I suggest you get your grimy hands off me!"

The man pulled away from Amber, not in disgust or fear, but rather annoyed that the conversation didn't go exactly how he would have liked. He straightened his outfit and said, "Hey, if you want help finding this thief, I'm sure we could work together."

Amber could only think of Kylis, the source of her anger at the moment. Although he had stolen nothing physical from her—he had stolen her trust. She shook her head and looked at the man as if he were a pathetic fool and replied, "Not on your life. This kid is mine."

She turned and started walking away with a proud stride and heard the man mutter, "Whatever. Have fun."

Amber kept up her rough pretense until she turned the next corner. Relieved to find the street bare of any living locals, she leaned against a nearby wall and let out her breath, realizing she had been holding it since she left the creep. Silent tears fell as her heart rate returned to normal. She covered her mouth, afraid the internal screaming in her head would escape her lips. Her knees buckled as her body slid down the wall to the blood-stained ground. She wrapped her arms around her knees and tucked her head to her chest, muffling the sounds of her cries.

Amber hadn't realized how hard this whole plan was going to be. She thought she knew everything about Darmentraea from Kylis. But, as she well forgot, it's one thing to hear or even read about something; it's an entirely different story when facing it in reality. At this point, she didn't care what the Brothers were planning. For all she knew, Ambrose may already be dead. Galaseya felt like a long-forgotten dream—one she wished she could instantly return to.

Her cries receded to mild sobs when a cold hand touched her arm. Thinking it to be another creep, Amber's head shot up as she came eye level with Kylis whose eyes were full of concern. He said nothing but gave her a kind smile. He didn't ask what she had seen during her time alone, but given what he knew about the city, it wasn't hard to figure out. He silently released her arms and gently pulled her to her feet. He stared into her bloodshot eyes as pity overwhelmed him. He had known from the beginning she would never be ready for the horrors within the Dark City. At times, he too had a hard time stomaching the atrocities.

"Don't worry, we're not all bad," assured Kylis in a low tone. "Sorry for abandoning you. It was the hardest choice I had to make."

"How could you?" asked Amber, her voice cracking from the strain of crying.

Kylis shook his head, feeling ashamed, "I had to. You've seen the inhabitants of the City. Have you seen anyone being genuinely friendly? Our cover would have been blown."

Amber opened her mouth to speak but was quickly interrupted by the sound of shattering glass echoing off the metallic buildings. Kylis looked at Amber, panic in his eyes as he said, "I won't leave you again; you have my word. Come on, we need to hurry."

Kylis didn't give Amber the chance to argue as he grabbed her hand tightly and pulled her along, running through the streets and taking sharp turns with ease. Not once did he let go of Amber's hand; his grip remained the same, proving to her he intended to keep his word.

Soon, the surrounding scenes gradually changed. The once blood-covered ground turned a more natural color, and the piles of corpses that littered most of the streets were nowhere in sight. In fact, even the living seemed scarce the farther on they ran. The condensed buildings disappeared as Kylis skidded to a halt in front of a large, out-of-place black metal manor. It wasn't made of the same material as the other buildings. It looked cleaner and more structured, as if this building held some kind of importance many years ago. For a place that was seemingly abandoned, someone took great care of it. The square manor looked to have belonged to a large family, perhaps a leader at one time.

"Are you coming?" asked Kylis, nearly at the entrance.

Amber shook her head and said, "No, this is wrong. Where are all the people...the bodies...the buildings? What happened here?"

"I'll explain inside. It's not safe out here," Kylis said as his eyes nervously shifted toward the darker corners of the city.

It's a trap. It's got to be. He is a Darmentraean after all. Maybe this was his plan all along? Could he be in league with the Brothers? But why would they need a powerless human to help them? This doesn't make sense...I shouldn't be following him, but I...I can't help it, Amber argued with herself as she entered the foreboding mystery house.

The entry way wasn't too impressive to Amber, that is, until she craned her neck up and looked toward the ceiling. For reasons beyond her understanding, the entry way was actually the bottom of a turret. The cylinder-like room stretched to the sky by at least three stories. The top of the room held an unusual glass-like ceiling. Amber assumed the original owners of the house intended the room to be for decoration, but this still seemed odd to her, as these people appeared unlike any of the other Darmentraeans she had seen so far. She walked through the empty, dusty house, noticing a large stone-like fireplace in each room. The building felt so familiar to Amber, yet she couldn't place exactly where she had seen it—perhaps a vague dream she had had as a child; or maybe it reminded her of the old Victorian houses on Diraetus. Either way, the building felt eerie. And with each step she took, more questions arose.

As they reached the kitchen, Kylis stopped in front of the large stove, which had metal pots and pans dangling from above it. He clapped his hands together and said, "Okay, story time."

Amber stopped by what appeared to be a sink and crossed her arms, "You have my undivided attention. What's going on?"

"This building belongs to the Elders. As far as the citizens of the Dark City are concerned, this manor is cursed. People have tried coming here for thrills, but none ever came back. Little is known of the first Elders, but from what we do know is this was the first building made in the city. I guess you could compare it to that of the White House or even Buckingham Palace. But the real rulers are through this door," said Kylis opening the door next to the stove and grabbing a lantern off a wall, "This is the only entrance to the Elders' hideout. Over time the citizens of the City filled in all the tunnels, as they didn't want any unwelcomed visitors in their City. The Elders made sure their secret place remained safe. Follow me, they're all waiting for you."

As Kylis lit the lantern, Amber hesitantly followed him into the pitch-black tunnel. The bobbing light guided her around the precarious twists and turns deeper in the underground. Neither of them spoke as they traveled through the maze-like tunnel; however, their minds were full of so many thoughts and fears of the situation at hand. By the time the lantern stopped moving, Amber could have sworn they had traveled deep within the planet at least by a few miles. Amber watched as Kylis blew out the light. Just as she was about to ask the reason for the darkness, she noticed a pale blue light emanating from around the corner, casting a glow on her friend. He smiled as he explained, "Now, you're going to have a lot of questions. Most can't be explained all at once and some we can't explain at all."

Amber walked closer to Kylis as he stretched out his arm and continued, "Welcome to the Beacon of Hope!"

There was that word again. Beacon. Somehow she felt that phrase and the word in the various parts of the City connected to something far deeper than any of them knew. Brushing this strange feeling aside, Amber followed Kylis's gesture and proceeded toward the dull blue light, where the strongest and deepest vision waited to greet her.

16

Hundreds of voices echoed around her as the scene slowly formed. The vision brought her back to the Dark City; however, this time its appearance and ambiance were quite different from what she had already seen. She stood outside the black manor yet again, but there were no signs of the crowded buildings or even a hint of violence. The land stretching out before her held many holes, which led to the labyrinth of underground tunnel systems reaching all around the planet. The people, on the other hand, appeared to be working well together, setting up temporary homes around the holes, although most wore expressions of sadness. But she couldn't blame them; they seemed to be struggling with building a civilization, as if they had just arrived on Darmentraea. Off in the distance, Amber noticed a massive metal heap, which would soon be the crowded and violent City she was originally introduced to.

But it wasn't just the people and the surrounding sight that seemed different. Even the darkness on the planet seemed different. The world had a blue tint, similar to the color she had seen engulfing Kylis, just before her vision began. The air felt clearer, and at times she could have sworn she saw the wild creatures at the edge of the nearby forest watching these strange invaders. Generally, the animals wouldn't think twice about killing a human in their sight. Something felt off to Amber as she stared out at the unusual scene. Something drastic had made Darmentraea go from a planet of darkness to one of evil.

The voices of the crowd soon dwindled down to murmurs as the Darmentraeans' attention shifted toward the black manor, where a tall, thin man stood proud. Clearly, he was the leader of the citizens, and he seemed well-respected. He said a few words of what appeared to be encouragement as smiles formed on the faces of the people. Amber couldn't identify what he said, as her vision seemed more focused on the situation rather than what the people said. But after all the visions she had, Amber knew that they only showed her what was important. The leader finished his speech to the people and walked back into his beautiful home while the citizens pumped their fists in the air as if cheering him on.

The scene quickly changed as Amber soon found herself inside the huge house. Except for a few pieces of odd furniture, which Amber assumed may have come from the metallic wreckage, the house seemed quite barren of anything that would make it a home. In her peripheral vision, Amber noticed two small figures running from one room to the other. She turned her head and smiled as two young boys ran around the vicinity, playing some kind of game. There seemed to be an age gap, as one child looked nearly in his teens, whereas the youngest child looked barely seven. Their mother quickly came out, telling the kids to be more careful, as any concerned mother would. At that moment, Amber caught the names of the children. The youngest was called Crais and the eldest—Dugon. Her eyebrows furrowed in confusion, wondering why she had never seen this part of his life in the last vision of him. Maybe he forgot about it. Or could it have been something he knew, but kept well-hidden, even from her?

Her focus changed when the scene moved on to the two boys fast asleep in their shared bedroom. At first, it didn't seem significant to her, until a golden glow enveloped Dugon's sleeping figure, making him disappear completely. The Brothers had left every memory of Dugon to torture the family in some sick way.

In the next scene of the vision, Amber watched as Crais grew up into a decent young man. By the time he reached his early twenties, both his parents had passed away, and by default, he became the next leader of the Darmentraeans. This is when everything seemed to go wrong. Crais wanted nothing to do with leading anyone; the young man could barely handle his own family. The pressure became too much for him, as more and more people came to him with their problems hoping he'd be just like his father. Crais was no more a Darmentraean than Amber was.

Finally, the day came where the pressure of his father's legacy became too much for Crais to bear. The one citizen who, Amber noticed, pestered Crais the most came to him yet again, this time more adamant that the young leader help him. Unfortunately, everything escalated so quickly it was almost a blur. In a fit of frustration, Crais killed the citizen and quickly ran back to his house for safety after realizing that there were many hostile witnesses. The vision moved inside the house, and Amber saw Crais kneeling down next to a young boy whom Amber assumed to be his son. A name—Danin. That was the only thing she caught from the entire hasty conversation. Just as Danin rushed off toward the kitchen, the front door burst open with a mob of enraged citizens, all carrying some kind of weapon. Amber turned the vision toward Danin, as she didn't need to watch what came next for Crais and his wife—their screams of terror were enough to paint a gruesome picture in her mind. The young boy managed to escape the bloody scene and traveled blindly down a tunnel that he knew led to other parts of the planet, although any time he had previously journeyed through the maze, his father had always guided the way with a lantern.

Soon, the young boy reached a place that he had never seen before. If Amber had to guess, she'd say the massive, dome-shaped room was the near the center of the planet. Its blue glow felt homey, and there were veined marble columns all around the room. It really brought a whole new meaning to an inanimate object being alive. The room felt like the heart of the planet—Darmentraea at its purest form. As the crying child cautiously walked into the large cavern, Amber noticed it begin to change physically—providing a more hospitable environment for the child to reside in. It was as if this magical bubble knew the child's dire situation and that he needed help. After a taking a moment to calm down, the boy rubbed his stomach, realizing how hungry he was. Suddenly a piece of the cavern wall opened to reveal a tunnel, which Amber assumed led to another part of the planet.

As the child looked all around him in awe, a speck of hope spread across his face. Amber felt the vision end as one by one people began filling the massive cavern—fast-forwarding the scene through the years. Crais certainly had a legacy. His son was the last of the Grunewalds on Darmentraea, and when the vision ended completely, Amber saw exactly what he had created. He didn't just save his family from being completely eliminated—no, he built an entire civilization.

She stood in the middle of an enormous underground city. Kylis looked at her with some concern, but he wore a smile that told Amber he was also impressed. The others in the cavern had different expressions. Some were confused, while others seemed leery of her. But a select few had a difficult time concealing their fear. After all, the only power they had seen like that came from the Brothers. Amber glanced around at her estranged family and guessed there to be generations upon generations of Grunewalds within the room.

Out of the crowd emerged a tall young man, roughly in his mid-to-late twenties. He stood tall, and his tight t-shirt emphasized his large muscles—numerous tattoos ran the length of his arms. His short brown hair spiked at his forehead, and his dark blue eyes stared at Amber. He crossed his arms and said, "Welcome to our Beacon of Hope, Amber. I'm Jalerydin. Now that you pretty much know everything, let's cut to the chase."

"Hold it, I have some questions," said Amber, hoping her demanding tone wouldn't cause a riot.

"Oh? I thought your vision would have explained everything," said the young leader, curiosity shining in his eyes.

"Hardly, it only gave me more questions," Amber pointed out. "First, how could you have known I would have a vision?"

"You're famous here. Kylis has been incredibly helpful in keeping us informed about you and the rest of the family on Galaseya. This cavern is full of memories, we took a chance and figured you'd at least get something from it. But judging by how spaced-out you looked, I'm going to guess you got more than you expected?"

Amber looked at her surroundings, momentarily forgetting that there were hundreds of other people in the room, still staring at her. She noticed a group of kids at the edge of the large circle that the people created around her. The younger children stood behind the eldest brother, and based on the absence of their parents, Amber assumed they had come to their untimely end. The brother cared much for his younger siblings, as he discreetly held them back behind him, afraid of what Amber could do. On the other side of the circle, she noticed a sweet-looking couple who stood quite close to each other, trying not to show any signs of concern, but the young woman held her man's hand far too tightly.

Amber looked back to Jalerydin as other Elders of the

Grunewalds came out of the crowd and took their places beside him. That's when she noticed something unique about these leaders. They wore a symbol tattooed on the left side of their necks. It was an image that appeared more symbolic than anything else. A raindrop took up most of the design, which transformed at the bottom into thin branches with leaves at the tips. On the top of the drop stood three flickering flames on each side with the tip of the drop standing tall in the middle. In fact, as she scanned the crowd again, she noticed the oldest brother of the children and even the young woman's man had the same tattoo.

Kylis remained by Amber's side as he didn't want her to feel alone, but in her peripheral vision, she noticed Kylis was one of the leaders as well. But his symbolic tattoo appeared smaller than the others. Judging by the size difference of the other marks, Amber realized that it was a position in rank. Kylis seemed to be on the lowest end despite all he did for the Elders. With her power, she could see how the other members felt about him—Kylis was just another errand boy for them. It didn't feel right to her. Kylis looked at her, concerned she'd be angry, but she just shook her head and gave him a small smile of understanding. She had every right to be mad at him for being so secretive, but after the vision and what little she gleaned from his role with the Elders, everything made sense. She had a lot of questions for Kylis, mainly why this mark was important, but that was a question she would have to ask at a much later time.

She looked back at Jalerydin, who appeared impatient, as if they were all on some kind of invisible time crunch. Still skeptical about everything, Amber continued the conversation. "Yeah, you could say that. But there are still some things I don't get. Does Dugon know anything about this?"

Jalerydin explained. "Rydan and his daughter, Saraleast, have been helpful in keeping all of us connected.

As you know, Saraleast put herself in those computers that Kylis has in the cave—that is the only means of communication. She is, in a sense, our lifeline. Without her, those screens would be rendered useless. When Kylis found Ambrose, we knew he was the one to stop the Brothers; after all, we have spied on them long enough to have heard of stories of a strange child becoming a Darmentraean. Ambrose began having visions of you, and that is when we decided to take action. At first, we didn't know what to do, but then Saraleast came to us, explaining she had the power to go back and forth between the planets and said she could help us. We didn't have many other choices, and we knew she could be trusted. From that point, she communicated with her father that we needed help. I believe he sort of already knew. As for Dugon, I don't know what he knows, there never seemed to be a good time to explain that his little brother's legacy lived on. I figure he feels as empty as Crais did, but without understanding why. Maybe one day we can all meet and talk. But now, we need to get to work."

As the leader began to turn, Amber stopped him, taking the lead of the situation. "No, I'm not finished yet."

All eyes were on her, completely surprised by her forwardness toward their leader, someone who could easily kill her without a second thought. Even some gasps and murmurs swept over the crowd as he turned back to her with almost a look of appreciation that someone dared challenge him. "Is that so?"

"Yeah, it is," said Amber defiantly. "Tell me, how the heck did you all manage to hide from the Brothers? They are the planet; shouldn't they know about your little hideout here?"

Jalerydin laughed and replied, "Simply put, the Brothers are only part of the planet. Think of it as a human. If a person is born with a deformity or some kind of incurable sickness, you can't wish the deformity or disease away. You may be able to alleviate symptoms it may cause, but that only does so much. But believe me, that doesn't mean the Brothers haven't tried getting rid of us. They've tried blocking us from returning to the surface many times, but the cavern knows we are trying to help restore the Balance. Now follow me. There's something I need to show you."

The finality in his voice revealed to Amber that her question-and-answer time was over for the time being. She silently followed him through the crowd as the people parted for her, still nervous about her presence. Due to his height, it was hard to see where Jalerydin was leading her. But as he moved off to the side and the crowd made room, Amber immediately saw it—on the wall of the cavern, displayed like a mounted animal head, hung Ambrose, in an uncomfortable spread-eagle position. At first glimpse, it looked as if he were dead, but when Amber slowly moved forward, she noticed his chest rising ever so slightly. He was in a deep sleep as his body was gradually becoming part of the wall. His skin even blended in with the color and strange design of the walls. Amber felt her stomach squirm at the thought of the mental games the Brothers put Ambrose through.

"How long has he been like this?" asked Amber, her eyes glued to her brother's sleeping figure.

"He showed up here right as you arrived on Darmentraea," one of the other leaders spoke up. "Before that, the Brothers captured him just as you got out of your illusion."

"And you're just bringing me here now? I could have saved him a month ago instead of trying to fit in with your culture!" exclaimed Amber as her frustration rose.

The eldest child of the family of children stepped out and crossed his thin arms. A vest, similar to the one Kylis wore, lay snug against his chest, a few tattoos peeked through the fabric. A black gauge was evident in his left ear, while his right ear was riddled with piercings. His black eyes challenged Amber as he snapped, "Do you even know how to save him?"

"Jozderin!" yelled Jalerydin.

"No, he's right," said Amber looking at Jozderin. "I barely have enough power to see visions. I can't even get back to my own planet. I have no idea how to save Ambrose, but that doesn't mean I'm not going to try."

Jozderin's glare softened as a hint of appreciation crossed his face. He said nothing as he continued to look at Amber, trying to find any sign of something to question. When the crowd hushed, Amber reached her hand out, nearly touching Ambrose, when a thought struck her and she immediately pulled away.

"What's wrong?" asked Kylis.

"Doesn't something feel off to you guys?" asked Amber facing the crowd.

"You're on Darmentraea, what do you expect?" asked Jozderin, as a rumble of chuckles spread throughout the crowd.

Ignoring his sarcastic remark, Amber continued, "Why here? Of all the places the Brothers could trap Ambrose, why put him in *your* living space? If I manage to rescue him, there is a chance that something bad will happen. I don't know how many confrontations you've had with them, but from what I've seen, they don't give away freebies...they don't provide a way to escape without some kind of consequence."

"We know," said Jalerydin somberly, "we haven't personally dealt with them, fortunately, but we have seen what they can do from a distance. More than likely, this is a trap for us. But this is a chance we are all willing to take."

"Amber, I don't think you really get us. We all have sacrificed so much for you and the Balance of this solar system. Jozderin and his siblings lost their parents not too long ago because they were defending our secret location from outsiders," said Kylis as he turned to the couple across the circle. "Hashjen and his wife Mikali lost their parents while they went hunting in the forest, trying to gather food for us. And I...well, my story isn't important. You see, we have all sworn to protect not only you but anyone in danger. Killing other Darmentraeans is the hardest thing for us, as we consider them family in a way. What matters the most right now is that you and Ambrose leave here and somehow get to Galaseya. The Balance of our worlds is in your hands because only you have the power to save us."

No pressure! thought Amber as she turned her focus back to Ambrose. She stared at his pale face and for a moment wondered what horrors the Brothers were putting him through. *Is this how my family felt when I was asleep? Could he be in a dream-like state, trying to fight his way through? Is he just like the rest of them and only concerned about the Balance? Could he really care about me as he sounded before?*

Amber shook all these doubts and worries away as she reached out toward Ambrose's hands. Her fingertips lightly brushed his wrists, when suddenly his hands wrapped around her wrists in a vice grip. His eyelids flew open, revealing glowing, sapphire-colored eyes. Electricity flowed through Amber so much that it felt almost painful.

Her grip loosened slightly as the pain grew too much to bear, but at that moment a female voice reverberated off the walls of her mind: *Amber, my name is Khyra. Let me help you.*

Suddenly Amber felt the strongest surge of power she had ever felt. The new source did more than just help Amber; she could feel her own abilities recharging. Amber noticed in her peripheral vision that a golden light, which enveloped Ambrose, now spread like glowing veins throughout the entire cavern. Ambrose slowly regained normal strength as the wall released him, causing him to tumble into Amber's arms. That's when all Amber's fears came to life. An earthquake of a magnitude unlike any other rumbled through the cavern. Screams of fear and pain ricocheted off the crumbling walls. She didn't dare turn around to see the catastrophe that the Brothers' trap inflicted.

The voice returned to Amber, telling her something she had already planned: *Save them, Amber, you have the power! Save them all and get home!*

Holding her power on full force, Amber glanced over to the crowd. Some scattered toward any exit that they could find, whereas others like Kylis, Jozderin, Hashjen, and Jalerydin stayed where they were—all hope lost. She looked back at Ambrose and then closed her eyes, exerting all her power toward those still trapped in the room. The more she focused her ability, the weaker she became. As blood streamed from her nose and ears, Amber knew she was overdoing it, but she had to get them out of harm's way, even if it was elsewhere on Darmentraea. Her vision got blurry as she pushed for one last surge of energy. *Galaseya!* was the last thought in her mind before a bright white light consumed her senses.

17

Ringing...a constant ringing. Nothing like the tinkling of a delicate bell, but that of one being the lucky survivor of an explosion. But unlike a typical war zone, there was no sign of smoke. In fact, there seemed to be no odor at all. The atmosphere felt clear, but this wasn't enough evidence for Amber to believe her crazy plan had worked. After all, the cold, smooth stones that pressed against her stomach felt similar to the ground in Darmentraea, but these stones were not scattered haphazardly like most of Darmentraea; these felt structured.

Did it actually work? Am I home? Did everyone get here safely? These thoughts raced through Amber's head as her eyes shot open. Through her blurred vision, she saw many Darmentraeans shielding their faces from a bright light. Then, like a flick of a switch, the bright light dwindled down to a mere glow—just enough for the Darmentraeans to be comfortable. The bearers of the darkness stepped forward into Amber's line of sight. Just as usual, the Sidhe came in the nick of time. They stood in the light facing Amber, and as her vision focused, she noticed everyone in the room staring at her.

Feeling slightly embarrassed, Amber slowly lifted herself from the ground, noticing a warm hand resting gently on her back while another hand grabbed her arm, helping her to her feet. Amber didn't know what to expect, but it definitely wasn't a hug from Hunter. She squirmed away from his embrace, still uncomfortable around him, and turned to see Jermiar, who no doubt had used his ability to give her energy. Silently, Amber looked around to see the faces of the Darmentraeans who had been trapped in the hideout. She did it! Everyone was safe, and somehow they had managed to get back, not just to Galaseya, but inside the darkest room of the palace...although she suspected the Sidhe had something to do with that, given their impeccable timing.

Moments later, the rest of her family and some guards came to see what all the commotion was about. Amber suspected that Hunter and Jermiar either happened to be in the area or just got to the room first. No one said anything at first. The Galaseyans' and the Darmentraeans' eyes were locked—all equally confused. The Sidhe looked slightly amused by the human reactions but saved them all from a horrible awkward silence by speaking up.

Levendria stepped forward and said, "Well done, Ameliana. Your rescue was fascinating."

She glanced at the Darmentraeans, who simultaneously gave her a look of appreciation, except for Jozderin, who still had an air of skepticism about him. Addressing the crowd, but still looking at Jozderin, hoping to give him more reason to trust her, Amber said, "Thanks, but I...I can't take all the credit. Someone helped me."

"That's not even possible...is it?" said Mason.

The Sidhe shifted nervously as Vaeris said, "Indeed. In fact, we know of whom you speak."

"Vaeris is correct. The woman has been through quite an ordeal, most of which even we cannot fully comprehend," said Analira.

"Care to elaborate who *she* is?" asked Amber, annoyed by their elusive words.

"Khyra," said Levendria simply. "She is Diraetus' Protector."

"Okay, well, we kind of figured there was a Protector on Diraetus, but what makes her so different and powerful?" Amber asked.

"She is the reason the Protectors even exist. Khyra has been alive far longer than even Rydan. Of all the people who wish to restore the Balance to the planets, Khyra has dedicated her entire immortal life to doing so. She has, as you humans say, her finger on the pulse of the situation and probably knows more than any of us," said Vaeris.

"So why hide if she wants to help the cause?" asked Jalerydin bravely.

Levendria spoke up again, hesitation in her voice. "The beings on Diraetus, known as the Scientists, are in many ways more ruthless than the Brothers. As you know, the Brothers enjoy mind games with the people of their world. The Scientists perform horrible experiments on their humans, such as making them think they are on a planet called Earth. We assume that that is where Khyra and her people originated."

A wave of hushed murmurs spread throughout the crowd as the other Sidhe looked at Vaeris, surprised by her unexpected announcement. Amber spoke above the crowd, silencing them all. "Wait, who is she really, and why did she come all the way over here?"

"Vaeris has already said far too much, as we all know the walls have ears," said Levendria as her eyes shifted up, referring to the Brothers. "We cannot say any more of her true identity; she will have to explain herself, as it is not our story to tell. You must find her. I believe that now is the right time. She would not have contacted you in such a way if she were not ready."

"I don't know how!" said Amber, in exasperation.

The Sidhe faded away as they simultaneously said, "You will."

"Do they always do that?" asked Hashjen, his scared face contorting in confusion while his tongue played with his lip ring.

Amber nodded "yes" as Iethreor came barreling into the room, a look of fear plastered on his face. Some relief passed over it as he saw Amber. "Amber, you must come with me. The cameras are dying!"

Without explanation to the Darmentraeans, Amber ran out of the room after Iethreor. She turned sharply around corners while calls from the others came from behind. When she reached her bedroom where the computer was, Sphinx dove under her bed, hiding from the others who came behind. Amber slid into the chair and started frantically pressing buttons, hoping the fading screen would stabilize. Nothing worked. All they could do was hopelessly stare at the screen. Suddenly, two distinct images came across the screen, and by the sudden gasps of surprise from the others, Amber knew she wasn't the only one seeing them.

The first image was of a strange house made out of the branches of two massive trees and surrounding thick vines. The house stood in the midst of a dead forest, but there was no telling where the location was. Moments after the house appeared, a bright, tan-colored light showed through, in its center was an image of a young woman with short and spiky brown hair, lightly colored skin, and hazel eyes. Behind those eyes lay over a thousand years of fear and grief. Amber read her expression clearly. This was Khyra, and she just gave them their only clue as to how to find her. The screen faded out for the last time—its life support, Saraleast, lost forever in the dark Abyss.

Silence swept through the room. Rydan stared at the blank screen—a mix of emotions plastered on his face. Amber half expected him to be in hysterics, but not a single tear escaped his eyes. He, like everyone else, was mentally prepared for a scenario such as this, but never once did they really think it could happen. Not to them. Now the Darmentraeans were completely cut off from their world, left unprotected from the Brothers. Yet again, all eyes turned toward Amber for answers.

"There's no time to waste," she started. "We have to find Khyra. We have to restore the Balance before the Brothers have a chance to destroy it."

Days turned into weeks, and Galaseya was left in peace. At first, the Darmentraeans found it difficult to adjust to the atmosphere and light on Galaseya. Some even became sick just as Amber had seen in her vision of Saraleast as a child. But Rydan made a cure for this situation should it ever occur. He explained that that was what his fruit was initially for as he too experienced complications with the transition. But after the fruit's destruction, Rydan concocted a safer method should any other Darmentraeans unexpectedly arrive.

The new arrivals certainly missed their homes and families they left behind. Many worried about the chaos that would erupt on their planet, and they began to feel hopeless. To Amber's surprise, the animals of the woods sensed the hurt that the Darmentraeans felt and at first were extremely cautious about their new guests. But eventually, the creatures warmed up to them and tended to the newcomers. At first, the adults were scared of benign creatures, as they were far too used to those on Darmentraea. But the young children, who had never experienced the horrors of the creatures on their planet, found the animals friendly.

The new Darmentraeans started to get used to their temporary home. They kept to some of their ways. Clothing and mannerisms didn't change all that much. Although they could easily walk about the land, the Darmentraeans preferred to only go out and explore at night. This also provided relief to Amber, as she didn't know how the Darmentraeans would react to the village people and their way of life. That was an unnecessary disaster, in her book. But while everyone tried to adjust to the new events, the members of the palace returned to their regular routine—helping the village people and maintaining order.

Seeing how she understood how traveling between worlds worked, Amber thought about traveling to Diraetus in hopes of finding Khyra. She knew that it was a shot in the dark: after all, if the Sidhe didn't have any idea where she was, how could she have known? Amber couldn't shake the feeling that Khyra was still trying to reach her, but if it was through her dreams, as most messages came, nothing was received. The only thing she dreamed about since the event were random woods, all of which seemed peaceful, but had nothing in common.

One evening, however, more answers to this puzzling mystery came. Amber found herself lost in her own thoughts while sitting on her windowsill, when suddenly a figure entered her view, sitting down in the grassy field. Jozderin. This was the fifth time Amber had seen him coming outside, staring up at his planet. Next to him sat a little fawn that she often saw trailing along beside him at night. An invisible force compelled Amber to sit with him during his time of solitude.

"What do you want?" snapped Jozderin as Amber reached him.

The young man never removed his eyes from Darmentraea as Amber kindly responded, "I was just coming out here to see if you were okay."

"Why wouldn't I be? My planet's there, and I'm here, I can't go back, and there's no telling what happened to the rest of my family," he replied—his tone laced with sarcasm. The young fawn placed its head on Jozderin's leg as he started stroking its small, fragile body.

"Jozderin, I'm sor..."

"Don't be," he interrupted. "You almost killed yourself trying to save us. I'm not mad at you."

Feeling out the situation a bit, Amber sensed the silent cue that she was welcomed to continue. She sat down next to him and said, "So then, what's the real issue...aside from the obvious?"

Jozderin stopped petting the animal, resting his hand on its head, and turned to Amber. His eyes watered as he said, "Me. I'm the problem. Just before my parents died, I promised them I would look after my other siblings, that I would protect them at whatever the cost. But back there, when you came to rescue Ambrose and ultimately us, I felt powerless. All I could do was stand there holding the rest of my family close while the world around me literally fell apart. Do you have any idea how that feels? Knowing you are strong and can save people, but having to rely on someone you don't know to do your job?"

Amber stared at Jozderin as he turned his face away, hiding the tears that streamed down his face. A small smile appeared at the corner of her lips as she replied quietly, "Yeah, actually I know what you mean. That's exactly how I felt when I first got here. My power was just starting to peak, and Kaleya was relentless. She drove me to seek help from people I didn't trust, let alone knew."

"Right, I remember that now." said Jozderin sheepishly. "But you figured out your power and were still able to bring your family together and your world! I can't do anything, I have no special gift, and I've never been great at resolving conflict...just creating it."

Amber placed a hand on his shoulder and said, "That doesn't mean you're useless, Jozderin. We all can contribute something to make our worlds better. You just have to trust in yourself and the loyalty you have toward those you care about. In my experience, even loyalty can go great distances. You're the kind of person I'd want on my side for any battle we face."

"Thanks," he said with a faded smile. "Not to change this emotional topic, but what *is* your plan? I know you haven't been keeping yourself locked away in your room for some kind of break."

"To be honest, I have no plan at the moment. We have to wait for either the Brothers or Khyra to make a move and currently both sides are silent," said Amber, in a frustrated tone.

Jozderin stared off into space, contemplating on her words. The little fawn trotted off into the woods, seeing its job was completed, at least for the time being. "It's kind of odd that Khyra would randomly stop talking or at least sending messages to you after the rescue on Darmentraea. If she's really hiding as your Sidhe say, maybe she's sending hints?"

Suddenly, flashes of various woods from her more recent dreams ran through Amber's mind, giving her sort of a mental whiplash. Within each forest stood one common element: a hut made of trees and nearby vines. She peered into the recesses of her memory and noticed something disturbing about these woods. They weren't random but were woods near every place that Amber had lived on Diraetus. Khyra had followed her, and the last image on the computer screen was the final clue as to where the mysterious woman currently resided. The ocean through the trees, the various evergreens—Khyra lived somewhere in Ipswich.

"Amber, is everything okay?" asked Jozderin, who seemed to have been calling her attention for some time.

"I...I got it...I know how to find her...I need to get Ambrose. We have to go now!" said Amber jumping to her feet.

"Last I checked he was in your grandfather's library doing some kind of research," said Jozderin, his last few words drowned out by the wind whistling in Amber's ears as she ran at full pace toward her home.

No matter how many telepathic calls she sent Ambrose's way, she only received silence, meaning either he was ignoring her or their connection was only strong during stressful times. Amber managed to get to the library in record time, but before she entered the massive wooden doors, the sound of an altercation within the room stopped her. Her inner instinct told her this was a conversation that needed to be overheard. She leaned her head closer to the partially opened door and listened in.

"You're so full of it, Chris, she has every right to know!" came Ambrose's voice.

"Do not condemn me! I have been trying to tell her for the last year of living in Galaseya. There just never seemed to be a most opportune moment," Chris said defensively.

Ambrose threw up his hands as he turned to face the partially open door, where his eyes met Amber's briefly. "Christolar, there will never be an opportune moment to tell the sister you practically *raised* that you are part Sidhe."

Amber knew she should have been more surprised at the news, but given all the other secrets her family held, this announcement seemed typical. She continued listening in, hoping to get an explanation but was met with a quick telepathic message from Ambrose: *I'm sorry, Amber. You had to know now. The Brothers are coming, and they're planning something huge. The more you know, the better you're prepared.*

When are they coming, Ambrose? Amber asked.

A loud explosion interrupted whatever message he intended to send back, but instead replied, *Now!*

Amber turned around and ran outside to where the chaos erupted. She met with Jozderin and many other family members who were staring out in shock at the village—blue and white flames emerged from the houses, but not one bit of the ground in danger of the fire. This was a scare tactic, as no planet could truly harm another, as it was written in their own code. The screams from the people resounded all around as two tall figures emerged from the flames and started toward the palace at a relaxed pace. Just as Ambrose warned, the Brothers had arrived with the intent to destroy. As they approached the palace, every window of the massive structure blew out, raining shards of glass on the family below.

The Sidhe were nowhere in sight, possibly dealing with the chaos in the village below. With her Protector abilities fully charged, Amber threw up a powerful shield, blocking the intruders from attacking the family and their home. Martheykos stopped at the sparkling, golden barricade and gave Amber a condescending look. With a nasty smirk, he took his hands and cut through the shield like a hot knife through butter. A blue light spread through the shield as it crumbled to the ground, exactly as the windows had.

"Please, you really think that little shield can hold us back? That's cute," said Martheykos.

Seconds after their arrival came a wave of multicolored lights that took the same path as the Brothers, extinguishing the flames rising from the village in one sweep. The lights came down and landed with grace right beside the Brothers—in the form of the Sidhe. Martheykos rolled his eyes just as a child who didn't get his way. He heaved a disgruntled sigh and whined, "Oh, you always ruin our fun!"

"Why are you guys here?" asked Amber, crossing her arms.

Petraylin spoke up and said, "Why, the truth, of course. We both agreed you ought to know of the final secret that your family kept from you all these years. About Chris."

Amber and Ambrose exchanged nervous glances. Fortunately, Amber already knew what they had to say, so it really wasn't a surprise to her, but she needed to play their game still. She had to know what their plans were.

"Why should I believe anything you say?" she spat.

Martheykos looked around at the familiar faces of the Darmentraeans and smirked as his eyes gazed upon the crowd, falling back on Amber as he said, "Unlike the rest of your cowardly family, we aren't afraid to tell you the dark truths of who they really are."

Amber looked at Chris. The blood drained from his face to the point that he looked deathly ill. She turned back to the Brothers and glared at them, saying, "Whatever secrets my family has, they'll tell me on their own time. And honestly, I don't really care what it is. Nothing you or anyone says will change that, either."

"Oh really?" asked Martheykos, thoroughly enjoying this new challenge. "So the fact that Chris is a Sidhe doesn't faze you? Wow, you're more forgiving than I thought...or foolish—not really a difference there."

Amber had never found herself good at acting but tried putting on the best confused expression she knew how. Fortunately, the Brothers bought it, as Petraylin continued where his brother left off. "I don't know, Martheykos, she still doesn't look that surprised. Maybe we should explain how he became one and whose fault it was."

This time her confused expression wasn't faked. She accepted the fact that Chris was part Sidhe, but why would it be anyone's fault? That's when Amber looked to the Sidhe for answers, but Levendria merely warned the Brothers, "That is enough! You are not welcomed here, Martheykos and Petraylin. Leave at once."

"Nope, don't think so," said Martheykos, waving his hand as a wave of crystal blue water formed into an icy throne behind him. He leisurely sat down. "We're sticking around for the show!"

Chris moved toward Amber and stopped when he stood only a few inches away. He looked down at her and formally spoke to her, just as the majority of her Galaseyan family did.

"Amber, I made a mistake in not telling you sooner. Although I did not expect to tell you my story in this manner. Yes, I am for all intents and purposes, a Sidhe, but you must understand how it happened. When mother was still pregnant with me, she fell gravely ill. The Sidhe did everything to keep the both of us alive, thinking me to be the Protector of Galaseya. That is why they put their power into me before I was born. Without their power, I would not have survived. In truth, I am biologically no more your brother than Sphinx is a dog."

Amber stared in awe and silence as Chris transformed into his real form—half human, half-Sidhe. He looked similar to how he had on the road to Ipswich, but this time less human. His opal-colored eyes, white spiked hair, and silver, glowing body were the only indicators revealing his otherworldly side. Amber looked from Chris to the Brothers, whose mouths formed into the nastiest grin she had ever seen.

At that moment, a flash of a vision came through, but this didn't come from her own power, as her visions were limited to the planets. The feeling with these visions was from the same source who helped her escape Darmentraea—Khyra.

The images came at warp speed as Amber tried to decipher them. The first showed the Darmentraeans on the planet growing darker and then the Brothers opening the Portal. The Darmentraeans made their way over to each planet, causing whatever was left of the Balance to be completely eradicated and making Diraetus and Galaseya just as evil as Darmentraea. Total takeover. That's all the Brothers wanted, and if Amber had to guess, the Sidhe knew of this plan too, but because of their connection to the Brothers, they were backed into a corner.

The images ceased, and Amber returned her gaze to Chris, trying to act as normal as possible given the situation. Chris returned to his human form, thinking Amber was too afraid to look at him. She had to warn her family of the vision, but obviously now wasn't the time. No, she needed to play her part and act it out. That's what the Brothers expected. Her only option was to try to send a telepathic message to those who were on the same wavelength.

She looked at Chris with horror still, as tears fell down her cheeks. *Chris, anyone, if you can hear me...I'm not angry, I already knew. Follow my lead, lives depend on it. I'll explain later!*

No one responded, except for Chris, who gave a slight sign of a wink. All that mattered to Amber was that he knew what she was about to do.

"I can't believe you! After all this time of raising me, you throw this bomb in my face? Chris, you had plenty of time to tell me!" she exclaimed.

"Amber," said Stephria, "what Christolar did wasn't right, but he is truly sorry."

"You're kidding me, right? What was so hard about telling me this? So what if he's different? I wouldn't have seen him any other way. After everything we've been through, it seems that none of you really know who I am. Some family you are!" said Amber, as genuine tears streamed down her face—the accusations she spewed tearing her heart apart.

"What can I do to make it up to you?" asked Chris, still following her lead.

"Forget me...all of you. I'm done with this. We will never be able to accomplish anything with these lies," said Amber, backing away from her family.

"Amber, what are you talking about?" asked Marsacor, with a silent look that he had received her mental message.

She looked at her old and new family, every one of them wearing a look of shock, except for a select few Darmentraeans, who deemed this reaction reasonable. Her heart ached with pain as she glanced back at Chris and hissed, "I'm saying it's a shame you couldn't take mom's place."

Under the strenuous circumstance, Amber had no idea if her plan was going to work. With all the strength she could muster, she tried to activate her Protector abilities and transformed into a cloud of smoke. She saw the scene before her vanish as she disappeared to Diraetus—her heart laden with grief at walking away from her family.

18

Whitecaps crashed against the rocky Ipswich bluffs as seagulls soared overhead, their screeching calls matching the gloomy late spring evening. A storm brewed on the horizon as sheets of rain fell upon the dark blue waters. Thunder roared in the distance as Amber felt tears fall from her cheeks. She hated herself for hurting her family, but the Brothers had given her no choice: it was play their game or die.

Amber lifted her face as the rain came pouring down. Seconds later another sound of thunder rumbled overhead, but when Amber looked up to see the expected lightning bolt flash across the sky, she instead saw a large, pale blue beam of light strike down to the earth mere feet from her. As the light faded it revealed a figure—Ambrose. With quick reflexes, he straightened himself and approached Amber.

"Amber, that was incredible! The Brothers bought it, they left moments after you did. Don't worry, Marsacor, Rydan, and Chris are explaining everything to the family. No one is mad at you."

"I am! I just verbally destroyed them, and for what? To follow a plan that may not work out?" exclaimed Amber.

Ambrose grabbed Amber's hands and said, "Hold it, you're not making any sense! What plan?"

Amber quickly explained the vision that Khyra had shown her, as the blood slowly drained from Ambrose's face. He said, almost in a daze, "So that's what they've been struggling to hide all these years. I knew something major was going on."

"We've got to find Khyra. She's our only shot at stopping their domination!" said Amber frantically.

Ambrose checked her peripheral vision and whispered in a low tone, "We have company."

Her heart sank when she turned to see a young couple staring at them—a cellphone recording their entire conversation and possibly their entrance to the Bluffs. The two shook with fear from the encounter and began backing away slowly into the woods. Amber reached out a hand to reassure them and a familiar brown glow emanated from her hand, striking the young girl to the ground.

"Julie! Julie, are you okay?" asked the young man, putting the phone in his pocket.

The young woman looked at him with a confused gaze. "I think so, what happened? Why are we on the Bluffs again?"

"For our one-year anniversary, don't you remember?" asked the young man in fear.

"No, you told me this morning you wanted to go to the Bluffs for our anniversary, but that's it," Julie replied, getting to her feet.

"That was a week ago!" exclaimed the man.

"Charlie, who are these people? Are they friends of yours?" asked Julie with a smile, completely unaware of their arrival.

Charlie grabbed Julie's wrist and ushered her quickly into the woods, shouting back to the twins, "I'll make you pay for this!"

Ambrose pulled Amber into the woods on the other side of the bluffs, trying to put as much distance from the couple as he could. Amber didn't hear a word Ambrose said as they ran deeper into the woods, the pine trees completely engulfing them. He suddenly stopped and sat Amber down on a large tree root. She stared at her hands in shocked silence while Ambrose kept trying to get through to her. As gently as he could, Ambrose took his twin's shoulders and shook her. "Amber, snap out of it! You have to listen to me!"

"Ambrose, I didn't mean to, I swear! I...I don't know how to control that!" she exclaimed frantically.

Ambrose took Amber's chin and tilted it so their eyes met as he said, "Just as our family has limitations with their powers. We, the Protectors, have anti-abilities which are controlled by emotions. What happened back there was an accident, okay? Let me show you."

He held up his left hand as a navy-colored smoke rose from his palm and into the air. He directed it towards a nearby flower, which immediately wilted as the smoke wrapped around the plant. "I have the power to instantly kill," said Ambrose.

He lifted his other hand as a baby blue-colored smoke came. He noticed a nearby squirrel struggling to move after an attack with another creature. The baby blue vapor stirred around the creature, as did its counterpart, but instead left the squirrel happily chattering away, seeming to say thank you. "I also have the power to heal."

"Whoa," said Amber, as she looked down at her hands and saw a dark brown color rising from one and a gold color from the other.

"Now focus, we have to get out of here. I know a lie when I see one and that guy was dead set on revenge. We don't know what will happen. The sooner we get a hold of Khyra, the quicker we can get home," Ambrose said, helping Amber to her feet. "Because the Mask doesn't work on us, it's going to be hard to find where Khyra is located. Tap into your own memory and lead us in the right direction."

Hesitantly, Amber moved forward through the dense woods, her twin never leaving her side. At first, it was challenging to figure out where the main town of Ipswich lay, as with every turn she was greeted by more pine trees and occasional boulders. Fortunately, the formation of the land replicated the Mask, so certain natural landmarks were identifiable. As they climbed down rocks and skidded down steep, leaf-strewn hills, the twins finally reached the downtown district, only to be met by a twisted sight.

Hundreds of people walked all around them. Some appeared to be walking up invisible steps into local buildings, others drove invisible cars, and the majority of these people walked straight through massive trees and boulders—every person seemingly ignorant of his or her spectral behavior. Amber couldn't help but wonder how Chris and the others could handle seeing both the Mask and through it. Just within the half hour of being on Diraetus, the sight gave Amber a headache.

"I've seen this from the cameras on Darmentraea, but it's so strange seeing it in person," said Ambrose in awe.

Amber walked further into the midst of the crowd, dodging low branches and stepping over jutting roots. "This is some kind of Mask!"

"A Mask I get, but no amount of a mental Mask can make someone go through a solid object. Even we can't do that," he replied.

"I agree," said Amber, watching a local talk to an invisible child. Her stomach turned as she realized that if these people believed they were on Earth, then there was a likelihood that some people from Earth were embedded in the Mask.

"I wonder how we look to them," said Ambrose, watching two children play in what seemed to be an invisible yard.

"It's all part of the Mask. We look no different than anyone else." she replied solemnly, her heart breaking for those who had families with the Mask people. "Come on, we've got to keep moving."

They wove in between the trees, dodging the locals who merely went about their daily routine. On a few occasions,

Amber noticed some police officers walking their beat, but apparently they didn't see anything too out of the ordinary with the twins. However, before the two made it out of the downtown district, they accidentally passed by the police station, where dozens of officers stood outside readying themselves for what appeared to be a manhunt.

That's when Amber saw him, the young man from the bluffs. His eyes passed through the crowd before coming to a stop on the twins. Charlie's eyes widened in horror as he pointed to them, shouting for the officers to get them. Ambrose didn't understand his sister's panicked expression until he put a hand on her shoulder, getting her attention. He got more than he bargained for as the world around him drastically changed and he not only saw the city before him but also the angry officers.

Amber, I see the city...how is that possible? Ambrose asked in confusion.

I don't know, something we will have to figure out later. Now, run! he heard Amber shout in his mind.

I knew the kid was mad, but sheesh! Do the police usually react that quickly? asked Ambrose as they ran up a hill.

Amber quickly responded back, *No! Even a legit criminal isn't found that quickly. I think the Scientists have something to do with this speedy response.*

Ambrose heard the officers racing after them and knew that some of them might no doubt even be in a vehicle trying to catch up to them. *Amber, we don't even know what these Scientists are really like. If they're anything as their experiments show, I don't think we want to mess with them.*

Amber came to an abrupt stop as three officers pulled in front of them in their invisible cruisers. As a few other men came up and bound their wrists, Amber whispered to him, "I don't think we'll have much of an option, Ambrose."

A rough-looking man read them their rights while

another officer muttered, "We have some people very interested in meeting you two."

Although Amber was easy to force into the cruiser, Ambrose couldn't see anything without his sister's help. The officer started to complain about his insubordination until Amber quickly thought of a believable lie, saying that Ambrose was blind and she was his guide when he didn't have his walking stick. Naturally, the officer responded in a suspicious manner, but after testing her claim, he decided not to press it further, as they were in a time crunch.

Amber reached out for Ambrose, as he didn't exactly know where to step into the invisible vehicle, but as Amber's fingertips wrapped around his arm, he slid into the cruiser. She held on tight to Ambrose, as letting go would make the Mask disappear, causing him to fall out of the car and requiring a hard explanation. The ride looked very weird and, at times, downright terrifying, as Amber saw both the Mask and through it. Sometimes trees would plow through the cruiser as they drove down the partially visible roads. Boulders and trees flashed by as phantom buildings stood in their place. Seeing Diraetus this way made Amber feel as if she was caught between two opposing worlds—both with the same landscape.

For some reason, which she could only attribute to the Scientists, their destination lasted only a short time. When the twins were pulled out of the vehicle, both noticed that they were in front of a pristine glass skyscraper in what appeared to be the heart of Washington, D.C. The Mask felt so powerful in this whole area that even her ability to see through the disguise didn't work. She let go of Ambrose temporarily and, judging by his surprised expression, he saw the foreboding building as well. To keep up with the pretense, Amber held onto Ambrose's arm after the officers adjusted her handcuffs to comfortably guide her brother.

They walked into the grand building as the officers

handed them off to higher-looking officials who looked more threatening. Amber looked around at the employees of the expensive-looking establishment and noticed something off about many of them. Several of the workers had a strange orange glow about them. Each of these people took a quick glance at the twins with almost a hidden warning look. They must be the Scientists the Sidhe spoke of. If she were the average person, these strange beings would appear like any typical government worker. For the life of her, she couldn't understand their motive for wanting to fit in so well, whereas the other planets wanted to be themselves or rather close to it.

The moment the government officials led them to the elevator and pushed the button to the highest floor, Amber knew deep down they were in serious trouble with someone greater than general law enforcement. There was no telling what that kid from the bluffs had told the Ipswich police, and if the Scientists knew who Amber and Ambrose were, chances of their leaving the planet without a nasty fight were slim.

"Radio silence," Amber whispered to Ambrose. He remembered the Scientists in the lobby and understood that their telepathic communications had to be put on hold for the time being.

A large oval table stood in the middle of a large room to which the officials led the twins. Surrounding the table sat other members of the government, who stood when Amber and Ambrose entered. On one end of the room a massive screen hung mounted on the wall, possibly for various conferences or videos calls to the president and other countries. Off to the side were two-way windows, the kind Amber always saw in all the crime shows she watched when she had lived a normal life. The people behind these windows could be anyone from other officials to psychologists, although, given the circumstance, she was betting on the latter.

Among the staff, Amber noticed one woman standing by the head agent. She had fair skin, dark brown hair, and dark green eyes, but the leader looked completely different. He had darker skin, deep brown eyes, and short black hair. Judging by their intimacy, Amber gathered they were either married or at the very least in a committed relationship. However, this seemed odd, as most businesses didn't allow couples in the same department. She overlooked that when she noticed the same orange glow around the woman. The only defense Amber had right now was to play dumb and act like a typical citizen of Diraetus.

"Can I ask why you brought us here? Do we need a lawyer, because I can do that if needed..." started Amber, in a believable panic.

"Look, you're not in trouble, we just want to ask you some questions," said the lead agent in a thick Southern accent. "Please sit down and tell me what your names are."

Amber and Ambrose slowly sat down in the chairs they were offered, and Ambrose followed Amber's lead, cautiously replying, "My name is Ambrose Oak, and this is my twin sister Amber."

The leader looked at Ambrose as an expression of realization flashed across his face. "Right, I was told you were blind. My name is Levi Bates, and I am the head of the United States Homeland Security. You were brought here today due to an incident in Ipswich, Massachusetts, where you reportedly appeared on the bluffs in a...beam of light?"

The leader looked at some papers, making sure he read the report correctly. He then tossed the paper back down on the table and said, "Care to explain this accusation?"

No one dared to move, as all appeared unnerved by the twins' presence. Continuing with their façade, Amber said, "That seems a bit far-fetched, don't you think?"

"You see, that was our first thought, but then we saw the video that the kid took with his phone. It was kind of hard to argue with the evidence," Bates said. "So, let's try this again. What happened?"

More lies. It seemed lying became not only part of Amber's everyday life but part of who she was as a person. One day she hoped there would be no more lies, and perhaps the Masks would not be necessary, but now wasn't the time for a drastic change like that. She looked all around at the men and women government agents who all awaited her answer.

Amber's eyebrows rose in mock fear as she said, "Okay, we...we were shooting off firecrackers. I know it was illegal, but today's our birthday, and before our parents died, we always shot off fireworks to celebrate...it's a tradition we wanted to keep alive for them."

"Wait a second, if you're twins, why do you have different accents?" asked a female agent, her eyes narrowed, matching the skepticism in her voice.

"Oh, well..." started Amber, her lies running low on fuel.

"I went to school abroad in Germany and then studied a few years in Russia," interrupted Ambrose. "Languages have always been my forte, and I picked them up rather quickly. It was only a few months ago that Amber and I met up after several years of being apart. Today was the first birthday we were able to celebrate since we were young."

"Yeah, and it was ruined over stupid accusations that made us out to be terrorists," said Amber, hoping to turn the tables on them.

The agents murmured amongst themselves, unsure of exactly how to proceed with this situation, as the answer the twins gave was not what they expected. However, while Bates' wife spoke to him he nodded at the appropriate times, seemingly listening to her concerns, but really his eyes were deadlocked with Amber's.

Something about Bates seemed familiar to her. She didn't recall seeing him in a vision or even mentioned on TV. This familiarity felt different, almost like a surreal connection. That's when she saw it: something in his eyes seemed different somehow. Amber could somehow see that, deep within the recesses of his mind, he saw beyond the Mask. How did this government agent with a Scientist as a wife not show any indication that he saw the world differently? Maybe that's why this Protector married him, to make sure he stayed in line. It wasn't as if they could throw Bates into an asylum and say he was crazy—that would raise too much suspicion that even the Masks couldn't conceal.

Amber thought about the other agents in the room and wondered if any of them had spouses who were the Scientists in disguise. Her staring contest with the lead agent continued when Khyra sent her another message, but one that was so faint even the Scientists couldn't pick up on it. It didn't contain a lot of information aside from the fact that Bates had always wondered if there happened to be more to the world than what the Mask revealed. Khyra didn't have to explain to Amber what she had to do next: guide the leader to the truth. But with the Scientist breathing down their necks, that would prove to be a difficult feat.

Then an idea came to Amber, one that would be risky, but it was her only shot.

Amber withdrew from the staring contest and crossed her arms, acting annoyed with the constant murmuring. She spoke up above the noise and said, "With all due respect, if you aren't going to throw us in prison, can you just give us a fine for the firecrackers and let us leave?"

All went silent, each contemplating the next step. To the twins' surprise, the Scientist spoke up and said, "If I might put in my two cents, perhaps letting them off with a warning would be the best idea for now. After all, the couple's story conflicts, seeing as the girl claims the video didn't happen. Their testimony wouldn't hold up in any court of law. Our department would be the laughing stock of all law enforcement."

"I'm sure we'd all like to return to our duties, but firecrackers are still dangerous and could have hurt someone. Some kind of punishment should be involved," said a tall, man with tan skin and dark brown hair.

"Agent Wiles, I understand your concern, but I think in this case we should do what Hannah said and send them off with a warning," said Bates.

The agent didn't seem thrilled about his leader's opinion but moved behind some people in the crowd, hiding his disapproving expression. To Amber's surprise, Bates made an unusually forward move and extended his hand out to Amber, saying, "We'll never bring this up, and you won't hear from us again. No hard feelings?"

Amber's hesitation wasn't at all insincere. She looked at the Scientist, Hannah, expecting to see a warning look, but instead found her to have a pleasant expression. Amber glanced at Ambrose, who continued his blind act. This was her only shot at sending a message along to Levi Bates, a message only he would be able to receive.

"Miss Oak?" asked Bates, his hand still extended.

She focused her memory ability on transferring everything of her life from the moment her mother died to the present day. This happened to be one of the largest risks she had taken, but it was necessary. There was no telling if he would receive the message, how it would be received, or if he'd do anything about it. But Khyra's message seemed clear: this was the only step to take to proceed, and the Diraetus Protector held all the cards at this point.

She accepted Bates' handshake, feeling a small surge of energy flowing from her body into his. She stared into his eyes, hoping to see at least some kind of acknowledgment that the transfer worked, but if it did, he showed no sign.

"Thank you, now if you'll follow my men outside, they'll bring you home," said Bates with assurance.

Amber took Ambrose's arm and walked toward the door where they met two Scientists disguised as ordinary police officers. They took off their handcuffs and led them through the door. The second the doors shut behind them, Amber and Ambrose found themselves immediately back in Galaseya in front of the palace. The Scientists had warned them all right, but in their own discreet way. Unlike on the other planets, these guys seemed to want nothing to do with anything or anyone outside of their jurisdiction. Her only hope now was that somehow the memory had landed somewhere in Levi Bates' subconscious and would soon surface. But at this point, what happened to him was out of her control.

Right now she needed to proceed in finding Khyra, starting with explaining her sudden departure to the family she deserted.

19

"Are you sure we made the right choice in letting those kids go yesterday?" Levi Bates asked his wife the next morning.

She hurried around their large kitchen, preparing their two children's lunches and getting their breakfast ready, as she replied, "Yes, Sweetheart, I'm positive. Besides, I highly doubt they'll be an issue again. You saw how scared they looked when they came into the room."

"I understand what you mean, but something seems off about both of them, and I just can't put my finger on it," said Levi as he gulped down the rest of his coffee.

Hannah called for the children to finish getting ready for school. Not a moment later, two kids came running down their large staircase, their school uniforms on and backpacks dangling from their arms. Levi smiled as he remembered that today was Friday, the day of the week children most looked forward to. He watched in amusement as his children wolfed down their cereal, barely stopping to even taste it.

"Stevie, Kaitlyn, slow down, you're not going to be late," he said with a slight chuckle.

His children looked up guiltily and returned to their food, following their dad's suggestion. Levi moved over to the coffee maker, finished off the rest of the brown liquid and asked his son how his science project was going.

The eleven-year-old shrugged and said that it was nearly done, but Levi saw so much of himself in Stevie, he knew that shrug really meant the science project was nowhere near finished. On the other hand, seven-year-old

Kaitlyn seemed overly excited for her class's talent show.

Moments like these made Levi feel proud that his children grew up the way they did. He hadn't had it so lucky at their age.

He turned to his wife and gave her a goodbye kiss as she said she'd be in the office later that morning. The kids ran out the door with their packs securely on their backs. Levi grabbed his briefcase and keys and started toward the car. The moment he closed the front door behind him, he stopped on the stone steps of his house, frozen in shock.

Two unusual objects hung in the vast blue sky. One massive planet hovered over his world so close he could see the black surface in between the thick blue clouds. Another one, much smaller than the first, glowed so brightly it could easily be mistaken for a sun, but it wasn't. In between the rays of light that seemed to explode from the surface, there were a few patches of land with miles and miles of bright blue ocean surrounding them.

Kaitlyn called for her dad's attention, but as he tore his gaze away from the bizarre sight, he looked around to find he and his children stood in the middle of a vast forest—no sign of civilization in sight, except for his neighbors, who went about their daily activities seemingly ignorant of the thousands of trees standing in place of their homes.

"Dad, are you okay?" asked Stevie.

Levi looked at his two children, who seemed to have a hazy, brownish glow around them. The light pulsated as Stevie and Kaitlyn shifted uncomfortably where they stood. Levi shook his head and rubbed his eyes, hoping this weird episode would disappear. Fortunately, it worked, but just as with the two kids from yesterday, he couldn't shake the strange phenomenon.

As Levi drove his children to school, he reflected back on his life and all the times he noticed strange things about the world. The forest wasn't too unfamiliar to him, as he used to imagine vast forests in the major urban areas, but were they really his imagination? This certainly didn't feel like it. He tried brushing off the strange feeling and the incident with the strange kids from the other day. He needed to keep his head in the game today, as mounds of paperwork and reports waited for him to sift through. Lately, he was way behind on his workload as other situations that came up took precedence.

Finally, his routine returned to normal and soon the episode from this morning felt like a mere dream as he walked through security and clocked in for what he knew would be an unreasonably long work shift. He rode up the elevator to the top floor of the building and within seconds of exiting the lift, one of his closest friends came charging up to him.

Levi laughed at his friend's excited behavior but was glad to see him as well, as his friend was working on a case out of state. He shook his friend's hand and said, "Hey, Mitch! When did you get back?"

"Oh, just this morning, actually, but I had to write up my report, so I came in a bit earlier today. Got a lot on your plate?" asked the big man.

"Yeah, I'll be glad if I don't pull an all-nighter here," said Levi, shrugging.

"You mean, you don't do that every night? If I didn't know you had a wife, I'd say you were married to your work!" joked Mitch.

"Hilarious," said Levi sarcastically. "So tell me how the case went, heard it was a tough one."

Mitch began relating his story, emphasizing certain parts with exaggerated hand gestures as he usually did, but then another strange thing happened. The people walking around them started to slowly disappear, with only a couple dozen people remaining. The last person to vanish was Mitch himself.

Levi stared around and looked down the empty halls of his office. It felt as if the people who disappeared had never even existed. Could that be true? Were the disappearing people somehow part of the strange vision he had seen as he left the house? The forest, the planets, the invisible people—all were connected.

Just as before, he shook his head and rubbed his eyes, bringing him back to the only reality he knew. Mitch continued speaking, his friend's strange behavior not fazing him in the least. Levi's heart pounded in his chest, the throbbing nearly hurting him. He interrupted Mitch's one-sided conversation and excused himself for a meeting he was running late to. Mitch gave Levi a curious look as he watched his friend walk away with haste. He shrugged his shoulders after figuring that Levi was having a rough day. But in reality, that was a major understatement.

His meeting seemed normal. People started piling in one after the other, quietly conversing about the subject that was to be discussed. But when his wife came into the room, his entire world came crashing down.

At first, she appeared as he always saw her, but then her body disappeared, replaced by dozens of what looked to be golden lights, each one surrounding a small, brown ball. They reminded him almost of the shooting stars he had seen as a child out in the country. Hannah returned to her human form as she approached him with a loving smile and a gentle hand on his shoulder—something she normally did every time they met at work.

Somehow, he managed to direct the meeting as he usually did and no one was the wiser, not even his wife. But every part of him just wanted to run out of the room screaming from the insanity he had endured the day before. No, he knew he had to wait. All of this began when he met that girl and her twin. In fact, he started to wonder if she actually intended for this to happen. The rational side of him refused to believe that this young woman had some kind of magical power—he had never liked anything involving fantasy or science fiction. To him, the only importance he saw in the world were facts and tangible evidence. Yet the things he had seen couldn't be ignored no matter how hard he tried.

He even went as far as going out to the bar that evening, where all the local law enforcement went, just to drown out the day's events. Of course, he never drank unless a stressful event led him to that; he generally liked to keep his wits about him. Naturally, Hannah asked where he was off to before he left after dinner. For once in their fifteen-year marriage, his trust in her began to dwindle. He remembered his friend Mitch from earlier in the day and used him as an excuse, saying they were to meet later on that night to watch a football game. Although Hannah wanted to spend time with her husband, or so it seemed, she shrugged and reluctantly let Levi off the hook.

At the bar, he greeted some old friends and saw the bar owner, known as O'Malley. He was a kind Irishman who always supported the police force and local government. He started Levi off with his usual shot of whiskey. O'Malley didn't even have to ask Levi what happened that day—the exhaustion on his face was enough to tell him he'd have to call a cab at the end of the night.

After each shot, Levi found his problems of the day slowly fading away, but by the fourth shot, they all came rushing back in the form of a strange young woman. She casually walked up to him and set her half-finished Bloody Mary next to his empty shot glasses. Levi turned to get a better look at the woman and was surprised that she had even made it through the door without being questioned.

She wore baggy cargo pants held up only by a thin canvas belt. A tight, dark green tank top reached just above her navel, exposing her flat stomach, which, like many other parts of her body, were riddled with various scars. Unlike many of the women he encountered on a daily basis, she wore no makeup but had a clear and beautiful complexion. Her brown hair was styled short and spiky, almost unkempt, but it was her hazel eyes that drew him in—eyes that seemed to contain years of pain, secrets, and knowledge. She looked down at his shots and smirked as she sarcastically said, "Can I buy you another?"

Despite his drunkenness, Levi knew how to keep his wits about him. He chuckled and politely said, "I think I'm past my limit, but thanks."

The woman took a sip of her drink and said, "I assume you don't often come here for a drink. Rough day?"

"Yeah, you could say that. I think my job is making me go crazy," Levi replied with a slight shake of his head.

"Well, I'd imagine being the head of the DHS would make anyone go crazy," said the woman matter-of-factly, "especially if you can see through the Mask."

"I'm sorry...Mask?" Levi asked, forgetting about the fifth shot the bartender placed in front of him.

"Yeah, you know the people disappearing, weird planets appearing—oh, and can't forget how some people look like they're made of little light flares. Not many people can see that. Those who do generally are put in a mental institute. At least that's what the Scientists have resorted to doing, seeing how they can't control all of them," said the woman, as if this was a normal conversation.

"Who did you say you were?" asked Levi, dumbfounded by the woman's boldness.

"I didn't," said the woman, extending a friendly hand. "The name's Khyra."

Levi introduced himself and asked, "What can you tell me about this Mask?"

"Not much else, the walls have ears, I'm afraid," she replied, returning to her drink.

"Do you mean these Scientists? Who are they and what do they have to do with the planets?" he asked, hoping his voice didn't sound too panicky.

Khyra shook her head and said, "I was hoping Amber's message would have made things clearer, but I guess not. Like I said, I can't say a whole lot other than that you're in extreme danger—you and your children."

Just like any law enforcement officer, Levi saw this comment as a threat toward his family. But before jumping to conclusions or accusations, he calmly replied, "Me and my children? Why not my wife?"

"She's part of the reason you're in danger," said Khyra in a quiet, serious tone. "In fact, all of your friends at the meeting with the twins are in the same situation. Their spouses, along with yours, are brainwashing you. They are trying to stop you from seeing the way the world really is."

Levi reflected back on how he had felt toward his wife earlier in the day. For Khyra to know any of this information and the things he witnessed, she would need to be psychic. He took a deep breath and said, "If we are in as much danger as you say, then tell me, how are we supposed to escape it?"

"Ah, great question, yet one I can't answer at the moment," said Khyra, standing up from her seat. She gulped down the rest of her drink as if it were water and dropped some cash on the counter, then turned to Levi before leaving and said, "When the time is right, find the children."

The mysterious woman walked away, leaving Levi fully absorbed in what she said. He was looking down at the last whiskey shot before him when Khyra's words penetrated through his drunk mind. Now he had a reason to take the woman in for interrogation: a real threat was made against his children and those of his team members. He slapped the dollar bills down on the counter and ran out of the building, hoping to catch the young woman.

But as he barreled out the door, he nearly ran into a lamppost and came to an abrupt stop on the sidewalk. He hung on for support while his blurry eyes scanned the streets for her fleeting figure, but she was nowhere in sight. He raised a shaking hand towards the sky, hoping his signal would hail a nearby cab. When a bright yellow car pulled up to the curb, Levi tumbled into the car, mumbling his address to the driver, who didn't dare ask any questions about the haste in the agent's voice. As the cab swerved around corners and passed other vehicles, Levi's stomach turned in every direction. Fortunately, time flew rather quickly as the car pulled up to his house. The driver refused the money Levi offered him. The amount he gave didn't match what was owed, and based on how drunk and sick the agent looked, the driver took pity on him and said the fare was on him. Levi muttered a thank you as he stumbled out of the car and up the driveway.

His mind swarmed with confusion. He always had a strong stomach and could hold his liquor. This sickness made no sense to him, but the fear and adrenaline coursing through him on top of being drunk, just made things worse. He took a few deep breaths, as he didn't want his wife or children seeing him this panicked or drunk. He had learned a few techniques over the years that helped with controlling anxiety and calming oneself down. Fortunately, it worked, but it didn't get rid of his pounding headache.

The first thing he did as he entered the house was go to his children's room. To his relief, found they were sound asleep in their beds. Even his wife was curled up in their bed when he entered his bedroom. Finally, life returned to normal. As he stepped into the shower, he watched the water go down the drain along with the craziness he had experienced that day. But no matter how relaxed his body felt, his mind repeated the day's events so fast that sleep didn't come easily to him. Deep in the recesses of these thoughts, Khyra's intimidating words crept to the forefront of his thoughts, overwhelming his mind until he drifted off to a dreamless sleep.

"Levi! Levi, wake up!" Hannah screamed frantically.

Ignoring the pain pounding in his head from a horrible hangover, Levi made an evasive maneuver out of bed. He brushed passed Hannah and raced down the hall, knowing exactly what the problem was. His fear was true. Both of his children had disappeared. His wife came sobbing down the hall after him, saying in a choked voice, "I woke up only a half hour ago, and they were gone. Where could they be?"

Beyond her tears and quaking voice, Levi heard something else—something that she hid very well. But with panic running through his mind, her secrets were another matter he had to figure out later. Without responding to her or even calming her down, he rushed to his cell phone, making calls to every member of his team. His fear increased as they all replied with the same story as his—their children were gone. Levi threw his phone across the room in a fit of rage. Mentally, he beat himself up for being so drunk the night before and not paying attention to the things Khyra said. How could he find the children if no leads showed up?

You know where to find them, Levi, echoed a familiar voice in his head, *follow your instincts.*

Anger welled up within him as he realized Khyra was somehow telepathically speaking to him. Was this some kind of a joke to her? Did she want money? Could she be friends with that Amber girl and they were trying to take over the country? All of these questions came with no logical answer—no, something on a much larger scale was going on. None of his team members would understand any of this, so he humored Khyra and allowed himself to follow his instincts by trying to peer through the Mask.

It was as effortless as turning on a light switch. He had had it in him this whole time, but all it had taken was for a strange woman to show him the truth. The world appeared so bizarre to him, and he knew that finding the children would be incredibly challenging, so he occasionally reverted to his original vision. Although his life turned upside down, and he wasn't sure whom to trust, he had to keep up appearances. As he left the house to go on the search, he promised his wife that their children would be found. She stood in the front doorway, watching her husband text his team to meet at headquarters before jumping into his SUV and peeling out of the driveway.

By the time he reached his office, the sun had begun to peek over the horizon. He rushed into the meeting room, where he found his team gathered together, doing as much research as they could. Within his text message to them, he had asked them to start finding everything they could about the mysterious woman. But based on their frantic expressions and the dozens of empty coffee cups in the trash can, they had burned their candles at both ends—their efforts proved futile.

A young officer named Nick approached Levi and said, "Sir, there's no record of a woman like that existing. Did you get the last name?"

"Sorry, Lipinski, she didn't go into much detail about herself," said Levi, feeling foolish for not keeping himself sober.

"Then how are we supposed to find our kids?" asked Rachel Smyth, sitting down with a coffee cup in her hand.

The other team members stopped what they were doing and looked up at their leader, despair and exhaustion plastered on their faces. Quickly he formulated an encouraging pep talk, but just when he was about to deliver his message, a mysterious figure materialized in front of them. His jaw dropped as Khyra stared at them all bringing an entirely different message.

"Don't bother trying to research me. As far as anyone's concerned, I don't exist," started Khyra. "Besides, I'm not who you should be afraid of."

"Aren't you the one who threatened our kids?" asked Allen Richards.

"Threaten? Hardly. I was warning your leader of the impending doom that's coming. Although with his drunken mind, I'm surprised he heard anything I said," replied Khyra with confidence.

"Sir? You never mentioned you were drunk when you spoke with her," said Trevor Wiles respectfully.

Avoiding this possible catastrophe, Levi changed topics and asked, "Who should we be afraid of, Khyra?"

"Uh, hello! The Scientists! Man, you really need to keep up!" she replied, her tone full of annoyance.

"What is she going on about?" asked Nick, staring at his commander with slight suspicion.

Levi began ignoring the questions from his team, focusing on his conversation with Khyra as if they were the only ones in the room. He stared at her, wishing he could see through all the secrets that she hid. He recapped the conversation, connecting what few dots there were. "You mean to tell me that you're protecting our children from the Scientists who you claim are all of our spouses? So what? Are you going to kidnap the children and hide them forever? If these Scientists are as horrible as you say, how can one woman protect twelve children, or for that matter hide them?"

Khyra smiled, glad that Levi was beginning to understand the situation, but found it humorous how little he really knew. She shook her head. "Ah Levi, you're right. However, you're also completely wrong. Everything you stated is just skimming the surface of the real issue at hand."

"Then why don't you enlighten us," demanded Rachel with a glare.

"I would love to, Rachel, but as I told your commander, the walls have ears and the Scientists will stop at nothing to prevent you from seeing the truth of the world you live in. That is why I have your children. They are the key to restoring Balance to this world. When you find the children, you will have your answers," Khyra explained calmly.

Ending her cryptic response, Khyra faded away, leaving everyone but Levi confused. He knew what needed to be done, but at the same time, his training told him to never give in to terrorist demands. Then again, dealing with a magical woman and other planets wasn't exactly in his Academy training either. He addressed the group and filled them in more on everything that had occurred yesterday and how he believed Amber and her brother were somehow involved, however remotely.

Naturally, many scoffed in disbelief, but then, after his team argued and murmured to each other, they realized they didn't have many other leads at the moment, and they probably wouldn't get any. It became a unanimous agreement to follow what was there and never to speak of it to anyone outside that room. But the more they discussed the options and theories before them, the weirder it felt to them.

"Am I the only one who feels like we're in some weird science fiction novel?" asked Trevor, who started rubbing his temples to ward off an oncoming migraine.

"Yeah, I have to agree with Wiles," said Allen, shaking his head.

"Okay wait. I understand what you feel, because believe me, it's beyond strange to me, too," Levi assured them. "But what do we know so far? Khyra has power. The Scientists are a terrible force to be reckoned with and probably have powers as well. What we see here isn't real, and in fact, we're seeing through a Mask put on by said Scientists. Our children are in danger, and Khyra is trying to protect them from the Scientists who just so happen to be our spouses. Our children have the answers to who the Scientists are, and somehow Amber and her brother are wrapped up in all this," said Levi, pacing the floor.

"Right, you forgot to mention our kids are hybrids, then," said Nick sarcastically.

Levi put a hand to his head, frustrated that nothing made sense, at least regarding reality. That's when he heard a voice, but not from anyone in the room.

Look through the Mask, follow the children! Khyra's command echoed in his head. Levi tried shaking off the words as he walked toward the window and stared out into the early morning sun. The city below was just starting to wake up as cars whizzed by going about their usual business—a reality he deeply missed. Suddenly, the bustling morning routine faded away, as miles of trees and hills popped up in its place. Near the horizon, a bright light, almost like a flare, shot up in the sky. It hit him, hard. This sign was meant for him. To find the children and Khyra, he needed to follow the signs—signs which only could be seen through the Mask.

He turned around to face the silent room of hopelessness and said, "Do you all trust me?"

Exchanged glances of concern and confusion rapidly spread throughout the room, but eventually, they all nodded their heads in agreement, waiting for their leader to continue.

"Good, then follow me, I know how to find them."

After a comment like that, one would think that his team would be asking millions of questions, but all of them knew the answer wouldn't be logical or something they wanted to hear. So they remained silent as they followed him out the door and piled into a few government vehicles, starting toward a nearby national park.

Levi parked as close to the origin of the flare as possible, but the rest of the way required a good hike in the woods. His team didn't seem enthusiastic about this idea. However, they also knew an unknown time constraint hung over their heads. With his newfound vision, Levi searched through the Mask for any sign of an unusual light flare. Occasionally a sign came guiding him toward the right direction, but it wasn't a constant thing. He suspected this was mostly due to Khyra's fear of the Scientists.

As they turned around bends in the trails and periodically took shortcuts off the beaten path, they managed to find their way deeper into the woods to an area that seemed forgotten by the outside world—a perfect spot for someone in hiding. A warm breeze swept over Levi's body as he quickened his pace to a run, knowing deep down his children were just at the end of the path. He came to an abrupt stop as he came to a dead end clearing, where Khyra stood at the edge with all the children surrounding her. Some of the younger ones clung to her as if she were their mother. The midmorning sun shone through the colorful leaves, casting an almost fantasy-like glow over the entire area.

Khyra stared at Levi and smiled as she calmly said, "Glad you made it."

"Answers. Now," was all Levi could muster through his gasps for air.

"Dad, we can't really tell you, we can only show you," said his son.

"Stevie's right, but we need to hurry before the Scientists find us," said Khyra, as her hazel eyes scanned the area.

"What makes you think these Scientists won't find us wherever we go?" asked Trevor.

"Where we are going they have no power over us. We will be protected," said Khyra, her voice sounding more impatient.

Levi thought for a moment back to everything he saw in his visions and replied, "Would this place have anything to do with the planets in my first vision?"

"You're right," she replied, "the people on one of the planets are waiting for us. We need to go now."

"I can understand why they'd protect you, but why us?" asked Rachel.

Khyra opened her mouth to speak, but immediately fell silent as her eyes stared past the agents toward the trees behind them. The children crowded closer to her for protection. Levi turned around and saw their spouses—Hannah leading them.

"Oh, don't stop on our account, Khyra. Please tell us all why you think Galaseya will protect not only these people but you. A woman who I thought we killed over a thousand years ago," she said, her tone laced with acid.

"Guess you didn't finish the job," Khyra replied with a glare.

Levi and his team stood on the sidelines while Khyra and the Scientists continued their verbal shootout. None of the agents was sure which side to choose as both began making compelling arguments.

"You just had to intervene, didn't you, Khyra?" asked a man who, judging by Rachel's expression, was her husband.

"You've spent the last two thousand years with your heads in the sand...trying to avoid an inevitable battle! And for what? To control a race of beings that have never belonged to you?" exclaimed Khyra, getting to the heart of the matter.

"We were merely curious about the human race. We wanted nothing to do with the disagreements between the other planets," said Hannah.

"Yeah, well, while you let your curiosity run rampant—that so-called disagreement has turned into chaos. The Brothers have been planning a galactic takeover. So this is your problem too!" Khyra replied, as her voice echoed throughout the clearing.

Hannah exchanged nervous glances with her group as she replied, "The last we knew, they wanted nothing to do with us either."

"And that's where I come back to the whole 'head in sand' thing," Khyra replied sarcastically.

Nick stared at the next woman who spoke, realizing that it was his wife. In a snobbish manner, she said, "You forget one thing, Khyra. We are the planet, and you are a human residing here. You belong to us—what we say goes."

With the Scientists sounding more murderous and Khyra less crazy, the agents inched their way over toward their children.

Khyra ignored their presence and became angrier with the Scientists. "Wrong. You gave up that right when you started messing with the Balance. You don't own the people. We never asked to come to this planet, let alone solar system. So now you have a choice to make. Be the planet you're supposed to be and protect yourself from the Brothers or get out of my way!"

Hannah looked taken aback by her demand and said, "Who are you to tell us what the Balance wants?"

The children, who hung onto Khyra, took a step back as if they knew what would happen. The young woman's wardrobe changed, as the bottom of her tank top grew a long, sheer brown lace that reached to her waist. From the back of her cargo pants grew the same material, reaching down to the ground like a natural train full of glitter and various colored leaves. Her hair sparkled, and her hazel eyes glowed, looking more inhuman. She opened her mouth to speak and out came a voice so powerful that the trees quaked. "Because I am the Balance of Diraetus and these are my people!"

A bright white light engulfed the senses of the agents, and within seconds they all stood with their children and Khyra in front of a massive and ancient palace, one that resembled those of Europe, but felt different in a way. Levi looked around him and saw that the palace sat in the middle of a field with the forest surrounding it. Behind them lay a large, bustling fishing village—the people either ignorant of the group's presence or just used to it. Suddenly the palace doors opened with a creak and out came a number of individuals who Levi assumed to be the residents of the building, based on their fancy outfits.

The last to arrive was none other than Amber and her twin, neither of whom appeared at all surprised by the group's sudden arrival. The twins approached the foreigners, and Amber smiled, glad everyone made it safely, and addressed them.

"Khyra, it's good to finally meet you in person."

"Likewise, Amber," Khyra replied with a confident voice.

"Levi, I'm glad you, your team, and children are safe," Amber said in a serious tone.

"Amber, where are we?" he asked fearfully.

She nodded her head, realizing that this would take some getting used to, and replied, "Levi Bates, welcome to Galaseya. We have much work to do and a lot to explain. Let's get started!"

20

After their arrival, many things took place nearly all at once. One by one the family introduced themselves to the newcomers as the servants gradually brought them all to their rooms—each one prepared in advance, courtesy of Khyra's constant communication with Amber. While they rested Amber, her family, and members of the palace gathered together trying to figure out what their next step would be, as they had a lot of explaining to do.

The Sidhe quickly sneaked in on the conversation while the others rested. Up until this point, they knew of every move that needed to be made to restore the Balance, but now there was no advice that they could give. Amber got a strange sense that there was more to their silence than they let on. She brushed it off, though, as she didn't want them to disappear for another lengthy time. Right now she needed all the help she could get, as there was no telling what the Brothers were planning.

However, the Sidhe left the conversation moments before Levi and the other Diraetans came into the palace library, Iethreor leading them. Amber and her family took turns explaining some of the smaller details to what Levi and his team already knew. This included enlightening them on some of the history of the planets and how their family got wrapped up in it all. Granted, Levi and the agents interrupted many times, but Amber found it odd how the children just stood around, silently observing the situation. Khyra had previously told her in one of their many telepathic conversations that the children already knew of their destiny from birth, but still, their presence weighed heavily in the room.

When all was said and done, and everyone was caught up with the latest news, Rydan spoke up from his own silence, as he had remained in the corner the entire time, mostly watching the children. He addressed the parents, saying that all the humanoid version of the planets will disappear when the Balance is fully restored, meaning their children may not make it either. With their permission and the permission of the children, he suggested that he may be able to find a way to save them. Of course, there was much deliberation over this offer, but Stevie and Kaitlyn, who were now the unspoken leaders of the children, approached the Alchemist and agreed to do the testing before the adults had a chance to stop arguing.

Levi and his team came to a sudden, disturbing revelation. These children were no longer theirs. Sure, they were their flesh and blood, but now they started opening up, revealing wisdom far beyond their years. Levi sighed and shook his head; first his wife betrayed him, and now he was losing his children to some unforeseen force. He looked at Rydan and asked him to just be careful. No sooner did Levi say that than Rydan was already halfway out the door, with the children following right behind.

But unfortunately, he didn't get too far with his research. Rydan would stay up for days just to find a cure for these children. Amber often passed his room where he was coming up with a formula, and many times she could have sworn he was talking to himself. For some reason, saving these children was important to him, but Amber suspected that may have something to do with spending so much time with the children.

This wasn't the only thing that changed in Galaseya. The Sidhe removed the Masks from all the other agents, which spooked them quite a bit and made some of the original skeptics believe. While their parents adjusted to their new sight, the children were often found wandering the palace grounds, and to everyone's surprise, the young animals would escape the protection of the forest and play with these strange humans. These strange occurrences made many of the family members question whether the Balance had been restored, but the Protectors knew something else was up—that this was merely a stepping stone toward their end goal.

But as the weeks progressed, that next stepping stone seemed to drift farther away, that is, until one day in particular, when many of the family members and agents met in Jermiar's library. He pulled out dozens of books, hoping to find their next step or at least a possible idea as to what the Brothers were up to.

But Khyra didn't take part in the research. She stood in front of one of the large windows staring out onto the field, her mind in a far-off place that seemed to drain her of all emotions except sadness. Amber stared at her new friend, wishing she could break through the walls Khyra consistently threw up. But that was an invasion of privacy that even Amber didn't dare break.

"I don't get it," said Jalerydin. "We have all the Protectors, the hybrid children, their human parents are safe, and the Brothers are quiet. So why isn't the Balance restored?"

"Or is there a possibility that it's already been restored?" asked Rachel.

"No, because...we'd see a lot of changes, not just here, but on the other planets," said Ambrose, with a strange pause as if he had almost said the wrong thing.

"Now what? We have no knowledge as to what the Brothers are planning, and I have no doubt the Scientists are still quite put out with what Khyra did," said Hunter, his eyes shifting toward the woman at the window. "Besides, am

I not the only one who feels like we are in a stalemate?"

"What do you mean?" asked Kylis, whose eyes looked from Hunter to Khyra.

"I am only saying that I find it strange how we have had no leads since Khyra's arrival," he replied accusatorily.

Khyra remained as still as a statue with her eyes glued to the outside world. Breaking the uncomfortable silence that seemed to suck the air out of the room, Amber replied, "I hardly think that's her fault. She can't exactly know what all the planets are doing at once, and it's not like they've been open before."

Amber hoped this comment would at least warrant some kind of response from Khyra, but she refused to move. Then a sudden warm breeze blew past all of them, following the familiar voice of Levendria. "It was not as if we did not wish to be more open. Am I right, Khyra?"

Although the Diraetans had seen the Sidhe on several occasions, they still felt a twinge of fear and awe in their presence but just didn't show it too much. The Sidhe floated down the stairs and toward the group as Amber said, "Khyra, what is he talking about?"

"Tell them, Khyra, it is time they understood the gravity of the situation," said Vaeris.

"Why? So the Brothers can hear it all and ruin any chance we have of saving everyone?" she suddenly exclaimed, turning toward the group as a single tear fell from her eye.

"They already know you're keeping something from them, Khyra," said Kaitlyn, coming in with her brother and the other children. Rydan following behind them with a look of exhaustion. The girl continued, "Whether you verbalize it or not won't matter. The Brothers will eventually find out, it's only a matter of time. But they will destroy everything on their way to finding the truth. At least if you speak up now, fewer lives will be lost. Please, Khyra, tell them about Earth."

"Wait, so Earth is real?" exclaimed Levi.

Khyra swallowed a lump in her throat as more tears came. She looked at Levi with pain in her eyes as she replied, "It was. I...I can't—"

A thought came to Amber as she walked over to the woman in hopes of comforting her and gathering more information. She put a gentle hand on Khyra's shaking shoulder and said, knowing she'd understand what she was going to do, "Please, let me help."

Khyra turned her tearstained face to Amber and looked into her kind eyes. She sighed, closed her eyes and nodded her head reluctantly, knowing this was the best way to explain her story. Amber silently signaled for Jermiar to come over to boost her ability. He too seemed reluctant to want to know, but with another, more persistent look from Amber, he walked over and grabbed her hand. Within seconds, the library transformed around them all, bringing them back to a long-lost civilization.

They first saw Khyra's family life, which seemed to have some conflict, but nothing that was very clear to them. She had a father, mother, and three older siblings. Both her parents were brilliant chemists with a massive corporation. They gave her everything a child could ever want. But material things never impressed her. She seemed to want to be with her family more than anything. Unfortunately, her relationship with them deteriorated after she became an environmental scientist. Her family moved from their home in London to build another branch of their company in Portland, Maine. She grew up and received her master's in meteorology and astrobiology. It took a while for someone in the science community to notice her. She often published papers to get noticed, and one day someone finally heard her voice. The largest scientific organization in America called her in one day for a job opportunity.

The more Amber and the others watched Khyra's life progress, the more they began to question why she was so distraught. But then, her life in this new position as a lead scientist on a project made a turn for the worse. In the Earth year 2010, she and her team were comparing the Earth to other planets when they noticed an unusual anomaly within the Earth. It started in the large cities of the world, where the most pollution occurred and then began to spread. It was as if the planet couldn't handle any more of the trash and destruction the humans placed on it. So the world fell apart. The next part of her life went by rather quickly; just like the beginning of the vision, there were parts that seemed fuzzy, aside from everyone dying off. There was no way of fending off this extensive destruction.

In 2017, what was left of humanity on Earth boarded a massive spaceship that some Siberian engineers had been constructing over the last three decades, leaving their gray and desolate planet behind. Some believed that the world would somehow renew itself and they might return home. However, Khyra knew the truth. Although her immediate family died within the first year, her cousin, the Marshall of the Royal Air Force, managed to be among the few to escape. On a few occasions that the visions showed, Khyra and her cousin didn't seem to get along. His name was John Oak.

No one really knew how long they were on the ship as time dragged on. The ship had an autopilot and could detect nearby earth-like planets. If Khyra had to guess, that ship became their home for at least seven years before they came across Galaseya and the other planets. The galaxy in which they arrived was enormous; Khyra believed that at some point it may have been barely visible from Earth on certain nights. The planets themselves sat at the very edge of this galaxy in a small solar system. According to the screens Khyra glanced at, Darmentraea sat farthest away, followed by Galaseya, and Diraetus. Each planet had its own orbit. The dark planet circled both Galaseya and Diraetus. Diraetus circled only Galaseya and for some strange reason, Galaseya's orbit seemed much too large, as if there were an invisible planet in the center. But just outside of the solar system floated a rather dead-looking planet that Khyra believed to have been the missing center of Galaseya's orbit.

Their ship never intended to go anywhere near the planets, but an invisible force pulled them into the solar system. From there, they stood still, not leaning toward any of the three worlds before them. This gave Khyra plenty of time to look at the other planets and see if they were fit for human life. But the more she looked into them, the stranger her discovery became. Each world seemed alive in a way, almost as if it had a hidden heartbeat. The surface of the planets changed, whether it was land mass changing or mountains randomly shooting up from the ground. Although each one was a perfect candidate for the weary travelers, something felt almost repulsive to her.

The leaders of the expedition, John Oak, and Lukas Grunewald, gave her the honor of naming the surrounding planets and galaxy, as Khyra seemed the most interested in the research aspect. She looked at the Earth-like planet and noticed how most of the planet consisted of land rather than water, the opposite of her world. She thought of the word "dirt," which is where the name Diraetus came from. She then turned to a golden planet whose outer atmosphere seemed to be a type of sun for the other two planets in the solar system, and she thought of a name so beautiful that the word itself seemed to glow—Galaseya. The third and final planet felt cold and evil. Only two words came to her mind when she looked upon the blue and black-colored planet, which acted as the moon for the other two. Dark and demented—Darmentraea. The name of the galaxy she felt was quite fitting—Chronosalis after the god of time. This specific location seemed stuck in its own realm of time far different from Earth's solar system or any of her neighbors.

Khyra presented her findings to the leaders and others of the expedition but cautioned that something still seemed off about the planets, aside from their odd readings. She tried mentioning the lonely planet off in the distance and guessed that it was the probable cause of the strange imbalance in the solar system. She didn't have a meaning for the name she decided on. It was hard to identify anything about the planet, as it was almost too far away to see. However, she felt a name would be useful in the future. This world, which would soon be forgotten, was called Heirsha.

Unfortunately, the leaders of the expedition didn't pay attention to her warnings as they, like everyone else, were tired of living in a metal box. They missed the fresh air, the sounds of birds and other creatures; to them, this was only the means of escape. Oak and Grunewald began making plans for who would go to each planet, making it a rule that they were to keep their calendar of months and days but starting from Year 1—something to remind them of their home world. Someone else brought up the idea that they should all keep their family surnames in honor of those who had died.

But after these decisions were secured in the minds of the team, their plans of escape quickly changed when their spaceship started breaking down from years of use. The people had to hurry to the escape pods, each one hoping they'd land on at least one of the planets. Grunewald, as well as other people from Germany, Russia, and a few

Americans, fell on Darmentraea. Oak, along with most of the British scientists, landed on Galaseya, and everyone else went to Diraetus. They would never hear from each other again.

Khyra felt a twinge of sadness at never hearing from her cousin again, but soon the other people she came with became her family. However, they weren't alone on Diraetus. A few months after their arrival, Khyra came in contact with the Scientists. They wanted to understand who these new creatures were and began experimenting on her in the most gruesome ways, which is where her many scars came from. Unknowingly, the Scientists changed her entire being and put some of their power into her. She managed to escape from them after many years, by faking her own death. Some of the Scientists didn't really believe she was dead, but after several years of total silence, they decided to come to that conclusion.

But the Scientists gave Khyra more than just powers. They gave her insights as to what they and the other planets were doing. She began noticing that this solar system particularly thrived on Balance, which was slowly deteriorating over time. She dedicated her entire life to trying to restore this Balance, as humanity would cease to exist without it. Often, she found herself reflecting back on the mysterious dead planet outside the solar system, wondering if that had anything to do with the Balance being initially thrown off. She waited for years, knowing that if she had powers, then the other planets would soon gain someone like her, someone from her own family.

The vision soon ended as Amber, along with everyone else, stared silently at Khyra, who now sat on the ground sobbing uncontrollably. Amber reflected back on the vision and noticed some areas that seemed obscure—elements that Khyra hid for probably good reason.

Surprisingly, Chris stepped forward, the only one to actually even begin to understand the sorrow Khyra felt. He had felt the same way when his mother died. He crouched down and put an arm around her, quietly saying, "Khyra, that was not your fault. Your intentions were as pure as any. How were you to know the pollution would have led to Earth's destruction?"

"I...I didn't. But...my father did!" she exclaimed through tears.

"What do you mean?" asked Levi.

"My team and I tried to find ways of stopping the pollution from spreading, but it was a mutation. It grew on its own even after the...source of the pollution ended. The water of the world became toxic, air unbreathable, and plants began dying—everyone lost hope. I'm sorry! I should have seen this before, I should have stopped my father! I'm the reason you're all in this mess!" she exclaimed, self-hate radiating out of her voice.

"You may blame yourself, but we don't," said Jozderin. To an extent, the Darmentraeans understood her situation and the guilt she felt too. "You and your team did everything you could to preserve human life. You might be the reason we're here, but you're also the reason why we are alive. All we can do now is move on and work together to restore this Balance. Maybe your theory was right, maybe Heirsha is the key to restoring the Balance."

Wiping the last tears from her bloodshot eyes, Khyra stood up and said, "You don't get it, Jozderin. Yeah, we may have figured that out, but so have the Brothers, and there's no telling what they're going to do next. We have a dead planet and no way to bring it back into orbit."

"Wait a second—if that planet originated from this solar system, then that means one of us is the Protector of it," said Kylis. "Maybe they're the key to bringing Heirsha back."

"You're forgetting something. If the planet is dead, then

whoever the Protector is, their power is dormant," said Khyra solemnly.

"So, what? Wait for the Brothers to do something drastic? By then it'll be too late," said Amber.

"Maybe...or maybe that will give us enough time to stop them," said Khyra, her mind wandering elsewhere again.

Over the next several days, Rydan found a cure for the children and even Chris, who, Amber verbalized, was in the same situation as the children. Fortunately, the treatment seemed to work without any side effects. He and the children soon joined the others as they all began to go over the new information—all frequently wondering who the next Protector was.

But the only thing they got out of this was a village full of sick people. The people on Galaseya were all relatively healthy. This sporadic sickness just reminded Amber that the Balance was deteriorating even more. This dilemma brought some of the family out of their homes, and because of their abilities, many of the people were healed almost instantly—all except one.

Among the family members who went into the town to help was Kylis, who caught the virus quite quickly. But no matter what Ambrose did or what Rydan concocted in his lab, Kylis grew sicker. While Ambrose and Rydan kept an eye on Kylis, the Sidhe, who were already well informed about the discovery of the new planet, periodically popped in to update them on what the Brothers were doing. Naturally, they couldn't find anything, since the Brothers, for once, kept their plans top secret. This worried everyone the most.

Kylis's health did not improve in the slightest. Most of the time he lay in bed with cold sweats and an aching body. At first, his sickness didn't seem to be a concern to most people, but when it continued consistently for over a month, everyone's attention moved from the Brothers to Kylis. Of course, he protested the attention, but all were strangely intrigued by it.

According to Rydan, the virus was on such a large scale that everyone should have contracted the sickness by now, especially himself and Ambrose, yet all were well. Rydan took samples from Kylis in hopes of pinpointing the origin of the illness, as he was now convinced it was no longer the flu that had afflicted the villagers. Even Khyra in the many years she lived had never seen anything so persistent before and grew concerned that it was a mutated virus that wiped out her people.

Kylis's sickness soon went from flu-like symptoms to something surreal. His body began to reveal deep wounds with no sign of a source. Kylis's body bled so much that his bed sheets had to be changed at least twice a day. Everyone wondered how he was still alive. These wounds were the only thing Ambrose managed to heal, but they became so frequent he gave up coming in to look on his friend and instead, began sleeping in a chair in the room. This took quite a toll on Ambrose, as he already started dealing with severe headaches and strange visions of the Brothers.

Whatever they were planning involved the Portal from Darmentraea to the other worlds. Khyra and the other Diraetans quickly returned to their world to prepare for the worst, wishing the others good luck before they left. After evacuating the villagers to a safe-house village deep within the woods, the Grunewalds and other Darmentraeans voluntarily took their positions at the pier where their Portal stood.

All this time, the rest of the family tried to make Kylis as comfortable as possible. Khyra began wondering if there was more to this sickness than what they saw. She brought it to everyone's attention that perhaps the Brothers had something to do with this and maybe Kylis was the Protector to Heirsha, although many people disregarded that, as he didn't show any possible signs of being a Protector. Still, she kept to her intuition, watching out for any visible signs of her claim. As if things couldn't possibly get any worse, the Brothers decided to pay them all a visit.

All the Oaks, aside from Ambrose who insisted on staying by his friend's side, were holed up in Jermiar's library, scanning more of his books in hopes of finding anything that may help Kylis and stop the Brothers. Suddenly a gust of icy cold wind blew throughout the large room, scattering papers and throwing ancient books everywhere. The beautiful mural painted on the ceiling cracked, and some family members lost their balance, falling from the ladders which were fastened to the wall. When the wind died down, Amber looked around at her family, who fortunately only sustained minor cuts and bruises from the ordeal.

"Well, that was entertaining," said Martheykos' acidic voice.

"You really ought to keep yourself organized," mocked Petraylin with a sly smile.

Without thinking, Amber immediately looked at Jermiar, who grabbed the edge of a nearby table to pull himself up to a standing position, rage etched into his face. He caught Amber's warning look and against his better judgment, kept quiet, letting her handle the situation.

"What do you want now, Martheykos?" she asked, refusing to sound afraid.

He callously brushed fragile papers off a chair, ripping them in the process, while he sat down, making himself at home. "We just wanted to pop in and see how you all were doing. You know, like any good neighbor would do."

"I highly doubt you came to just visit," snapped Rogalar.

"You're right, we actually came to give a warning...well, not so much a warning as an announcement," he replied.

"You certainly got our attention. What is it?" asked Amber, trying not to sound too interested.

"Oh, nothing too much really, just that we're planning to destroy whatever's left of your precious Balance and take over the solar system and soon the galaxy," said Petralyin, sounding rather bored.

"Is that all?" asked Chris.

"Far from it," said Martheykos, with a knowing look at Chris. "In fact, we are mere moments away from that happening."

"So let me get this straight, you want to destroy the Balance, the very thing this entire solar system thrives on, and then what? Take over the rest of the planets? To what end, Martheykos? You'll always want more and more until you not only destroy the planets but yourself in the process. Is that what you really want to do?" asked Amber, hoping her point would get through to him.

Martheykos and Petraylin laughed as Martheykos replied, "You misunderstand me. Destroying the Balance will only destroy the planets as you know them. The worlds will remain, but their personalities will change. Galaseya and Diraetus will just be another Darmentraea."

Amber stared at him in shock, her mind flooding with so many questions, yet only one came out. "Why? Why is domination so important to you that you are willing to risk everything?"

"That Balance has been in control for far too long, stifling Darmentraea from becoming what it's supposed to be. Feared. Respected. Worshipped. All Petraylin and I want is what is rightfully ours," Martheykos exclaimed as his body shook with every word he spat.

Seeing the situation growing out of control, Petraylin spoke up and said, "Martheykos is right, but honestly, our business shouldn't be of any concern to you. After all, you have greater problems on your plate."

Martheykos' shaking immediately stopped, as he looked at Amber with dark, cold eyes and continued Petraylin's comment with a wicked smile. "How's that little friend of yours doing? Kylis, is it? If I were you, I'd go check in on him. He doesn't have long left."

Before anyone else could speak, the Brothers quickly formed a cloud around them and disappeared without a trace. No one had to ask what their next plan of action was, as they all started for the door, with Amber leading them to Kylis's room. Along the way she caught a glimpse of Hunter and the other Grunewalds staring at her—a worried expression grew on each of their faces. Some of the Darmentraeans who knew Kylis well left their post to join in on the race to Kylis's room.

By the time they reached his bedroom doors, Amber found Iethreor and Flaedar staring into his room, sadness masking their usual happy faces. She brushed past them and entered the room. The smell of sickness and death hit her like a tidal wave. Ambrose stood rigidly at his friend's bedside. Not one muscle moved as he looked down on Kylis. The sight was almost too much for even Amber to handle, as Kylis's youthful appearance somehow degraded, his entire body looking deformed and deflated—every bone in his body crushed.

Forcing herself to look away from his body, Amber walked over to her brother's stone-like figure and wrapped her arms around him. He didn't hug her back, as his mind and body were still in shock. The only thing coming from him was a single tear falling down his cheek.

Suddenly the room grew darker, as the light from the outside world went out. They all ran outside to fend off whatever was coming through the Portal. Even Ambrose snapped out of his frozen state to aid the others, mostly out of anger at the Brothers. Three things were certain to everyone right now: Kylis was the last Protector, Heirsha was destroyed, and both were the last shred of hope they had for restoring the full Balance.

Twenty minutes. The longest twenty minutes of their lives, staring at the Portal, waiting for the unknown to happen. All around them their world crumbled. Darkness engulfed them, while freezing cold winds whipped at their bare skin. Lightning struck nearby trees and parts of the palace, threatening to strike them next. Yet all refused to back down from the fight. Amber looked at her family, new members and old coming together to fight a common enemy. In a sick sense she found it poetic, something the great poets of ancient times may have written about.

Suddenly, her focus shifted back to the Portal as figures jumped through it, with their weapons ready to sink into the nearest victim. Just as their feet hit the Galaseyan soil, the darkness around the world and its accompanied storm dissipated, as the planet's light returned. The Darmentraean army dropped their weapons; confusion replaced their hatred. With it came utter shock as their eyes looked past the family and toward the palace. Nervously, Amber turned around, and surprise swept over her.

Emerging from the palace was Kylis, healthier than ever before. But he looked much different than before. His once black hair had turned a dark shade of auburn. His dark brown eyes glowed green, and his usual Darmentraean attire was replaced by a more natural look, with various colored leaves as a shirt and soft-looking bark for pants, while his feet remained bare. Immediately Amber looked up into the sky and saw the most comforting scene—a third planet hung high in the heavens, entirely covered in greenery. She looked back at Kylis as he came toward them with a smile.

He stood only a few feet away from the crowd as he explained, "Heirsha's back. The Brothers tried to destroy it by exploding it, but a small piece of the force of the solar system brought a little piece of it back into orbit, and the rest of the planet followed, completely repairing itself when all came in."

Amber glanced at her brother, expecting him to be overcome with joy at his friend's resurrection, but instead, he couldn't stop looking at his new makeover, or rather what little he saw of it. His hair went from dark brown to black-blue. His eyes were no longer light but glowed a bright, almost neon blue. His wardrobe was unlike anything Amber could imagine, as his top reminded her of water, flowing with every move he made. His black pants merely emphasized the various shades of blue in his top.

Khyra and the other Diraetans showed up, and as with the other two, Amber stared in awe at her own new appearance. Long, silky white hair flowed down to her waist, as her hazel eyes now shone a silvery-gray color. Her original clothing looked like rags in comparison to the white gown, which cascaded down her body like a cloud. Almost too afraid to see her own appearance, Amber hesitantly looked down and noticed the most unusual dress flowing around her body, a dress made of fire. It flickered with every slight move she made, all the while staying aglow. She touched the flames, which only licked her fingers without leaving a mark. An invisible shield protected her skin and anything around her from catching on fire. She then caught a glimpse of herself in a nearby puddle, and her jaw dropped as she took in her golden hair and fiery red eyes. She smiled, knowing that the Brothers would never appear again, but then a horrifying realization came to her. If one thing happened to one planet, then the others would be the same.

"Chris!" she exclaimed looking around at her family members, most of whom couldn't look at her.

She looked toward the Oak house, then toward the castle. Neither place showed any sign of Chris. Tapping into her connection with the planet, she felt the energy the world gave off and found herself looking toward the woods in the direction of the royal cemetery. Without even thinking, Amber transformed herself into a fireball and shot toward the cemetery, rematerializing in front of the gravestones, the rest of her family following suit after her. Her face turned pale and silent tears streamed down her cheeks. Chris lay there in the midst of the tombstones, grasping on to his last few breaths. Amber dove to her brother's aid and held him in her arms, just as he had with their mother, what felt like centuries ago. He looked up into her red eyes and smiled as he choked, using words familiar to her, "You did it, Sis!"

"But the kids are okay, they made it!" she exclaimed, looking around at the children, who stood by their human parents with sorrowful eyes.

"You would have never agreed to this if you had known the truth," Chris said weakly.

"So you knew this would happen?" asked Amber, now looking to Rydan for an answer. He couldn't look at her but held his arm up against the tree, his face buried in the crook of his arm to hide his tears.

"Not at first, believe me," said Chris, distracting Amber from her anger toward Rydan, "but then Rydan noticed something off about the difference between the children and me. We had the same 'disease,' if you will, but different causes. They were born with the planet power. I...I needed it to live."

"Why didn't you tell me? I'm sure..." she started.

"Amber, I made Rydan promise to not tell you. You would have spent far too much time trying to save me when it's really humanity you needed to save. They need you, Amber," whispered Chris.

"No...no, Chris, I need you! I can't...I can't do any of this without you by my side. I won't!" she cried.

"Amber, look around you," said Chris. Amber turned her head and saw her entire family and friends, nearly everyone shedding a tear. Some who cried had never showed any sign of remorse before. In some way, Chris affected everyone. Amber returned her attention to Chris. Despite his pain, he was smiling, his natural pearly white teeth coated in red as he struggled to say, "You have everything, Amber. Always have and always will."

"Chris, why? Why do all of this if you knew your death was inevitable?" asked Amber, begging for a reasonable explanation.

Chris gave a weak smile as he replied, "Because, we're all connected. We're all family. Never forget that, Amber."

"What...what do you mean?" she asked, her voice well above the normal speaking range.

"It's not something I can explain even if I had the time. But know this, you'll understand soon, and when you do, you'll understand why I gave my life. I love you, Sis, don't ever think otherwise. Keep doing the work you were born to do. Repair the worlds and restore humanity to what it's supposed to be!"

With those few words, Chris exhaled his last breath as his life force finally left him. Amber held him close, rocking him back in forth, as if that would bring him back. The cry she let out was unlike anything her family had ever heard. Ambrose came to his sister's side and pulled her away from their brother's corpse. She clung on to her twin, hysterically crying. Many wondered if the tears would ever subside.

They did subside, but not until after his burial. Unlike Renalia's burial, Chris' was not as extravagant, but Flaedar, being the new ruler, permitted Chris to be buried in the royal cemetery, as his deeds were just as noble as those of any proper royal. To the family's surprise, some of the animals of the woods—mostly the bears—came out of respect for the fallen hero. Although Khyra wanted to attend his funeral, she and the other Diraetans had much chaos to deal with after the Balance was restored. The moment it returned, every Mask the Scientists put on the people was instantly removed, creating mass confusion and, needless to say, anger.

Life went on, and the Darmentraeans who intended to come for a fight on both planets were eventually integrated into society as their new world's effect on them changed their mindset. The family spoke a lot about fixing the worlds and helping the inhabitants, but Amber felt that her life had no meaning anymore. She became almost numb to the growing problems in her world and the others. Problems on all planets became more than only three of the Protectors could handle. They needed Amber's ideas too, but they also needed her mind to be cleared.

A week after the burial, they found Amber standing on a ledge of the high mountain, staring off at the ocean, her mind full of sorrow and regret. Ambrose put a cold hand on her warm shoulder, shocking her back to reality.

"Hey, what're you thinking about?" he asked rhetorically.

"Everything...and nothing," she replied in almost a monotone.

"No one can blame you for how you're feeling right now, but we've all visited the other planets, and there's a lot to be done that only we can do," said Kylis gently.

"I know, I'm...I'm just not ready," she stammered.

"Will you ever be?" asked Khyra, getting to the heart of the matter.

Amber's gaze grazed the treetops until it came to a stop in the area where the cemetery lay. She closed her eyes and said, "No, no I don't think I will."

"So you're just going to stand up here for the rest of your immortal life staring out at the ocean and let the other worlds fall to ruin?" asked Khyra.

"She's right, Amber, don't you want to find out what our brother died for?" asked Ambrose.

Amber's eyes shot toward Ambrose. *"Our brother."* Ambrose had never spoken of Chris in that way. As far as Amber remembered, her twin had never really talked to Chris at all. This was yet another example of the impact Chris had. She stared at Kylis saying, "There's a lot of problems out there, you say?"

He silently nodded, hoping Amber would break from her time of sadness even for a moment. Although that sadness still lingered in the depths of her heart, she reluctantly and bitterly replied, "What's one more adventure, right?"

Epilogue

Years went by before all the planets were repaired after the initial change. Twenty-two years, in fact. Galaseya was the only planet that didn't have to change too much, as they were used to change. But with Amber's new look, they were a little afraid and didn't quite know how to react to her. Flaedar, on the other hand, had seen this situation coming and explained what her role was and that she ranked even above him in authority. Naturally, Amber wasn't too keen on his announcing this. The people began to kneel in respect while bringing their hands close to their abdomens and bowing their head almost to the ground. This ritual never ceased to bother her, but the people, with their deeply rooted beliefs, felt it necessary.

Although they accepted her role, it took them about a year to accept that they weren't alone in the universe. Despite their curiosity about the new people, they resumed their normal routine after a few months. Khyra noticed some of the Diraetans were quite receptive to the idea of becoming new trading partners with Galaseya and expressed this thought to Amber. The Galaseyan Protector thought this would be good for her people. Khyra quickly located the Portal on her planet, which was set in the area that Ireland once stood, or what the Mask made to appear like Ireland. The Portal sat between two natural rock formations in the middle of a grassy field.

With the Balance now restored, the Galaseyans continued to be a kind and benevolent society, but they no longer tolerated any disrespect from anyone. Fortunately, the Diraetans whom they came in contact with didn't feel the need to be rude to their otherworldly trading partners, so there was little or no conflict.

Stephria and Joyra were the only family members that really stayed on the planet. Joyra refused to follow the other Grunewalds in repairing the other worlds, as she never felt comfortable with change. Unexpectedly, Flaedar abdicated the throne willingly, giving it to his second in command, Iethreor. After the brutal murder of his entire family, Flaedar wanted to leave, knowing his services could be used elsewhere. When the time came, and Khyra needed help with leading her planet, he offered to be an ambassador for Galaseya.

Iethreor proved himself to be an excellent ruler, as he not only expanded the village, making life a little easier for the people without changing too much of their lifestyle, but he also sent people to explore what lay beyond the forest; some of the Oaks and Amber even offered to help search. To their surprise, they found several other villages about the same size as the village by the ocean. One, in particular, was home to Kaleya, who now lived a more pleasant life and even started a family. But she wasn't the only forgotten individual they found. With her memory abilities, she found one person who happened to be a long-lost family member that all presumed dead. Mattreylar Oak. Saraleast's husband.

After he had left the family in search of a new and less complicated life, he stumbled upon this small village and became its leader after many years. Not only was he surprised to see his descendants, but he expressed his remorse and guilt for leaving. He had no idea what had happened to his family or if they even lived, which was why he remained in the village he found. He wanted to make things right and offered to help unite the other villages with the port city.

With this newfound information, the explorers returned to give the news to Iethreor. He decided to personally meet the leaders of all these villages in hopes of establishing communication and new trade with them. Dirt roads were made through the woods at the same time, avoiding all animal habitation. Fortunately, the wild creatures never bothered this new development, approving of the uniting of the people.

While Galaseya spent most of its time with new discoveries, it took the people of Diraetus about five years to adjust to the changes. Within the first two years, all four Protectors were questioned incessantly by the people, who were still wary of these new beings, the changes in their land and the missing people. After a while, Kylis and Ambrose had to return to their planets, but Amber remained with Khyra. Jermiar ended up coming to Diraetus, feeling he would be of more use there than on Galaseya. Fortunately, the agents and their hybrid children became a great help in restoring trust of the remaining people of the planet.

Rydan's cure for the children allowed them to keep some form of power that no one was able to fully understand, but they managed to bring the civilization back to the way the humans remembered it. However, the people who were part of the Mask could never return. To Amber's surprise, a number of individuals whom she personally knew as neighbors and classmates were among the Mask people, including the three boys.

According to Khyra, Levi spent most of his time speaking with other people of the planet, trying to convince them that this change would be good for them. Some saw the change she already made with rebuilding their lands and welcoming new ideas and believed she was the best thing for them. Others were harder to convince. She promised to not intervene with their way of life as long as they didn't go about destroying each other. Naturally, some did start up minor battles, but she was quick to put an end to any conflict before it erupted into a massive war. She kept her promises, and more of the leaders of the various cultures began opening up to her position.

When the people began to relax a little toward Khyra as their Protector, they started showing her respect by bowing in her presence, as the Galaseyans did, though they didn't lower their heads. This was not something she demanded of her people, but it seemed the planet had a strange effect on them, making them see her as some kind of god. After speaking with Amber about this strange reaction, both realized Khyra's theory was right. Only the people who accepted the Protectors would react in this way.

The Diraetans began to take action and change the old history books. The writers of these books spent their time going to and from Galaseya to interview some of the family so their books would be accurate. To many of the people on Diraetus, it was as if they were beginning their entire livelihood over again from scratch, creating their own history. Although in many of the books they mentioned the Masks and what Earth was like from their memories, they wanted to rewrite their history for the sake of future generations. Unfortunately, it took much longer to get information from the other family members from Darmentraea, as Ambrose made sure his people remained on the planet. They were not ready to integrate into society, as many of them still had a wicked mindset. It took Diraetus a little over sixteen years to fully adjust.

Darmentraea, on the other hand, took the longest of all the planets to change—twenty-two years, to be exact. Ambrose had the most difficult time maintaining his world. It took him ten years to get the people adjusted to the new changes. In this time period, the land began to return to its normal state, that is, the world became less dark, and the animals that lived in the woods only hunted each other and rarely attacked humans. The people found the lightness and mild warmth of the world difficult to adjust to.

When the people became tolerant of that situation, they had to get used to this "kid" ruling over them. That adjustment in itself took another five years. He had to bring out his Darmentraean side quite a bit and show off his "talents" on many occasions to get the violent people to listen. But when the citizens adjusted to their ruler, they showed Ambrose even more respect as the Diraetans and Galaseyans did. They not only knelt before their "god," but sat up rigid, with their left harm hanging straight by their side and hand balled into a fist, while they placed their right fist over their heart, as in pledging their allegiance to him. About fifteen years later, some of the citizens began showing true loyalty to Ambrose, and not just out of fear. Then he decided to introduce the idea of the planets and individuals on them to his people. This took another seven years, as he wanted to be sure that the Darmentraeans were ready. In its entirety, this whole period took twenty-two years.

During this time, Ambrose wasn't alone, as the majority of the Grunewalds stayed with him to help the other people adjust. Even some of the Grunewalds who remained on Darmentraea gathered their forces together and pitched in. Amber often popped over to check in on her brother, and it was during these times that Amber and Hunter returned to speaking terms. Both hoped that after the worlds returned to a relative state of calm, their long-forgotten friendship might be restored.

Ambrose discussed his plans with Amber, after finding out their family was once again what it should be, or rather close to it. He expressed to Amber that he wanted to introduce the recuperated Darmentraens to the other planets, but some just refused to change. For this reason, Ambrose came up with an ingenious idea to turn Darmentraea into a prison. The personality of the planet itself would clean up anyone's attitude. With the new rule, Ambrose encouraged the citizens of the world to take buildings of the Dark City and make them more jail like. The corpses that littered the street were removed and thrown into the woods to be food for the animals, and soon the blood dried up, permanently staining the streets. Some of the worse Darmentraeans that couldn't be changed remained in the City, whereas others who were ready to integrate with the other worlds went to their chosen planets.

On the other end of the Portal, the Protectors waited for the Darmentraeans' arrival. With the personality of their planets, many of the former Darmentraeans changed. Diraetus' prisoners who could not be reformed and were given life sentences were brought over to Darmentraea. The Darmentraean Portal stood in the middle of the Brothers' house. Because it was erected with the Brothers' power, the house no longer existed, but with his power, Ambrose built another building around the Portal—one that was less gaudy. When the Diraetans started coming through, he grew concerned that some might escape thorough the Portal. And although it took some work, he made it so it only went one way and none could get off the planet without his permission.

Everything seemed to be working fine for everyone after those twenty-two years, but then many people grew incredibly sick, with so many people coming over to other planets. Here Heirsha came in to the rescue. When found, this planet was uninhabited, and the majority of the world was covered in mountains, trees, and other various plants. It literally became known as a planet of forests. There were some bodies of water, although they were small and hard to find. The largest body of water on the planet was roughly the size of Earth's Great Lakes. Everything on this planet had healing properties and could cure any type of disease known to mankind, from cancer to depression. The water also had some kind of healing property, but it was mostly used as a distillation for the other plants and herbs.

The atmosphere on Heirsha didn't sustain human life, so Kylis mostly found this place as his own personal sanctuary, and it was here that he began experimenting with various types of cures for all sorts of illnesses humans could ever encounter. The plants and trees on the planet were watered through an underground reservoir, connected to all the bodies of water. They had day and night cycles exactly like Earth's. In fact, the planet's original location in the solar system looked exactly like Earth's, with the moon and sun the same distances from the planet. Because of the reservoir, there was no need for rain on this planet. Unlike the other Protectors, Kylis' power only worked on the world, but it was only his remedies that made the human race healthier and live longer. Perfecting his cures took at least a good ten years before he was satisfied with any results.

When the worlds were at peace, and all that was left to do was to explore and improve the planets, Amber found herself back at the old royal cemetery which had lain forgotten for over twenty years. With a wave of her hands, the brush blew away, and the grass receded as if someone had just mowed it. She approached a small tombstone with a crude engraving on the front. Chris' name was etched into the stone with the tattoo image of the Elders shakily scrawled underneath—something, she found out, represented the Balance.

She sat by the stone sarcophagus and said, "You were right, I've learned so much about the worlds and the people living there. I now understand why you sacrificed yourself for humanity. They all are unique and have such differing views about life and how things should be run, but at the end of the day, they have one thing in common, and that commonality is what brings them together like a family. Flesh and blood. That's the one thing that can't change them. I...I feel like I never really knew who you were, Chris. And I'm sorry I never got the chance. You've taught me so much over the years and I know it's probably too late, but thank you! You protected me despite the fact there were days I questioned you. The worlds will remember you and the sacrifice you gave to save them. I'll make sure of it!"

Amber rose to her feet and stepped back. She pointed a delicate hand at the tombstone and the symbol disappeared, replaced by an epitaph that held the most powerful words she could think of to describe what her brother did: "Born to save humanity by protecting the only one who could."

For the last twenty years, her depression over her brother's death had never left, but she had an incredible support system that reminded her of what he died for. She walked away from the cemetery vowing to return on occasion to keep the cemetery clean. But Amber had so much more work to do, albeit the worlds were doing better than ever. However, if life had taught her one thing, it was that it's full of surprises and something always manages to pop up at the most inconvenient times.

Amber knew she had to be ready for anything that would harm the human race. Sure, people may be ungrateful at times, but Chris saw beyond that, and it was up to her to continue what he started all those years ago.

Acknowledgements

If I could personally thank every single person in my life for helping me with this book, this section would probably go the length of the story itself. But this book would have never been completed without the help and support of the people who came into my life, no matter how long or short that time might have been.

I would first like to thank my Dad who was my first editor. With the patience of a saint he walked with me through this book for sometimes hours on end, just to make sure it was perfect. From conquering fire breathing dragons and saving villages (at the cost of a lot of sheep) to reminding me that it is socially unacceptable to allow one's eyes to fall on the ground, my dad showed me the importance of striving for your best and to never take yourself too seriously

My mom, on the other hand, helped me from the other end of the spectrum. From the time I was a teenager, she always saw the potential in my writing and has always been my personal cheerleader, going out of her way to find new ways of helping me fulfill my dreams.

My grandparents never stopped supporting me, even during times in my life that were on the low side. They always tried to tell anyone who would listen about my writing. Their constant encouragement made me want to strive harder.

As for the love of my life, Jeffrey, who has always been willing to sit down and listen to my strange ideas regardless of how tired he is. His support and love transcends even the days where I feel like giving up. He's always there to remind me of how far I've gone and that I can make it another day.

Stephanie, my best friend in the world. She taught me what it means to be a true writer. She broke me out of my shell and taught me that it was okay to be a little bit on the odd side. She helped me get into the mind of my characters and make them come alive.

My managers and close friends, Marshall and Ben, made me see that it wasn't just my family excited about my writing, but others as well. They put in so much time just to show others my work. Their excitement encouraged me to get out of my comfort zone and show the world what I can do.

Many of my college friends and professors encouraged and inspired me in more ways than I can even count. Whether it be helping me develop a character or idea, or just simply listening to my ramblings.

Thanks everyone!

About the Author

Rebecca Cobban

Ceara Comeau started writing stories when she was twelve years old. Her writing career began with "Amber Oak Volume 1" and "Adventures of the Young and Curious". Both books were a compilation of short stories that were self-published when she was fifteen years old. Over the next few years, "Amber Oak Volume 2" was written and became self-published when she was seventeen. During her college years, "Amber Oak and the Missing Links" and "Amber Oak and the Master of Illusions" were born. After they were self-published, Ceara wrote another story separate from her Amber Oak world entitled, "The Lost Journal of Erika Traynor". That was the last book she self-published before graduating from college in December 2016. Later, she returned to the beginning and looked at her Amber Oak series. It was then that she decided to take the series she worked hard on all those years ago and rewrite it. It first started out as an eight book novella series, then to a trilogy, and then into one book, "Memories of Chronosalis.